PRAISE FOR *Maud Hart Lovelace*

"There are three authors whose body of work I have re-read more than once over my adult life: Charles Dickens, Jane Austen, and Maud Hart Lovelace."
                                          —Anna Quindlen,
                         New York Times bestselling author

"Slipping into a Betsy book is like slipping into a favorite pair of well-worn slippers: It's always a pleasure to live in Betsy's world for a little while, to experience her simple joys but also her (thankfully short-lived) sorrows."   —Meg Cabot,
                         New York Times bestselling author

"I reread these books every year, marveling at how a world so quaint—shirtwaists! Pompadours! Merry Widow hats!—can feature a heroine who is undeniably modern."   —Laura Lippman,
                         New York Times bestselling author

"I read every one of these Betsy-Tacy-Tib books twice. I loved them as a child, as a young adult, and now, reading them with my daughter, as a mother. What a wonderful world it was!"
                              —Bette Midler, actor and singer

"Some characters become your friends for life. That's how it was for me with Betsy-Tacy."

—Judy Blume, beloved bestselling author

"The Betsy-Tacy books were among my favorites when I was growing up." —Nora Ephron, Academy Award–nominated writer-director

"I am fairly certain that my independent, high-spirited grandmother must have had a childhood similar to Betsy Ray's. . . . As I read . . . I felt that I was having an unexpected and welcome peek into Granny's childhood—a gift to me from Maud Hart Lovelace."

—Ann M. Martin, creator and author of the Baby-sitters Club series

"Family loyalty and the devotion of friends to one another . . . for me are the defining characteristics of the Betsy-Tacy stories."

—Esther Hautzig, award-winning author, former director of Children's Book Promotion for Thomas Y. Crowell Co., and publicist for *Betsy's Wedding* in 1955

"I truly consider *Betsy and Tacy Go Downtown* to be the finest novel in the English language! I will never love any other books as much as I love the Betsy-Tacy books."

—Claudia Mills, children's book author, winner of the National Book Award and Golden Kite Award

"When I was growing up in the Bronx, I had lots of friends. But the girls I most enjoyed spending time with were Betsy, Tacy, and Tib . . . in the series by Maud Hart Lovelace . . . three girls full of good ideas, adventures and fun."

—Johanna Hurwitz, award-winning author of more than sixty popular books for young readers

"Maud Hart Lovelace and her Betsy-Tacy series influenced me very much when I was a girl; I identified with Betsy, who wanted to be a writer, as well as the friends' girl power."

—Lorna Landvik, *New York Times* bestselling author

"Heavens to Betsy! It was pure bliss to slip away and into the world of these turn-of-the-century Minnesota girls, their families, their friends, their loves. It had been many, many years since I'd spent time with the enchanting Betsy Ray, but after reacquainting myself with these classics, I now realize that one of the reasons I believed I could someday become a writer was because of Betsy's own infallible confidence that she would be a writer. Don't worry if you don't have a young person to buy these delicious books for—be selfish and give 'em to yourself."

—Mary Kay Andrews, *New York Times* bestselling author

"I grew up thirty miles north of Mankato, and trips to town were filled with mystery and magic because I was walking the same streets that Betsy and Tacy once walked. The Betsy-Tacy books . . . more than any other books, fed my dream of becoming a writer one day." —Jill Kalz, Minnesota Book Awards Readers' Choice Award winner

"At school visits, when kids ask what books I read as a child, I have only one answer: Betsy Tacy—the entire series. . . . Truthfully, I think those were the only books I read as a child. But they were enough to make me know that characters in books had true and honest feelings and that made all the difference." —Maryann Weidt, author of the Minnesota Book Award–winning picture book *Daddy Played Music for the Cows*

"As a Minnesota girl, I read the Betsy-Tacy books about a thousand times as a kid. I used to go to sleep at night with one of the books under my pillow whispering to myself about the girls, hoping I'd dream I was playing with them." —Anne Ursu, award-winning author

Carney's House Party
and
Winona's Pony Cart

The Betsy-Tacy Books

Book 1: *Betsy-Tacy*

Book 2: *Betsy-Tacy and Tib*

Book 3: *Betsy and Tacy Go Over the Big Hill*

Book 4: *Betsy and Tacy Go Downtown*

Book 5: *Heaven to Betsy*

Book 6: *Betsy in Spite of Herself*

Book 7: *Betsy Was a Junior*

Book 8: *Betsy and Joe*

Book 9: *Betsy and the Great World*

Book 10: *Betsy's Wedding*

The Deep Valley Books

Winona's Pony Cart

Carney's House Party

Emily of Deep Valley

Carney's House Party

and

Winona's Pony Cart

TWO DEEP VALLEY BOOKS

Maud Hart Lovelace

Illustrated by Vera Neville

HARPER**PERENNIAL** MODERN**CLASSICS**

NEW YORK • LONDON • TORONTO • SYDNEY • NEW DELHI • AUCKLAND

HARPER**PERENNIAL** ● MODERN**CLASSICS**

HarperCollins books may be purchased for educational, business, or
sales promotional use. For information, please e-mail the Special
Markets Department at SPsales@harpercollins.com.

Carney's House Party was first published in 1949 by Thomas Y.
Crowell Company. First Harper Trophy edition published 2000.

Winona's Pony Cart was first published in 1953 by Thomas Y.
Crowell Company. First Harper Trophy edition published 2000.

FIRST HARPER PERENNIAL MODERN CLASSICS EDITION PUBLISHED
2010.

Library of Congress Cataloging-in-Publication Data is available upon
request.

ISBN 978-0-06-200329-4

HB 04.10.2024

Foreword

I feel like I've known Betsy, Tacy, and all their friends my whole life, but the truth is we didn't meet until my early twenties. I was an editorial assistant at HarperCollins's children's division in 1994, and the series was being reissued with covers by Diane Goode. I can't remember if I first picked up *Betsy-Tacy* as a work assignment—a big part of my job involved reading books and writing catalog or back cover copy for them, a gig which seemed too good to be true—or whether it was one of the dozens of books I devoured on the long subway ride home and brought back to work the next day. I do know that by the time Betsy and Tacy had recovered from their rocky start at Betsy's fifth birthday party, I was hooked. I thought each new (to me) Maud Hart Lovelace book was my favorite until I encountered the next one. I felt forlorn when I finished *Betsy's Wedding*, the final title on the list of Harper Trophy's Lovelace reprints. That was it: The End. There were no more books in the series.

Or so I thought. A fellow editorial assistant, Susan Chang, told me there were three out-of-print companion volumes about characters who play supporting roles in the main books—or, in the case of *Emily of Deep Valley*, don't appear in the Betsy books at all. When I heard there was such a book as *Carney's House Party*, I shrieked. When I heard Harper-

Collins was going to reprint that book at long last, I shrieked louder. Carney is one of my favorite characters in Betsy's high school Crowd, and if ever a character deserved her own book, it is Caroline Sibley, that warm-hearted, capable, mirthful, intelligent girl whose home is the setting of so many lively Deep Valley adventures. Carney, with her one dimple and her eyes twinkling behind glasses. Carney, hostess of countless parties. Carney, one of the first girls (or boys, for that matter) in Deep Valley to learn to drive an automobile.

Part of Maud Hart Lovelace's genius was her ability to create real, believable, multifaceted, imperfect, likable characters—not just memorable eccentrics like the Ray family's "hired girl," Anna, with her quirky vocabulary and her penchant for invoking the perfect McCloskey family of her past, but everyone from teachers to townsfolk to the hordes of teenagers who descend upon the Ray house every Sunday night for Mr. Ray's famous onion sandwiches. Over the course of the Betsy books, we meet dozens of her friends, and each of them is a vivid, fully realized character with a unique and quite recognizable—but never stock—personality.

There's Cab Edwards, the affable neighbor boy who drops out of high school to take over the family furniture business after his father dies. Ralph Maddox, the gorgeous football hero who holds back for fear of damaging his handsome profile. Bashful Tacy who bubbles over with a rather impish spirit when she is comfortably out of the spotlight. Joe Willard of the swinging walk: proudly independent, stubborn, sensitive. Winona Root, mischief-maker, with her snapping eyes and white teeth, introducing a spark of competition into all the Crowd's antics.

And there is Carney. When Betsy first meets Carney, in

Heaven to Betsy, she isn't at all sure she's going to like her—and neither are we. After all, Betsy's mother is pushing Carney so hard.

> *Mrs. Ray never mentioned Caroline Sibley without adding that she was a lovely girl, which always annoyed Betsy.*
> *"Caroline Sibley is a stick," she said.*
> *"Why, Betsy, you hardly know her. I'm sure she isn't a stick. And they have such a big beautiful lawn, and there's always a crowd of young people there . . ."*

When Betsy does get to know Carney, she immediately realizes she has been unfairly prejudiced against her. Although Carney is indeed the kind of impeccably tidy and beautifully mannered girl a mother is bound to gush about, she is also frank and funny and not a bit pretentious. What she has is a zest for fun, and the kind of natural enthusiasm that is irresistible to her friends. Many of the Crowd's best in-jokes—*O di immortales* and the Triumvirate of Lady Bugs, for starters—originate with Carney.

When, at the beginning of *Betsy and Joe*, Carney goes off to Vassar, the Crowd misses her deeply. Evidently, so did Lovelace's readers. As Amy Dolnick recounts in the appendix to this volume, "It was Carney's popularity with readers that inspired Lovelace to expand her story after completing *Betsy and Joe*." The real-life model for Caroline Sibley was Maud's friend Marnie, a.k.a. Marion Willard Everett. (That's right, Willard—as in the name Lovelace chose for Betsy's true love, Joe.) And like Carney, Marion Everett went off to college with an unresolved romance hanging in the air. Lovelace touchingly captures the tender affection between Carney and her beau, Larry Humphreys, an affection that thrives even years after Larry has left Deep Valley, Minnesota, for sunny San Diego—a cataclysmic move that rocks Betsy's Crowd at the end of Carney's sophomore year.

When *Carney's House Party* begins, four whole years have passed. Carney has just completed her sophomore year at Vassar, and her world is full of questions. Is she in love with Larry? Is he in love with her? Or rather, would they be in love if they could see each other? Their correspondence has been faithful and affectionate, but neither one of them seems able to move forward until they see each other again—and with a continent between them, that seems all too unlikely.

But Carney has more matters to reconcile than her relationship with Larry. She is headed home for the summer, and her somewhat snobbish Eastern roommate is coming with her. Posh Isobel's arrival in dear old Deep Valley causes Carney to see her hometown—and her home life—with new eyes. It is a rite of passage most of us must go through, and what is refreshing about Lovelace's treatment of the topic is that her heroine is neither brooding nor cynical. Carney may be sorting out her personal ideals, but she is not at all self-absorbed. When she runs into a tangle of emotions, she is able to step back and examine them with candor and common sense. She approaches self-scrutiny with the same kind of energy that propels her circle of friends from one adventure to the next during what becomes a delightfully giddy summer of parties and houseguests.

All through the summer of her "house party"—for Betsy Ray and Bonnie Andrews have returned to Deep Valley as well, and as usual, the warm hospitality of the Sibleys attracts Carney's friends like a magnet—Carney is reassessing relationships and examining life. Like many a college student back home for the summer, she finds herself scrutinizing the little things that make her home uniquely *her* home: the way her father and brothers polish their shoes every Saturday night; the suspense around the table as her father's famous rarebit approaches readiness; the trunk of costumes in the attic that the young people raid for a masquerade—each article of clothing capturing some piece of Sibley family history. Carney cherishes these things and becomes aware of the love her parents pour into making their home a homey place.

The rigorous intellectual training she has received at Vassar prompts her to ponder the sort of traditions she wants to carry forward into her adult life. At times her present seems maddeningly full of unanswerable questions—Larry is coming for a visit! Will they click? What if they don't? And *what* is she to make of that happy-go-lucky Sam Hutchinson, who zooms around town unshaven in his Locomobile, recklessly lavishing generosity upon his friends and then, horror of horrors, telling shopkeepers to "put it on the book"? But Carney faces each question with frankness and interest, even in painful circumstances. It's that combination of honesty and enthusiasm that makes Carney one of Lovelace's most likable characters. She's a real girl, rapidly becoming a real woman: a woman with integrity and vision who doesn't look to others to solve her problems for her but instead faces them head-on, confident in her own ability to untangle muddled thinking.

Carney's high-school chum Winona Root—one of Betsy Ray's earliest friends-slash-rivals—is another of Lovelace's most vivid characters. From her first appearance in *Betsy and Tacy Go Downtown*, Winona, who is a composite of two of Lovelace's real-life friends, adds a dash of spice to every scene she inhabits. I suppose it's no accident that the word "dash" inserted itself into that sentence—Winona is always "dashing" somewhere with her eyes "flashing." The summer of Carney's house party, Winona hosts a gathering:

> . . . a jolly party. Winona's parties were just like Winona, full of careless gaiety. There were tables for cards but no one played much five hundred. They sang around the piano to Winona's dashing accompaniment. They played wild games, and raced up and down stairs and in and out of doors.
>
> Winona loved races, fights, and scuffles. She would be a teacher soon. She had learned how to assume an expression of gentle sweetness. But tonight her black eyes flashed and her white teeth gleamed. . . .

Dashing piano accompaniment! There it is again! I love this description of the nearly adult Winona. It gibes completely with Lovelace's depiction of the young girl who races Betsy to be the first kid in town to ride in Mr. Poppy's automobile, way back in *Betsy and Tacy Go Downtown*. It's especially fun to compare college student Winona's party to eight-year-old Winona's birthday party in the second book reprinted in these pages: *Winona's Pony Cart. Carney's House Party* was written first; *Winona's Pony Cart* takes us back in time to Winona's eighth birthday, when the thing she wants more than anything is her very own pony—just the thing for a girl who loves to dash around town, right?

It's not surprising that Winona begins the book in disgrace; a girl with that much dash is bound to get into scrapes.

In this case, it's because she has soaked her best dress trying to ride the bird bath like a horse. Her mother wishes she would be more sedate and dignified. On party day, Mrs. Root will come to find her own sense of composure challenged when she discovers her friendly, outgoing daughter has unexpectedly doubled the guest list. Later it is the dignity with which Winona accepts a fate she cannot control—her mother is dead-set against Winona having a pony—that causes her parents to reassess the situation. Likewise, Winona's openness and friendliness help her mother to look at people—such as the washerwoman's twin daughters and some Syrian children from the other side of the Big Hill—in a new way.

Indeed, if it is dignity and manners Mrs. Root wants to foster in her daughter, she could hardly do better than the example of the children from Little Syria. One of Lovelace's best themes is the slow unfolding of relationships between the German, Scandinavian, Irish, and New Englander residents of Deep Valley and the small community of Lebanese Americans over the hill—a subject she explores with great attention in what is arguably her finest book, *Emily of Deep Valley*. In *Winona's Pony Cart*, we get just a hint of these broadening perceptions; and just as Winona's mother gains a new understanding of her Syrian neighbors, Winona, too, gains a new perspective of a boy she would rather not have invited to her party, the seemingly odious Percy. Despite his aloofness and ruffled blouse, Percy proves to be quite courageous, keeping his head—and his seat—when a pony runs away with him.

Winona looked at Percy, thinking hard.

"Maybe," she thought, "if I were a boy, Mother would make me wear a ruffled blouse."

This subtle character growth is what Lovelace does best, and it is why her work endures. Winona—like Carney, like Betsy, like Joe, like Tony, like Tib, like Mr. and Mrs. Ray and Mr. and Mrs. Root and all the rest of our Deep Valley friends—is, to quote Betsy's commencement address, "essentially human." Betsy is referring there to the heroines of Shakespeare. I wish Lovelace had given us a peek at the rest of that address because I'd like to see how Betsy developed the thought. I suspect that what Betsy was getting at is that Shakespeare populated his plays with real, believable, imperfect, changeable people. They make mistakes. They puzzle things out. They struggle past their own weaknesses. They grow. As do the heroines of Lovelace, from eight-year-old Winona swallowing her tears and mustering gratitude for the presents she *did* get, to brokenhearted Betsy determinedly putting on a smile so as not to spoil Christmas Day for her family, to Carney searching her heart for her true feelings about Larry Humphreys.

I'm the mother of many daughters now—four of them, and two small sons—and as my girls grow to womanhood I hope they will become, to quote Dickens, the heroines of their own lives, facing life's challenges with Carney's integrity, Betsy's determination, and Winona's sense of fun.

They are reading my Betsy-Tacy and Deep Valley books to tatters, so I'd say we're off to a good start.

— MELISSA WILEY

Carney's House Party

For
BILL *and* TED

Contents

1

Sunset Hill

CARNEY WAS CLIMBING Sunset Hill.

Far below she could hear a group of her class-mates, like herself just released from examinations, singing as they strolled beside the brook.

"Where, oh where are the gay young Soph'mores,
Where, oh where are the gay young Soph'mores,
Where, oh where are the gay young Soph'mores,
Safe now in the Junior class."

Well, she had passed all her exams, she felt sure. But sophomores wouldn't be juniors, really, until fall. They were staying on for Class Day, seniors and sophomores being sister classes. Twenty-four of the prettiest sophomores, including Isobel, would carry the Daisy Chain. The rest had to pick the daisies, and there were awful rumors of a shortage. But then there were always such rumors, and always enough daisies in the end.

"They've gone out from their Soph'more Lit Oh,
They've gone out from their Soph'more Lit Oh . . ."

Carney began to hum it from force of habit, but she stopped because she didn't feel like humming. She had a problem to think out, which was the reason she was climbing Sunset Hill. She didn't like unsolved problems hanging over her, any more than she liked unpaid bills or unaccomplished duties. Whatever Carney Sibley had to do, she liked to do with efficiency and dispatch.

Sunset Hill was scattered on the lower reaches with small gnarled old apple trees and, of course, with evergreens. The spicy odor of evergreens was everywhere about the college. In the tall grass were red clover and white yarrow, buttercups and daisies like those the sophomores must gather next week.

Benches here and there invited one to stop and look at the brook, at the roofs of the college, at the flag on Main where Carney roomed with Isobel. But Carney wouldn't stop until she reached the top. There was a bench up there, with a view of rolling blue hills, to which she had brought all her problems during her two years at college.

She passed the ancient apple trees, which had been part of Matthew Vassar's orchard back in 1865. It was 1911 now, but the sophomores down by the brook were singing about him.

> "Oh, young Matthew Vassar was a boy of no
>   renown,
> He was born in merry England o'er the sea,
> He sailed across the ocean,
> In Poughkeepsie settled down,
> Where in course of time he built a brewery . . ."

And the brewery had made his fortune, Carney remembered. He had labored and prospered and when he came to dispose of his wealth it occurred to him that injustice had been done to woman's brains.

> "What a pity undeveloped they should be.
> So Matthew, Matthew Vassar
> Built a college then and there . . ."

The song died away, for Carney had left the sloping green meadow behind and was entering a growth of tall, dark evergreens. They were almost as tall as those down on the campus; the branches of the Norway spruces trailed on the ground like ladies' skirts. She passed the outdoor theatre, a green knoll with a semicircle of pines behind it on a lower slope.

How lovely Isobel had looked there, in her Greek robe and fillet, at the Founder's Day Pageant!

Carney reached the summit and her bench, made of wood and cement like all the Vassar benches, with V. C. carved on the side. The woodsy path went on, downward now, to a rendezvous with the brook in a green-gold glen. Sitting down in the aromatic shade, Carney looked off at the hills and felt at home. Hills also surrounded Deep Valley, the Minnesota town in which she had grown up.

She set herself at once to her problem.

"I believe I'll pretend it's a topic for Miss Salmon," she thought, a smile bringing a dimple into her left cheek.

Miss Salmon was her history professor and Carney admired her clear orderly thinking. Miss Salmon would analyze the problem like this . . .

Not having a notebook and pencil, Carney addressed a chipmunk, peeping out from under a blackberry bush.

"One. Why don't I want Isobel to visit me this summer?

"Two. Are my reasons valid or invalid?

"Three. Decision."

The chipmunk ran away, and no wonder, Carney thought. Put into words, her dilemma was astonishing. Isobel was not only beautiful, but charming. Fascinating, the girls always called her. And Carney liked her. She had been as flattered as she was surprised at Isobel's suggestion last spring that they room together. But in spite of living with her—happily, too—through the whole year, Carney didn't want her to come to Deep Valley.

She knew that Isobel wanted to come. Not that she had said so! She had subtly insinuated the idea—by looking eagerly at Carney's home pictures, by animated questions about the Deep Valley Crowd. Carney herself was direct to the point of bluntness, and she was always irritated by Isobel's circumlocutions.

"She's so *Eastern*," Carney thought resentfully, and was immediately aware that Miss Salmon would not approve of such a label. There were plenty of frank Easterners and devious Westerners, of course.

Carney tried to search out the cause of her inhospitality.

"I'm not jealous of her," she began.

This was true. Carney had never been jealous in her

life. Yet she had been, she admitted, a little startled when Isobel was chosen for the Daisy Chain and she herself left out. In Deep Valley she was considered outstandingly pretty. Not that it had ever mattered. She just took it for granted.

She was pretty now as she sat under the pine tree. She had a dainty figure, softly pomped dark hair, bright eyes, and a skin as fresh as apple blossoms.

Part of her charm lay in her immaculate neatness. Her middy blouse was snowily white, the red taffeta tie crisp and spotless. Part of it lay in her bubbling gaiety, quenched now by earnest introspection.

Yes, she thought, having Isobel preferred to her had come as a bit of a shock.

"Though I ought to be used to shocks by now, after two years."

She had come to Vassar wearing, she realized, a mantle of complacency. She was a Sibley of Deep Valley, Minnesota. But no one at Vassar had ever heard of the Sibleys or of Deep Valley either, and they didn't know much even about Minnesota. Some girls thought there were Indians running wild in the streets out there.

Moreover, they thought that all culture and refinement ended at the Hudson. They were too polite to say so, but their opinion was implied in their kindly curiosity. They were astonished at how well she played the piano. They were amazed that her clothes were so modish, and it meant nothing to them when Carney explained that she and her mother had bought them in Minneapolis. They confused Minneapolis with Indianapolis and both cities seemed equally remote.

"They haven't any *idea* how nice the Middle West is," she thought, with a sudden longing for it. She had returned to Minnesota last summer feeling that nothing she had seen in the East was half so beautiful as that rolling green country, with its generous farms, its groves and fertile pastures, a tree-fringed lake around every turn of the road.

Of course, she liked the East, too.

She had spent a week-end with Isobel in East Hampton, glimpsing unfamiliar luxury, seeing her first golf course, eating her first shore dinner. (She thought lobster far inferior to chicken.) She had loved the Atlantic Ocean, the great crashing breakers drawing their ruffles of foam in proud retreat across the sands.

She was fascinated, too, by what she had seen of New York. It was as though, in that great city, folding doors were pushed apart and she was reluctantly introduced to wonders—Maude Adams in *Chantecler,* the Metropolitan Opera, Tschaikovsky's Fifth Symphony.

Miss Chittenden, Vassar's piano teacher, had been impressed with Carney's talent and had taken her to play for Matthew Lang. Carney was still stung by what he had said to her. But meeting the famous pianist had been important. It was one of the experiences which had molded her.

She could almost feel herself being molded, a piece of wet clay, in the powerful hands of the East.

She loved Vassar. She was proud that in two years she had made a small place for herself—not so small either, for she was vice president of her class. And she warmed when she thought of the fun she had had with the girls—Sunday breakfasts in their rooms, bacon bats down by the brook, the secret preparations for dedicating their Class Tree this spring. How they had fooled the freshmen!

"Just the same," she said aloud, "I'd like to see a few boys."

At home she not only had three brothers, but boys were barging into the house all the time. One went riding, or walking, or picnicking with a boy as freely as with a girl.

At Vassar, for some mysterious reason, boys were put in a class with poison ivy. No young man was admitted unless he came laden down with references and credentials. And then he was entertained stiffly in the parlor in sight of everybody!

Dances were unbelievably stuffy, beginning at four in the afternoon. And whenever Carney went down the Hudson to attend a dance at West Point with her old friend Tom Slade, she had to take a chaperon and it cost twenty-five dollars.

"Twenty-five dollars just tossed away!" she thought. "Tom and I have never felt romantic about each other."

Carney had never felt romantic about any boy, except Larry Humphreys. He had been her beau through her first two years in high school. When she was fifteen he had moved to California and for four years now they had never missed a week in writing to each other. Somehow he had kept her from getting interested in other boys although she had always had more than her share of attention.

Her friend Betsy Ray was visiting in California. Carney had had a letter from her, which she almost knew by heart.

"I've done gone seen him! And he's most attractive. I don't think you'll be a bit disappointed in him, Carney. Maybe you'll be a little afraid of him. I was. He always seems to be laughing at me, and he has a sort of . . . touch me not, I'm already spoken for . . . air. Now who has spoken for him, Miss Caroline Sibley?"

Carney shook herself.

"You came here to think about Isobel and whether you should ask her to come out to Minnesota," she rebuked herself sternly.

She had written to her mother suggesting Isobel's visit, secretly hoping her mother would settle everything by saying it was out of the question. But an answer had come today, and to her dismay it contained a cheerful acquiescence.

"The Andrews are back from Paris as you have probably heard. They are living in St. Paul, and I've invited Bonnie for July. Why don't you have Isobel come at the same time? It would be a sort of house party."

It would be a house party all right, Carney thought. But how much nicer to have just Bonnie! Bonnie had been her dearest friend before she went off to Paris. And Paris would not have changed Bonnie, Carney knew. She would be just the same. It would be Isobel who would seem strange and exotic in Deep Valley.

Carney had a sudden recollection of her home—the large frame house, its gray-blue paint faded; the wide vine-covered porch with its rain-washed chairs; the trampled side lawn where her brothers were allowed to play ball; the old barn transformed into a garage.

In Deep Valley the Sibley house was . . . the Sibley house. It was not the most modern or elegant in town but certainly one of the most important. Her father was the banker. He was a pillar of the Presbyterian church. His people and her mother's, too, had come from fine eastern families, and had helped to lay the foundations of society in the Minnesota town.

But they didn't have a tennis court or swimming pool. There wasn't any wicker or cretonne on the porch. And there was just Olga, the hired girl, in the kitchen, no white-capped maids such as she had seen at Isobel's.

It was a spacious comfortable home, with good furniture, her piano and her father's books. Over all the airy rooms it bore the print of her mother's exquisite housekeeping. But her father and brothers pressed their own suits and shined their own shoes on Sunday morning, and at the breakfast table they discussed the Sunday School lesson. Carney couldn't picture Isobel there; she just couldn't picture it!

"Good gracious!" she thought. "Am I getting ashamed of my home?"

Frowning, she brought herself back to Miss Salmon and the questions.

"I don't want Isobel to come because she's Eastern and I'm tired of the East. I don't want her to come because she's so grand. I don't want her to come because I want to be alone with Bonnie. I'm a selfish pig. She shall come."

With which announcement Carney jumped up and her dimple flashed. As always, her smile changed her look from demure primness to mischief. It showed white, slightly irregular teeth that folded in front into a piquant peak. It was irrepressibly mirthful.

Shaking out her white skirts, she started back down the hill.

As she came out of the pine woods into Matthew Vassar's orchard, she heard the long whistle of the west-bound train. Her thoughts always followed it for at least a fleeting moment half across the continent and home. Next week she would be on it. And in July Isobel would be on it, too.

The sun was getting low now. Down on the campus girls in middy blouses and skirts, girls in ankle-length cotton dresses, girls in gym suits modestly concealed by skirts and coats, were hurrying along the paths to their rooms in the various buildings.

"Where, oh where are the gay young Soph'mores,
Where, oh where are the gay young Soph'mores . . ."

Carney hummed skipping down the hill, forgetting to assume the dignity of one who was "Safe now in the Junior Class."

2
Isobel's Man

CROSSING THE PINE WALK which encircled the campus with a dim, pungently scented, green-roofed lane, Carney ran into her friend Sue. She almost literally ran into her, for Sue was advancing at a breakneck pace, her hair flying, her wide-set blue eyes big with excitement.

"Carney! I've been looking for you everywhere."

"Why? What's the matter?"

"You never could guess! Something absolutely thrilling!" She grasped Carney's arm. "Isobel," she announced dramatically, "is entertaining a man!"

"Jiminy! Who is he?"

"I haven't any idea. But they're down in the parlors. He's terribly handsome, sitting with his arms folded, looking scared. Isobel looks as cool as ice cream. She's talking and laughing away."

"You've been peeking?"

"Of course. Everybody has."

Carney's chuckle was a small explosion of mirth. "Come with me?" she asked.

"Sure. There are Win and Winkie," Sue added. "Let's get them to go, too."

Sue and Carney ran toward The Circle, an area quite properly round, rimmed first by pines and then by a border of flowers. The 1897 Class Tree spread its broad boughs in the center. Here croquet, tennis, hockey and basketball were played. There was a cinder path for track. At the Gate House, where equipment was stored, Win and Winkie were hooking skirts over their gym suits with that propriety decreed by Vassar's supreme authority.

They were tennis stars, roommates and great friends. Win was tall, dark and vivacious; Winkie was short, with thick braids of light hair bound about her head, and deceptively grave eyes.

"Win! Winkie! What do you think?" Carney and Sue cried together.

"I've stopped thinking. Exams are over," Winkie said.

"President Taylor has eloped with the Lady Principal?" offered Win.

"Don't be silly. This is important," said Carney, but she paused to let Sue deliver her own scoop.

"Isobel is entertaining a man!"

Win received the news with due excitement, but Winkie looked disappointed.

"What of it?" she asked, shouldering her tennis racket.

"We're going to peek. Want to come?"

"Not me. I want a bath before dinner."

"I'll go," said Win joyfully. "But oughtn't we to get Peg? She'll never forgive us if we don't."

They hurried into the back door of Main and into the elevator. Peg lived in a single alley on the fourth floor. There was a sign on her door.

"Engaged! Keep out! This means you!"

"Just ignore it," advised Win. "She's packing, but what's that compared to a visiting man?"

A barrage of knocks brought a reluctant turn of the knob, and the three girls shouted: "Isobel's entertaining a man! . . . They're down in the parlors . . . We're going to peek. Want to come along?"

"Of course," said Peg, annoyance giving place to delighted interest. She was a large, gentle girl with curly hair. "Just wait till I wash my hands," she added.

"Peg would wash her hands if she were running to a fire," said Carney.

"So would you," teased Sue.

"But a man! I haven't seen a man who wasn't faculty for weeks and months."

"Neither have I," said Win. "Not since I followed Peg's father all over the campus to smell his cigar."

"I almost swoon," said Sue, "when Carney puts on her father's dress suit for dancing in J."

"You're all nutty," said Winkie. "So long."

But Peg was ready now. Four strong again, they rushed back to the elevator.

Down on the second floor, they strolled with elaborate carelessness along the wide hall which ran from the dining room to the entrance stairs of Main. There were suites of connecting parlors on either side.

"They're sitting on the right-hand side," Sue whispered, and the girls turned their eyes to the right.

Isobel's guest sat in a horsehair chair; Isobel was opposite on a sofa. He was indeed a handsome young man, wearing a stiff high collar. But he had relaxed now to the point of unfolding his arms. In fact he was leaning forward looking at Isobel.

She had already dressed for dinner in a soft pale silk and was wearing her coral necklace and bracelets, the ones that came from Florence. Her golden brown hair was, as usual, slightly disordered, breaking at every twist into airy curls. She didn't so much as glance at the girls, but gazed at the young man with adoring interest. Now and then her low, lazy laugh floated out.

The girls traversed the hall once, twice, chatting with false vivacity and glancing furtively into the parlor.

"We'd better go now. She'll be mad," Carney whispered.

"He'll be leaving in a minute anyway; it's almost time for dinner."

"And we have to dress."

Reluctantly the four withdrew. But Isobel and her guest were not left unchaperoned for long. The elevator disgorged a group of freshmen.

"Is it true that Isobel Porteous is entertaining a man? Which parlor?" they asked.

Leaving Peg at her fourth-floor room, Carney, Sue, and Win proceeded along the corridor which was filled with the trunks, suitcases, and hatbags of departing students. It was enclosed by glass and looked out on the campus. Such corridors ran across the front of Main on every floor. Matthew Vassar had provided them so that his young ladies might take their constitutionals even in bad weather. A pioneer in many ways, he had believed that exercise was beneficial to young females. Unfortunately each corridor deprived a row of bedrooms of outside air. It was one of the reasons Carney liked rooming in North Tower.

They reached this retreat by a winding stair, which ascended all the way from the bottom floor and emerged into a small central hall with a skylight above it and doors all around. Carney and Isobel lived in the southwest corner room, Win and Winkie opposite, Sue alongside. These girls had been friends since they had met at supper on the first night of college, freshman year. Peg, too, was one of the group but she liked the comfort of the sitting room attached to the bedrooms in her alley.

The room Carney shared with Isobel was large, with two beds. It was furnished in golden oak which Carney thought very pretty, but Isobel had brought in her own mission oak desk and easy chair. There was a couch full of pillows, making a nest for Carney's doll. Suzanne, her beloved baby since childhood, was now the mascot of North Tower.

There was a tea set with a spirit lamp. A built-in cupboard held Whitman's Instantaneous Cocoa, sugar, crackers, jelly, and other supplies. On the wall were the banners of many colleges—Leland Stanford, a gift from Larry; West Point, representing Tom; Yale, from one of Isobel's flames. There were pictures by Burne-Jones and Maxfield Parrish, framed photographs of friends. Larry's photograph had the place of honor on Carney's desk.

The two windows were high and opened in. Carney crossed to one now and looked out, into the tree-tops and the rooftops of old Main. She wasn't romantic, like her friend Betsy Ray, but she liked living in Main.

It was the first and oldest building; originally it had housed the entire college. (Originally, she had heard, each room had been provided with just two hooks for dresses. When someone protested, old Matthew Vassar had said, "Why, that's enough. One hook for her everyday dress, and one hook for her best dress.")

It was a long brick building four stories high with groups of towers at either end. Isobel, who had been everywhere, said that it resembled the Tuileries. Above the main entrance, which looked down a tree-lined avenue to the Old Lodge Gate, was part of the original sign, "Vassar ——— College." That blank had once held the word "Female."

> *"An institution once there was*
> *Of learning and of knowledge,*

Which had upon its high brick front,
A 'Vassar Female College'...."

But the "Female" had blown off one time in a windstorm.

"Let's have a spread tonight," Winkie called through the open door.

"Fine!" shouted Carney, pulling off her middy. "We can pump Isobel about her man."

"What are you wearing?" cried Win. "She may introduce us."

"A clean duck skirt and waist. I'll be a vision in white."

"I'm going to wear my smocked blue silk," Sue chimed in. "And my lavaliere with the pearl drop. Do you think he would be impressed by pearls?"

"You idiots!" came Winkie's voice.

"Maybe he's been smoking cigars and Win can get a whiff of tobacco."

This brought gratifying shrieks of laughter and Carney, stripped to her petticoat and corset cover, went happily into the attic to wash. The tower bathroom was housed out under the eaves.

She was glad she had decided to invite Isobel to Minnesota. Diving into the white waist and skirt, which with her dark hair and rosy cheeks were becoming enough to please even Isobel's man, she planned to tell her at dinner.

But Isobel didn't sit at her own table that night.

After grace was said, the big dining room broke into uproar. It was even more noisy than usual, due, perhaps, to the enlivening nearness of vacation. The Vice-president of the Students' Association, whose duty it was to keep order, kept beating on a bell, but in spite of that shrill warning there was a clamor of voices.

There were ten girls at a table. The same groups ate together all year. But tonight there was an empty place at the table where the North Tower girls and Peg were seated.

"She's certainly bidding him a fond farewell," said Carney, serving the roast beef. The girls took turns serving, changing each week. Carney sat at the head of the table tonight.

"She's just being mean. She knows we're dying by inches," said Win, filling her glass from the tall pitcher of milk.

"Maybe she's so shattered by his departure that she can't eat," said Sue.

"Not Isobel . . ." but Carney broke off, for at that moment Isobel swept into the dining room with the handsome young man behind her. Not even glancing at her friends, she crossed to the table of the Lady Principal.

"Well, did you ever!" cried Sue.

"How did she talk Mrs. K into *that*?"

"I had a boy come to see me, he was a friend of my brother's that I'd known all my life, and we could only . . ." but no one was listening. The visit of Sue's brother's friend, a momentous event in its day, was entirely eclipsed.

"I wonder if she'll bring him to Chapel."

"Oh, please! Please! She'd introduce us!"

"What's for dessert?" asked Winkie. "Isn't this peanuts-and-maple-sugar night?" Peanuts-and-maple-sugar was an endowed dessert, the gift of some peanuts-and-maple-sugar loving alumna.

But no one answered. No one else cared whether it was peanuts-and-maple-sugar night, or ice cream night, or Tombstone pudding night. Everyone was watching Isobel conversing elegantly with Mrs. K, the Lady Principal, and assorted faculty members, and her guest.

"That Isobel can wangle anything!" said Sue, and Carney thought with amusement of the Minnesota visit. Well, Isobel hadn't wangled it exactly. Carney had made her own decision.

After dinner it was time to sing. Catching up scarfs or the light Liberty capes which were the fad that year, the students streamed out to the steps of Strong and Rockefeller Halls and sang until time for Chapel.

Step singing was a highly organized activity. Each class had song practise regularly. The juniors sang on the steps of Strong, with the freshmen down on the lawn facing them. The seniors and sophomores went to Rockefeller where the millstone from Matthew Vassar's mill served as a rostrum.

Carney loved these nightly sings. She had grown up with a singing crowd in Deep Valley. And the campus was beautiful at this twilight hour, with the lamplighter making his rounds.

The sky was still full of tinted clouds. The air smelled of roses and pines, and of those Norway spruces which stood like stately ladies with their trailing skirts about them. When the singing stopped for a moment, you could hear the thrushes calling to one another.

But the thrushes didn't have much chance when the Vassarites really got to going.

> *"The maidens fair could not enjoy,*
> *Their bread and milk and porridge,*
> *For graven on the forks and spoons*
> *Was Vassar Female College*
> *A strong east wind at last came by . . ."*

Carney liked that one. It was such a satisfaction when "Female" blew off the sign. And she liked the one about Matthew Vassar's brewery, and the one about Maria Mitchell, which went to the stirring tune of "The Battle Hymn of the Republic."

> *"We're singing for the glory of Maria Mitchell's*
> *name.*
> *She lived at Vassar College and you all do know*
> *the same—*
> *She once did spy a comet and she thus was*
> *known to fame . . ."*

Singing lustily, marching eight abreast, their song leaders in front, the girls crossed the lawn to the Chapel. They threw their wraps down at the entrance in a many-colored heap and filed inside.

Carney didn't mind the fact that Chapel was compulsory and held every night. Not that she was especially religious. But she liked to sit relaxed in the dim light beneath the gilded angels and orient herself for the coming day.

But tonight neither Carney nor anyone else was thinking of much but Isobel's guest.

He and Isobel sat in the special guest pew, near the front at the right, and everyone watched him. A man guest at Chapel was always the cynosure of eyes, and this one was so extremely handsome.

"He's like a Gibson man," Carney whispered to Win.

"She'll certainly introduce us."

"She'd better! The pill!"

"He'll be going away. There couldn't be a man on the campus after dark."

And the Guest did indeed take leave of Isobel outside the Chapel door. But although her Tower-mates hung about, within easy beckoning distance, she didn't introduce them.

"Stung!" said Carney as he lifted his hat and strode down the path to the Lodge Gate where a bobtailed trolley car bound for Poughkeepsie waited.

The girls fell upon Isobel.

"Who is he? Why didn't you introduce us? . . . How did you ever talk Mrs. K into letting him stay for dinner?"

"I have my ways," said Isobel inscrutably. "And as for introducing you . . . I wouldn't do it after the way you behaved this afternoon . . . parading up and down the hall."

"*You* paraded when my brother's friend came!" cried Sue indignantly.

"You even paraded when my father came," said Peg.

"You *would* have paraded if Tom Slade had come up from West Point the way he almost *did* come, and I'm going to have him come next year, and I won't introduce you even if you give me all your peanuts-and-maple-sugar," cried Carney.

"Are we having a spread tonight or aren't we?" interrupted Winkie, looking bored.

"A spread? How divine!" Isobel exclaimed. "Is it going to be in our room? Carney, I hope you tidied up."

"Well, if the room was tidied up, I tidied it," said Carney. "Tell us, now, who was he? I'll bet he was your brother."

"Brother! Brother indeed!" scoffed Isobel, her low laugh rippling as she pulled her lilac-tinted Liberty cape from among the capes piled on the Chapel steps.

3
The Dress Suit and Suzanne

CARNEY PUT ON HER father's dress suit for the spread.

"It was a stroke of genius bringing this to Vassar when Dad bought his new one," she remarked as she squinted into a mirror, creating an upturned moustache with a piece of burnt cork.

"The dress suit and Suzanne," said Isobel, "were your two big contributions to the Tower."

"I'm Tower mouse-catcher, too, don't forget. You effete Easterners! Afraid to take a mouse out of a trap! How do I look?" Carney asked, turning about with a swagger.

"Ravishing!"

"That's good. I'm your man, you know. Or didn't you? Girls!" she shouted, as the bunch began to file in, Winkie lugging a chafing dish. "I'm Isobel's Gibson man."

"What's your name?"

"Montmorency Abernethy." Carney's mirthful chuckle exploded.

The girls rushed up to pump her hand.

"We're *so* pleased to meet you."

"At last!"

"We're Isobel's dearest friends; she just forgot temporarily."

"Don't blame her for not introducing us, Mr. Abernethy. She's a little . . . the Green-eyed Monster, you know."

"Do we have any cheese?" Isobel asked Winkie, trying to act lofty.

"I bought some downstairs this morning." There was a grocery store in the basement of Main where supplies for spreads and Sunday morning breakfasts could be purchased.

Peg arrived with a plate of fudge which she had

made that afternoon behind her "Engaged" sign. She, too, was introduced to Mr. Abernethy, who looked at her long and ardently.

"Why haven't we met before?" he asked.

"Why, indeed?" replied Peg, rolling her eyes toward Isobel.

"Yes, why? . . . Why? . . . Why?" There was a chorus of whys.

"I'm ignoring you. I don't hear a word you say," Isobel called out.

Winkie took charge of the rarebit and Peg toasted crackers over the gas light.

"Who's going to make the cocoa?" she called.

"Not me," said Win, who was tuning her ukulele.

"Not me," said Isobel, who was rocking Suzanne.

"I'll make it," said Carney. "Where are the tea spoons?"

But the tea spoons had been packed.

"Never mind. I'll use a shoe horn. See how ingenious I am, my love," she called to Isobel. Turning her head, she dropped the shoe horn, stared at Isobel wildly and clapped her hand to her forehead.

"Ah me! I forgive you everything when I see you with that child in your arms . . ."

Isobel burst out laughing. "I give in, I give in," she said. The girls swooped into a circle on the floor about her. "His name is Howard Sedgwick. What else do you want to know?"

"Is he in love with you?"

"I hope so. He hasn't told me."

"Are you in love with him?"

"Um-m-m!"

"We are," replied Win, Sue, Peg and Carney. And even Winkie condescended to ask, "What's his college?"

"Harvard."

"Harvard!" There were screams of delight but it didn't matter. As a rule, after ten o'clock, it was necessary to be quiet. Seven-thirty to nine-thirty were study hours; from nine-thirty to ten noise was unrestrained; but after ten o'clock there was not supposed to be a sound except from the old watchman patrolling the halls.

It was different tonight with the last examination ended. Parties were going on all up and down the corridors. In North Tower after Isobel's revelation Carney and Sue did the Cubanola Glide. Sue, putting a feather duster on her head, improvised a scene from *Chantecler*. With Win strumming her ukulele, everyone sang:

> "Come on and hear,
> Come on and hear,
> Alexander's Ragtime Band . . ."

They switched from that to "Alma Mater," sung in parts. The bedlam was so great that not until the girls had left did Carney have a chance to tell Isobel about her mother's letter.

Characteristically, she blurted out her news. Carney was never able to be casual.

"I wrote my mother about your coming out to Minnesota. I had a letter today. She says it's all right."

Carney saw a flush cross Isobel's face.

She wondered, as she had wondered many times, just why Isobel wanted so much to come. Carney knew from her short visit there that East Hampton was very gay. There were plenty of men, and few of the restrictions which prevailed at Vassar.

To be sure, Isobel had no brothers or sisters and she wasn't particularly close to her parents, who didn't even seem particularly close to each other. Perhaps . . . though it didn't seem likely . . . Isobel was attracted by the home pictures clustered about Carney's bureau, by the frequent letters from her father, mother, and brothers which she often read aloud.

Carney had a sudden repentant realization that she might have framed her invitation more graciously.

"I think we'll have lots of fun," she said to make amends. "Bonnie is back from Paris, you know, and she's going to be there. Mother says it will be a sort of house party."

"What else does she say?" asked Isobel eagerly.

"I'll read you her letter," Carney offered.

Isobel reached for a dressing sacque and stretched out on the bed, and Carney thought, as she had often thought before, how beautiful Isobel was. She was a fine roommate, companionable, easy-going and obliging. She was reasonably neat, didn't borrow too much, and never lost her temper. But best of all, she was lovely to look at, morning, noon, or night.

Her loosened hair was a rich golden brown and fell into ringlets, large and small. Her curling lashes were the same tint as her hair, her skin was flawless, her eyes darkly blue. Her lips were mobile and were often curved in a faintly mysterious smile. But she wasn't smiling now. She was listening intently, and Carney was glad that her mother sounded so sincerely cordial.

Mrs. Sibley mentioned various girls whom Isobel would enjoy.

"I imagine," she wrote, "that Isobel feels she almost knows your Crowd. And now," she continued, "I must tell you about the Hutchinsons."

"Who are the Hutchinsons?" Isobel inquired.

"Listen, my child, and you shall hear," said Carney, returning to the letter.

"I'm sure," her mother wrote, "you've heard of the Hutchinsons of New Town. He is the big milling man. (Railroad and lumber interests, too, your father says.) They have bought the old Dwyer place out at Murmuring Lake. You remember that big white affair with two acres of water-front land. They have been remodeling and putting in gardens. It's quite the sensation of the county.

"They say that Bradstreet has decorated it. They say, too, that the Hutchinsons give very fashionable parties to which the men wear evening clothes and the ladies, low-cut ball gowns.

"Lots of 'they says,' but you can imagine how Deep Valley is talking. The son of the house drives about in a big Locomobile."

"The son of the house? The son of the house?" Isobel interrupted.

"Aha!" said Carney. "Do I see a gleam in your eye? I seem to remember that those Hutchinsons have a son, not too ancient. We'll never meet him, though. I don't run with that set."

"Oh, dear!"

"Never mind," said Carney. "The boys in our Crowd are very cute. Three or four of them have been to the U and Tom will be home from West Point."

"I'll manage," Isobel said. "I'm awfully glad to come, Carney. You're kind to have me." Something in her tone made Carney think Isobel was aware that she had had misgivings.

"That's all right. Glad to have you," said Carney, jumping up. She began to sort and stack the dishes which had been used at the spread. Carney would never go to bed after a party without washing the dishes. Isobel thought it was foolish and long ago had made her position clear. She didn't mind washing the dishes if Carney would leave them until morning, but Carney refused.

"My New England ancestors would haunt me," she had said. "And I don't mind doing it. I sort of like it."

So Isobel went to bed, and Carney filled a small pan with soapy water in the bathroom. She carefully washed the china, rinsed it and wiped it, and put the little tea table in its usual immaculate order.

Ready for bed herself, in a long-sleeved cotton night gown, her dark hair in two smooth pigtails, she went to turn out the green-shaded Welsbach lamp. But she paused, as she usually did, to look at Larry's picture.

Larry wasn't handsome in the Gibson-man style of Howard Sedgwick, but he was attractive. He had thick hair and a crooked, somewhat quizzical smile. Betsy Ray had said he always seemed to be laughing at you, but Carney didn't think she would mind his laughing at her.

It didn't seem four years since he had gone away,

their letters had kept them so close. And he had sent her so many things, gifts and souvenirs, which had brought California to her room.

In the closet was his crimson football sweater with the big S which she adored wearing for mystified Vassarites. In her jewel case was his last Christmas gift, a pendant made from an abalone shell. She wore it sometimes just to give herself confidence, that quality which she had had without knowing it at home and which, in the East, had been so hard to hold.

"I'll bet he's a lot nicer than Isobel's Howard Sedgwick," she thought, turning out the light.

The next day juniors and freshman departed, vacating their rooms for alumnae, and leaving just the sister class behind to companion the graduates.

Class Day began to occupy all energies. That Daisy Chain! Would there be daisies enough? Would the weather be rainy, or poisonously hot, or reasonably cool for picking them?

On the great day the sophomores were up at dawn, wearing middies, old skirts, and straw hats. They piled into wagons and went off to distant fields seeking daisies, and more daisies.

Returning with their snowy loads, they went to the gym. They put the daisies into tubs of water and started bunching them. Men from Saltford's, the Poughkeepsie florist, came out to help twine the chain.

When it was finished it was thick and white and luscious. The sophomores were very tired as they bathed and dressed. But when the Chain was forming, out on the lawn behind Main, their pride and pleasure banished fatigue.

The twenty-four, selected for their pulchritude, were dressed in long white gowns. They were lined up in a double row, and Saltford's men were looping the chain from shoulder to shoulder. The shoulders were padded with tiny pillows, for the daisy chain was heavy.

The girls had been carefully graded for height so that each pair matched. It was said that some pretty girl of average height might fail to be chosen because an exceptionally tall or an especially small outstanding beauty had to have a partner. There were too many pretty girls of average height.

"If you'd been either tall or short you'd have been on the Chain," Sue whispered to Carney.

"I'm not missed," Carney replied. "Isobel represents the Tower like a million."

She did. When the procession started across the lawn, none of the twenty-four carried the flowery burden with more dignity and grace. The dresses of the beauties trailed on the ground. The sun shone with June warmth, bringing out the smell of the pines and of the roses in the arms of the seniors. The seniors followed, two by two, until the chain opened out and they walked between ropes of daisies to a temporary grandstand under their Class Tree.

"How old is the Daisy Chain tradition?" Carney whispered to Peg.

"No one knows exactly. The first mention in the records is 1890, I believe."

"I hope they will still have it when my daughter comes to college," Carney said.

The next day, leaving the campus to the graduates, parents, alumnae, and the impending Commencement, the sophomores also departed.

Everyone looked strange and dressed up in traveling clothes. Girls, who all year had worn ribbons about their heads, were magnificent in halos. Winkie looked uncomfortable in a basket-shaped hat. They all wore large hats and fluffy, pleated jabots or flat bows at their necks, and suits with long jackets and almost trailing skirts. Lined satin boas were tossed over really fashionable shoulders.

Winkie shook Carney's hand. "Remember you represent Vassar on every occasion."

"Yes, Mrs. K," Carney replied.

"Be sure to write," said Sue, Win, and Peg.

"See you in July," said Isobel, kissing her.

They left ahead of Carney, for trains to New England, New York, and Long Island left earlier than that train for the West with whose haunting whistle Carney was so familiar.

After they were gone she finished packing. There wasn't much left to do, for Carney was always forehanded, but she put Larry's picture in her suitcase. That was always the last article packed and the first unpacked.

Picking up Suzanne she went out to the drowsy campus.

She visited her Class Tree . . . everyone said goodby to that . . . and looked in at the music building where she had had those wonderful lessons from Miss Chittenden. It had originally been a riding academy, and the students practised at pianos in old horse stalls.

"I'll be glad to get back to my stall," Carney thought. In spite of Mr. Lang she loved her piano.

She wished she could go down to the brook and up Sunset Hill but she didn't have time. She had to take her doll over to Professor Bracq's.

Jean Charlemagne Bracq, with his moustache and pointed gray beard, was a distinguished figure on the campus. He was an author and head of the French department. Nevertheless Suzanne always spent the summer in a bureau drawer in his bedroom.

His wife had taught Carney's mother back in Vermont, and the Bracqs had given a dinner party for

Carney as soon as she reached Vassar. As guest of honor she had been served first and she had been mystified by certain plates and forks. Being Carney she had spontaneously laughed. They had all become great friends.

"Now if I should be invited to one of the Hutchinsons' grand parties I'd know just how to act," she thought, dimpling.

Her thoughts were pushing ahead to home, for this afternoon, when the west-bound train whistled, she would be aboard it. She would be rushing off through New York State, eating in the dining car, tucked into a sleeper behind waving green curtains, looking out the window at the flying lighted towns. Tomorrow she would wake to her own midwestern country, and change at Chicago to the train which would carry her home.

Cradling Suzanne, she hurried across the campus to the Bracqs.

4
Deep Valley

DURING THE LONG TRIP Carney began to think about her reunion with Bonnie.

Bonnie had left Deep Valley the same spring the Humphreys had, and parting from her had been a wrench comparable to the parting from Larry. Her father was the Presbyterian minister, and the parsonage had been just across the street from the Sibley home.

For years the two little girls had played together and had gone to Sunday School together. Later they had belonged to the same high school crowd. Once, Carney remembered, they had had their best dresses made alike.

Like Larry, Bonnie had been a faithful correspondent. The friendship had not shriveled, as such friendships sometimes do into a mere routine of Christmas and birthday greetings. The thought of seeing Bonnie added to the satisfaction which filled her when she woke, after a second night in the train, to find herself nearing the final great landmark.

Carney always felt a lift of the heart when she crossed the Mississippi River. On the other side was Minnesota, home. The river was wide and full of islands where the train rumbled over the bridge. Carney looked out at the heaving watery expanse, the towering bluffs.

"They're more beautiful than the Palisades of the Hudson," she thought loyally.

The train struck off across southern Minnesota and the rugged hills melted into that undulating prairie she knew so well. Little lakes flashed past, and leaf-embowered rivers, and broad farms. The names of the towns grew familiar, and Carney stood up and put on her hat. She collected her purse and gloves and although they were still two towns away she waited in the aisle.

"Deep Valley!" the brakeman called at last and mounting excitement almost choked her. The porter brushed her. He carried out her bags. She was there.

She expected her family to be waiting for her, and they were: her tall, handsome father with his smiling eyes and trim, close-clipped moustache; her erect, dainty mother; her three brothers, Hunter, Gerald, and Bobbie.

Carney was impressed by how Hunter had grown up. He had passed some invisible sign post and entered her world. The eighteen months' difference in their ages which had been so important in the past was important no longer. Now, although he was only just entering his senior year in high school, even a college girl would look at him with interest. He was handsome in the same tall, smiling-eyed way his father was, but he looked less inflexible.

Jerry, the middle one, hadn't changed. He hadn't grown any taller. He still wore knickers, although he was a junior in high school now. A bookworm, he was absentminded and dreamy. He grinned at her shyly.

Bobbie, the nine-year-old youngest, would one day look like Hunter. But his eyes had a sparkle of mischief peculiarly his own. He pushed out of the crowd of relatives crying, "Hi! Sis! Hi! Will you buy some bluing? It's swell bluing and if I can sell enough I can win a baseball suit."

"Bobbie!" his father said. "Sister hasn't had time yet to greet her grandmothers."

Carney greeted both grandmothers, the white-haired saintly Sibley grandmother, and Grandmother Hunter who had a strong, plain, humorous face. She and Grandfather Hunter came from Vermont. They had followed their only daughter out to Minnesota.

Carney greeted uncles and aunts from both sides of the family, cousins and second cousins. Some of them she loved and some she didn't, but they were all part of her life. At last, she and her father, mother, and brothers piled into the family Maxwell.

Carney looked about eagerly during the drive home. Front Street, where the stores and hotels were, flanked the river. Residential streets with wide shady lawns ran parallel to it up the eastern hills.

At last they reached the Sibley home on Broad Street, and the big gray-blue house, with its bay windows and tower and the porch hung thickly with vines, looked just as she had treasured it in her heart all year.

"It looks natural," said Carney, who never overstated.

She went to the kitchen to greet Olga, the Swedish hired girl. Then her father and mother and the boys all said at once, proudly, "Don't you want to see the sleeping porch?"

Sleeping porches were new and very popular, and the male Sibleys had built this one themselves. You entered it from a window in the closet of the boys' room, and it darkened the bathroom deplorably, but it would hold two double beds and a single one. Curtains were hung between them. It was screened, and looked out into treetops.

"We thought your house-party guests might like to sleep out here," Mrs. Sibley said.

"Fine," Carney answered, her dimple flickering at the thought of Isobel climbing through the closet window.

A gang of small boys was waiting for Bobbie out on the spacious side lawn. He left her murmuring, "Don't forget what I said about that bluing, Sis. Ladies all use bluing." Jerry found a book and disappeared. But Hunter lingered a moment as though he were as delighted as she was to find that they had suddenly "grown together."

"I think we're going to have a lot of fun this summer, Sis," he remarked, before he went out to tinker with the auto. The Maxwell could always do with any amount of tinkering.

Carney went into her own room where Hunter had already left her bags. It looked just the same— or would as soon as she got Larry's picture out. The curtains and bedspread had been laundered and the windows freshly washed for her home-coming.

The furniture was of heavy bird's-eye maple—a high-backed bed, a bureau, a dressing table with a nest of drawers beside the mirror, a slender desk, a rocker and straight chair. Photographs of relatives adorned the walls which were papered with yellow poppies.

She took off her suit and put on a faded blue dress she found in her closet. It was a pleasure to wear something she had not had at school. She went slowly and happily down the curving stairs.

Front parlor, back parlor, library opened one into another by archways. They were lighted by broad windows and beyond lay the green expanse of lawn. Smilingly, Carney touched the family treasures in the what-not which she and Hunter had secretly named the "what-in-ell." She paused at her piano and ran her fingers over the keys. It had been, she noticed with pleasure, newly tuned.

Darting into the pantry, she found the doughnut jar. It ought to be full of freshly baked doughnuts. It was! She helped herself and returned through the back parlor to the library.

This was the heart of the house. It had not only the fireplace and Grandfather Sibley's portrait and a curving window seat, but Mr. Sibley's chair, a tremendous black, leather-covered arm chair, deep and soft with pillowy arms. It swung on a patent rocker and could be luxuriously tilted.

All the members of the family loved this chair. Jerry loved to read in it, his legs twisted beneath him. He vacated it promptly, of course, when the rightful owner came in. Mr. Sibley was definitely head of the house, but he was a benevolent disciplinarian. Carney remembered studying her high school Latin on her father's lap in this chair.

"No Dad and leather chair at college," she thought, sinking into the soft refuge. She leaned back, crossing her feet on the footstool.

Her mother came in presently and sat down near by. A New Englander, with all a New Englander's reserve, she did not put into words her pleasure at having her daughter at home. But it shone in her eyes.

Like Carney, she had sparkling dark eyes, and her small, heart-shaped face was framed in abundant dark curly hair. She had once been the prettiest girl in Chester, Vermont.

She had come west to visit an uncle, and Hunter Sibley, college-bred son of a wealthy pioneer family, would not let her go home without a large three diamond ring. She had accepted the ring, but she had never worn it in Chester. It was too ostentatious, she had told Carney, for that modest town. After her marriage, the beautiful ring had seldom left her finger. She was a devoted wife.

As a girl she had been gently artistic, embroidering, painting lilies of the valley and violets on glass. As a young wife she had painted china with a teacher three mornings a week. But after her children came she had channeled her talent into her housekeeping. She was happy that her daughter also valued domestic skills.

"It will be nice to see Bonnie," she said now.

"Won't it!" Carney replied.

"When is Isobel coming?"

"Right after the Fourth. Who's in town of the old Crowd?"

"Not very many," Mrs. Sibley answered. "The Mullers have gone to Milwaukee and the Biscays to the lake. Your Crowd isn't the same since the Rays and the Kellys went away."

Both families had moved to Minneapolis, a happy coincidence since Betsy Ray and Tacy Kelly were inseparable friends. But Betsy had gone farther. During her freshman year at the University she had had an appendicitis operation. About that time her step-grandfather had died in California and Betsy had gone to San Diego to stay with her grandmother.

"She's having a wonderful time," Carney remarked. "She's seen the Humphreys boys."

"Oh . . . has she?" Carney saw her mother's lashes flutter. Her mother wasn't, she knew, entirely easy in her mind about the faithful correspondence between Carney and Larry.

"Does she . . . enjoy them?" Mrs. Sibley asked.

"Yes. A lot. What boys are in town?" Carney changed the subject.

"Lloyd Harrington," answered her mother. "And Dennie, I believe. And Cab."

"Hunter can beau me around," said Carney. "Isn't he the handsomest thing?"

Mrs. Sibley's eyes sparkled more than ever. "He's not bad looking," she admitted.

She returned to the kitchen presently. There would be an extra good dinner, Carney thought contentedly, because she had come home. Boiled custard, probably. That was her favorite dessert. Again she stretched out luxuriously.

The soft June air came in through the open window along with the smell of freshly cut grass and the sound of Bobbie's gang at play. She was back in Deep Valley. She was safe-back-home in Deep Valley. Relaxed and peaceful, she closed her eyes.

Strange light touches on her arm, an eerie scamper, brought her suddenly awake. Tingling, she jumped to her feet and shrieked.

"What's the matter?" asked her mother, running in. Hunter came, too, and Jerry, with a book. Bobbie and his gang pressed against the screens.

Tiny white objects were running in all directions.

"Why, they're mice!" Carney stammered.

"They're my white mice, Sis," said Bobbie in an injured tone. "They won't hurt you."

"I know that," she returned defensively. "I was Tower mouse-catcher at Vassar."

Bobbie stared admiringly. "Were you? What's that?"

"I set the traps and took the mice out. The other girls were afraid to."

"Then why did you scream at Snow White and her babies?"

"You come and catch them!" Carney replied, laughing. She returned to the chair, tucking her feet beneath her.

Bobbie's white mice provided the most excitement she was to know for some time. The days fell into a quiet routine. It was wonderful to be home, and yet Deep Valley was different in a melancholy way, because she was out of high school. The pattern of life she had lived there for eighteen years had been broken.

Bobbie was busy selling his bluing and Jerry was reading all the books in the Carnegie Library. Hunter had his high school gang—he was going with a shy slender girl named Ellen—and Carney felt actually old with them. They looked up to her so. The boys still belonged to Deep Valley and Deep Valley to them, but Carney felt herself cut off.

She was busy with housework, of course. She had always been required to help Olga with the housework. All through high school she had baked a cake every Saturday. She had wiped the Sunday dishes, and cleaned her own room, even scrubbing the soft wood floor. She took over these and other duties now.

She and her mother made plans for the house party. With zestful efficiency they made out menus and accompanying grocery lists, memoranda of things which must be done. In the warm afternoons they crocheted or embroidered with grandmothers, aunts, or cousins. Carney attended her mother's sewing circle and played the piano for them. (She always cheerfully played the piano when asked to do so.) She practised. She played the organ Sunday afternoons at a Mission Chapel in North Deep Valley in which her father was interested.

Sometimes she went riding in the automobile with Hunter, or out to the movies with a boy. Lloyd, Dennie, and Cab all came to see her. But, as her mother had said, the Crowd was scattered. Everyone missed the Kellys and the Rays.

Fortunately Winona Root was in town. She was the daughter of Deep Valley's newspaper editor. Tall, dark, and dashing, she was always gay company.

"Have you seen that Hutchinson house yet?" she asked.

Carney shook her head.

"Well, have you seen the son and heir? Of course," added Winona, "you may have thought he was a comet the way he rushes through town in that big black Locomobile. He goes like a streak."

"It's a good thing he does," Carney answered. "This town needs stirring up."

It was stirred up by Ringling Brothers Circus as the Fourth drew near. Colored posters blazed all over town, and Bobbie was in a fever of excitement. He even forgot to sell bluing. He and Jerry were going together. Hunter had invited Ellen. Lloyd Harrington invited Carney, but she had already planned to take her grandmothers.

Rosy and smiling, in a crisp pink linen dress, she piloted them carefully into the big tent—the saintly white-haired Sibley grandmother and the chuckly Vermonter. She bought them popcorn and red lemonade. She bought them balloons.

They came early to see the animals and stayed for the chariot race at the end. They were enchanted with everything: the blaring bands, the crowds, the smell of sawdust, the brightly clad performers swinging from trapezes and standing on the backs of racing horses.

Grandmother Sibley liked the seals best. "They're so intelligent," she said.

Grandmother Hunter liked the clowns. "I love to laugh," she confided to Carney. "You have little enough chance in this world."

Carney liked it all but especially the grandmothers' shining faces.

"It was the most fun I've had since I came home," she wrote to Larry.

Her letter to Larry went off every week and every week one from him arrived. They were as regular as church and Sunday School. There was nothing sentimental in the correspondence. Her mother, overcoming diffidence, questioned Carney about it and she replied, almost indignantly, "Heavens! Larry and I aren't a bit mushy." Her mother would have found no romance if she had looked into the letters. But it would have been different if she could have looked into Carney's heart.

Carney had a cedar hope chest in her room. She had had it for several years. It held growing piles of white sheets and pillow cases, towels on which she had embroidered her monogram, napkins she had hemmed and doilies she had crocheted. When Bonnie and Carney were quite young they had started exchanging silver spoons at Christmas and on birthdays. They thought in this fashion to acquire a set of silver before they got married. Carney now had eight silver spoons. She polished them sometimes.

The hope chest had always belonged to a future dreamily remote. The house in which she would one day cook, set tables, and make beds was as vague in her mind as a cloud castle. The lord of the manor had never taken shape at all. But this June, as she sorted and arranged her cedar-scented linens, she found herself thinking about a real house and a real husband.

The husband, to tell the truth, was more real than the house. He had thick hair and a crooked smile. He looked like Larry.

"It's a good thing Isobel is coming," Carney thought, rousing herself abruptly out of day dreams. And that night, out on the sleeping porch, watching the stars glimmer through the trees, she thought it again.

"Why, I haven't seen him for four years! I may not like him, and he may not like me. Oh, I *wish* that I could see him!"

It wasn't likely, she knew. He couldn't afford a trip back to the Middle West while he was in college. And her father would think she was insane if she asked to go way out to California just to see Larry.

If Betsy would only answer her letter! It was odd that she didn't, for Betsy liked to write letters . . . or anything else. She wanted to be an author. And

Carney had asked her so many questions!

"There's nothing I can do about it and so I'll forget it," Carney thought. That was her usual philosophy. If there was anything she could do to alter a bad situation, she couldn't rest until she did it. If there wasn't, she put it out of her mind.

"I'll think about the house party," she resolved firmly, and turned over and went to sleep.

5
East Is East

BEFORE LEAVING FOR the station to meet Isobel, Carney looked around with satisfaction. Everything possible had been done to start the house party auspiciously.

The house was immaculate, and Carney's bedroom was as fresh as the sweet peas on the dressing table.

Isobel's rack in the bathroom was a snowy drift of towels. Olga had polished the silver. She had roasted a ham and baked a pot of beans; she had made a molded salad, two kinds of cookies, and a cake. The menus Mrs. Sibley and Carney had planned were written neatly and hung on a hook in the pantry.

On Carney's desk was an incomplete program for the month. It listed the beauty spots to which she wished to take the girls, and assigned dates for parties. Of course other people would give parties. She had left space for these and for spur-of-the-moment picnics, hikes, and drives. But dates were set for the masquerade at which she proposed to introduce her guests to the Deep Valley Crowd, and the luncheon her mother's cousins were giving, and Grandmother Sibley's thimble bee, and Grandmother Hunter's breakfast.

As soon as Isobel arrived gaiety would burst like the Fourth of July crackers which were still sounding in the street—or almost as soon. Festivities would wait for Bonnie, who came later in the week.

Carney went out to the automobile where Hunter sat behind the wheel.

"Gee, you look nice, Sis!" he said admiringly, inspecting her starched yellow lawn.

"Wait till you see Isobel."

"Is she really so good-looking?"

"Peachy."

"Then I'm glad I put on my best suit." He winked at her engagingly.

"And *I'm* glad the heat has held off," Carney remarked. Excessive heat was to be expected in Deep Valley in July. But the day was only pleasantly warm. She was glad to have Minnesota put its best foot forward.

Isobel had certainly put *her* best foot forward, in return. Her traveling suit of dark blue silk did flattering things to her golden-brown hair. It had a hobble skirt, too, and her peach-basket hat and chiffon boa were the very newest style. Her gaze, as it scanned the depot platform, was appraising, but it warmed when she saw Carney.

Smiling, she stepped down from the train to Carney's hug.

Hunter swept off his hat, showing his glossy dark hair, with a smile that was much like his sister's.

"Carney!" cried Isobel. "Why didn't you tell me about your brother?"

"I did nothing but talk about my brothers."

"But I thought they were all little boys!"

"Hunter grew up while my back was turned."

He tried to conceal his satisfaction and delight as Isobel continued to gaze at him, wide-eyed. Carney could see that Hunter would fall. It wouldn't hurt him; it would do him good, she knew. But she felt a twinge at the radiance of his face.

As they drove along the quiet, greenly arched streets, Isobel looked curiously about her.

"It's like New England!" she exclaimed.

"It was settled by New Englanders—and New Yorkers," Carney replied.

"And then the Germans arrived," said Hunter. "They built the brewery and the Catholic Church and the College up on the hill."

"And now the Norwegians and Swedes are coming in. If you're lucky you may be invited to a smorgasbord supper while you're here."

"What, no Indians?" asked Isobel. It was a joke between her and Carney. When they first met she had asked with interest about the Indians in Deep Valley.

Mrs. Sibley was waiting on the porch. She greeted the visitor with a mingling of middle-western hospitality and Vermont reserve. Isobel presented her with a large box of chocolates.

"You're so awfully good to have me," she said in her sweetest way.

Jerry came to shake hands, a finger keeping his place in a book.

"What are you reading?" Isobel asked.

"*Twenty Thousand Leagues Under the Sea.*"

"It's wonderful, isn't it? I can see the ocean from my bedroom window."

Had she read it, Carney wondered? She hadn't exactly said so, but Jerry was beaming with pleasure.

Bobbie rushed in and shook hands firmly.

"Pleased to meet you. Want to buy some bluing?"

"Bobbie!" said his mother.

"I've just been wishing I had some bluing," Isobel said with a smile.

"Maybe you'd like two bottles."

"I would."

Bobbie grinned widely. "Gee! Sis bought some, too. I'll have my baseball suit pretty soon now, maybe."

"I hope you'll get it while I'm here," Isobel said.

"She's certainly trying," Carney thought. But when the girls went up to Carney's room, and Isobel strolled about looking at the family pictures, Carney thought she saw that appraising look again.

Determined to have the worst over, she led the way to the sleeping porch. "We're bunking here. I hope you're agile enough to climb through a window."

Isobel glanced at her quickly as though to see whether she was joking. Then she lifted up her skirts.

"Why do we have physical ed. at Vassar?" she asked gaily as she climbed.

Carney flapped the curtains, hung on wire runners

between the beds. "The boys sleep over there. I warn you that they sing after they retire. They sing, 'All policemen have big feet,' and thump their stomachs."

Isobel burst into laughter. She strolled to the end of the porch and looked up through the treetops at the over-hanging hills.

"Is there time for a walk before dinner? Do we dress?"

Carney chuckled. "We don't have dinner at night in Deep Valley. It's supper. And all we do is wash our hands."

When they gathered for supper her father said grace as usual. Isobel seemed surprised, although she shouldn't be, Carney thought. At Vassar, too, there was always grace before meals. But after that brief hesitation, Isobel bowed her head more devoutly than anyone at the table.

Supper was good, served in Olga's best style. Potato salad was rimmed with crisp green lettuce in the cut-glass bowl. There was sliced cold meat, and tomatoes from the garden. There were raspberries and heavy cream with some of the fresh cookies.

The boys were scrubbed so that their cheeks shone. Mrs. Sibley had put on a silk waist. Carney was proud, too, of her father, not only because he was so well groomed and handsome but because he talked so well. He had read the new novel, *Queed,* which

Isobel had been reading on the train.

After supper Mrs. Sibley untied the satin ribbons of the candy box. Bobbie passed it, then took a handful for himself. Everyone looked at Isobel with pleasure.

"They certainly like her. Now if only she likes them! But you can't tell a thing from that sweet smile," Carney thought.

That night, waiting for the concert on the sleeping porch to end, Carney and Isobel caught up on one another's news. Isobel had had lunch with Winkie in New York.

"She told me to remind you that you represent Vassar on every occasion."

"How about Howard Sedgwick, the beautiful?"

"I haven't seen him. What's the news from Larry?" Isobel added quickly.

"Oh, his letters come along as usual. I haven't heard from Betsy Ray, though. She's out in California now, you know."

"Isn't she the one who wants to be a writer?"

"Yes. I'm sorry you won't meet her. She's a peach and her house used to be the center of everything. But some of the Crowd are around. As soon as Bonnie comes we'll start things going. Until then we'll do as we please."

What Isobel pleased, it developed next morning, was to drive out to Murmuring Lake.

"You've told me so much about it that I'm dying to see it," she said.

"Why, I'd love to take you. It's a grand idea," Carney replied. "Shall we picnic or have dinner at the Inn? If we picnic, we can wear old duds. If we go to the Inn we'll have to dress up—a little."

"The Inn," said Isobel, after a pause.

So she put on a lacy blue dress and Carney put on her pink linen, fresh from the iron. She tied a pink ribbon around her dark hair. Hunter, gazing at Isobel, cranked the Maxwell, and they were off with Carney at the wheel.

The road to Murmuring Lake led up Agency Hill and along a high rolling plain. Corn was knee-high in the fields. The meadows were tinted with white and yellow daisies.

"I never want to pick another daisy," Carney said. "Gee, how many millions we picked!"

"I certainly never want to carry another. That chain was like lead."

The road was dusty.

"I wish there were paved roads everywhere like there are on Front and Broad Streets."

"We're getting them now in the East."

"Do Eastern horses have more sense than ours?" Carney stopped the car to let a team of terrified farm horses pass.

At last they caught sight of the fleecy willows, cotton-woods, and poplars bordering Murmuring Lake. It was the largest lake in the county and enclosed by wooded shores except where farms had lakeside fields and meadows.

The lake today was like watered silk.

"There'll be water lilies over in Babcock's Bay. Shall we get a boat and row over after dinner?" Carney asked as they walked toward the Inn, a spreading white building rimmed with narrow porches.

"We might . . ." Isobel answered doubtfully, and Carney knew she had something else in mind, but she didn't know what it was.

The dinner was excellent, as dinners at the Inn always were, and when it was over the girls walked down steep stairs to the dock. Carney sniffed blissfully. She loved the fresh, yet fishy, smell of the lake.

"I wish we'd brought our bathing suits so we could go swimming. But we can go wading anyway."

"Wading!" replied Isobel, in a startled tone.

"Sure. No one would mind if we took off our shoes and stockings. It's wonderful to feel wet sand between your toes."

Isobel laughed. "I don't believe I'd care to."

"Well, how about the water lilies, then?"

"We might . . ." Isobel paused. "Or we might go to see that Hutchinson house your mother wrote about."

"Marvelous!" Carney responded with enthusiasm. "I've heard of nothing but that house and the Hutchinson son ever since I got home."

She led the way briskly back to the auto.

They took the leafy road around the lake. Glimpses of shimmering water flashed past. Summer cottages were ensconced among trees, and happy children in bathing suits were shouting.

At length Carney said, "That's the old Dwyer place up ahead . . . the Hutchinson place, I mean." She slowed the car.

Nearing the hedge which enclosed the property, the road swooped inland, yielding the waterfront.

"If we're going to see anything, we have to get out," Carney decided. So they halted the Maxwell under a tree and walked back to the entrance.

Inside at the left were a boathouse, a diving tower, and a dock where a launch and several canoes were tied. From this vicinity there came a sound of hammering, but no one was in sight.

A wide driveway curved upward through a green tree-shaded lawn to a big white clapboard house. It was almost concealed by foliage, but they could see a tower and many porches.

"Oh, I wish we could get a little closer!" Isobel said.

"Well, come on, coward!"

They advanced boldly through the open gate. At the right was a rose garden in midsummer glory. There were red roses and pink ones, yellow ones and white ones. They seemed to tint the very air, just as they filled it with fragrance.

"How beautiful!" Isobel cried.

"Old Mr. Dwyer liked roses, but the Hutchinsons have added a lot," Carney responded.

"Perhaps you'd like to look around."

Both girls started at the sound of a deep soft voice. It was a surprisingly soft voice, Carney thought, when she saw from whom it came. The young man wasn't tall, and not exactly fat, but he was definitely large. He seemed to be overflowing a khaki shirt, baggy trousers, and high hunting boots. He had several days' growth of beard and his pompadour of fine straight hair was unkempt, too.

"He must be a very good gardener," Carney thought, "or the Hutchinsons wouldn't let him go around looking like that."

Probably, she decided, he was a stable hand, or general handy man. He had come from the direction of the boathouse and there was a hammer in his hand.

"If the family wouldn't mind," Carney answered. "We're just dying to."

"Come in, come in," he urged. "The roses are

rather special. Every variety grown in the Middle West."

"I can see that it is an exceptional collection," Isobel answered. Carney was pleased to notice her graciousness. There wasn't a trace of condescension in it.

The big young man showed them over the rose garden rather thoroughly. Isobel was full of questions. She knew, apparently, a great deal about roses. She asked to see their Alice Longworths and commented on grafting. Carney trailed after them, stooping now and then to sniff a particularly delectable bloom.

Suddenly Isobel stopped talking. "You've been awfully kind. But we really must go now. Don't you think so, Carney?"

Carney burst into a chuckle. "I certainly do. Before the Hutchinsons come down and throw us out."

"See here," said the unshaven young man. He looked at her intently with very blue eyes. He had, she saw, a dimple in his chin. "Nobody's going to throw you out. I'm Sam Hutchinson."

Carney stared at him, and then her laugh bubbled so infectiously that he and Isobel laughed, too.

"Well! Why didn't you say so? I thought you were one of the stable hands."

With his hands in the pockets of his grubby soiled trousers he grinned broadly.

"I'm Caroline Sibley."

"I know," he answered. "I saw you at the circus. Did the old ladies enjoy it?"

"They loved it. And so did I. This is my house guest, Isobel Porteous, from Long Island, New York."

"Long Island, eh?" said Sam. He gave Isobel an appreciative glance. "You must like boats then? Want to see my new one?"

"He likes Isobel," Carney thought, delightedly. "What luck that we happened to come!"

They strolled down to the dock at the side of which a gleamingly new sailboat rested against newly nailed canvas bumpers which explained the hammering. He suggested a sail.

"Really," said Carney. "We can't. There's lots to be done at home. I've the second installment of a house party coming soon." Her brown eyes twinkled. "I'm awfully glad you happened to be a Hutchinson. I wouldn't have enjoyed going out on my ear."

Isobel gave him her hand and her longest, sweetest, most adoring smile.

Carney, watching, had a sudden revelation. All at once she knew why Isobel had suggested driving to the Hutchinson house, why she had wanted to come to Murmuring Lake in the first place, and why she had chosen the Inn where they would have to dress up.

> *"East is east, and west is west,*
> *And never the twain shall meet . . ."*

thought Carney, both amused and irritated.

"Why, she could just as well have said right out, 'I'd like to meet Sam Hutchinson.' I'd have arranged it. In fact, we couldn't have avoided meeting him long, he's so friendly. He's like a baby . . . hippo."

Which thought brought the dimple into Carney's pink cheek. She ran ahead to crank the machine.

"See here!" called Sam. "I'll do that. Don't spoil your pretty pink dress. I like pink," he added. "It's my favorite color."

"Good!" thought Carney, still dimpling. "I'll tell Isobel to wear pink all the time."

But she didn't speak as she relinquished the crank. She climbed into the car and took the wheel, still smiling.

"Baby hippo!" she thought, longing to tell Isobel who, looking her loveliest, watched admiringly the large young man's performance at the crank.

6

Bonnie

Isobel didn't think the "baby hippo" line was funny.

"He isn't a bit like a baby hippo. He's quite distinguished."

"Distinguished!" snorted Carney, as she backed the automobile into the dusty road and started back along the lake. "He's too fat and he needs a shave.

He's been needing a shave for a week."

"Oh, but he has an air," Isobel insisted.

"Did you think so when you thought he was a stable boy?"

"I never thought he was a stable boy."

"What?" cried Carney almost running over a chicken in her surprise.

Isobel was nonchalant. "Of course, I knew all along that he was Sam Hutchinson. He had a sort of . . . *savoir faire* . . ."

"So *that's* why you were so nice to him!" interrupted Carney.

Isobel flushed, and laughed. "Is that a polite thing to say? I'm always nice to servants."

"Yes, but not *that* nice," said Carney, laughing, too. "I didn't mean to be rude. I just admire your perspicacity, or intuition, or whatever it is. You Easterners! *East is east and west is west,* all right."

"And in the west," said Isobel, good humoredly, "you can't tell a Sam Hutchinson from a stable boy. Well, wait till you see him shaved!"

But he wasn't shaved when the Locomobile drove up in front of the Sibley house next day.

The girls saw it from an upper window, a huge black open car with the top collapsed at the back. They saw Sam hop out and swing up the porch steps, looking as unkempt as before, overflowing a faded checked shirt, greasy trousers and the hunting boots.

"What an outfit for calling!" said Carney, running to answer the bell.

But when she opened the door she forgave him. His eyes were crinkled with friendliness, and they were so extremely blue! His smile was winning, even through a stubble of beard.

"I have to drive out to Medelia. Thought you gals might like to go along. Miss Porteous told me she was here to look over Minnesota."

"He *does* like Isobel," Carney thought joyfully. Nothing could be more fortunate. The success of Isobel's visit was almost assured.

"Like a ride?" she called to Isobel, who was sauntering down the stairs.

"I'd love it," Isobel said warmly.

Hunter had emerged from the back parlor to see what was going on. Sam turned to him. "Wouldn't you like to come, too? Drive the Loco?"

Hunter's face broke into smiles. "Gee, yes!" he cried.

Now that was a nice thing for Sam Hutchinson to do, Carney thought, as she went to tell her mother of their plans. And Sam was as good as his word. After the car had climbed out of the valley, Hunter *was* allowed to drive.

"I'll sit with Hunter," Carney said brusquely,

which for her was subtle maneuvering. She changed to the front seat while Isobel sat in the back with Sam.

Isobel seemed to enjoy the look at southern Minnesota. They bowled along a country road under a cloudless sky. Sam pointed out the lacy corn, the rippling wheat, the fat cows in meadows full of clover.

"Isn't this better than Broadway and Forty-second? Honestly, now!"

In Medelia, a tiny town with dooryards full of hollyhocks and children, he drove to the main street and parked.

"I have to go to the mill, Hunter," he said, "you take the girls into the Candy Kitchen. See that Isobel orders a banana split." Isobel! They had progressed. "It's part of her education in Middle Westania."

The two girls and Hunter went into the Candy Kitchen, which smelled richly of chocolate. They were just attacking the banana splits when Sam came in, greeted the attendant heartily, and ordered one, too. They consumed the giant concoctions with riotous laughter. When they rose, Sam called to the boy, "Charge it, Joe! Put it on the book."

Carney turned to him, puzzled. "Haven't you any money with you, Sam?"

"Not a cent!"

"Hunter can pay."

"Of course not. I invited you in."

"But the boy doesn't even know who you are!"

"Gosh! Everybody knows me."

"But you didn't ask what this costs," protested Carney. "When the bill comes in, you won't know whether it's right or wrong."

"I'll never see it."

Carney began to feel irritated. "It's ridiculous to charge such a small amount," she said bluntly.

"It isn't a bit ridiculous. It saves nerve strain. I never carry money," said Sam, and to prove it he pulled his pockets inside out.

"What does it matter, Carney?" asked Isobel, laughing.

"It's just so silly!" said Carney, and Sam turned to grin at her through his stubble of beard.

Back in the Locomobile, they stopped at a livery stable, transformed into a garage, and Sam told the boy to fill the tank with gasoline.

"Charge it, Joe. Put it on the book," he said, winking at Carney.

Perhaps, Carney thought, he felt at home in Medelia because of his father's business interests. He wouldn't behave like this in another town. But on the way back they drove through a village where boxes of strawberries were displayed in front of the general store. Sam stopped.

"Half a dozen boxes," he called, without asking the price, and when the clerk brought the berries he said, "Charge them, Joe. Put it on the book." He didn't even give his name.

Carney gave him a withering glance. "Why six boxes?" she asked pointedly. "Your family isn't that big."

"Mom can use two. And I thought your mother might like a couple."

"And the last two?" asked Carney, weakening.

"Oh, half a dozen is such a nice round figure. And Hunt and I will eat them, driving home."

Carney was soon to learn that Sam had told the truth when he said that he never carried money. The son of the richest man in southern Minnesota, the crown prince, the heir apparent, he conducted himself accordingly. He and the big black Locomobile were known in every hamlet.

Isobel seemed really impressed. He hadn't gone East to college. In fact, his college had begun and ended with a year at the U. But he had traveled almost as much as she had; they discussed Europe and Long Island.

"It's astonishing," she confided to Carney, "to run into someone like that out here in the Middle West."

Carney didn't want to discourage this interest. Privately, she couldn't understand romantic feeling about anyone so burly and untidy. She hoped Larry would be like her father who was always spruce and well groomed, never seen without a tie.

Isobel was interested, too, in Bonnie.

"Are the Andrews French?" she asked.

"No. English. American now."

"What was the family doing in Paris?"

"Dr. Andrews was connected with the American church there."

"Isn't it a pretty far jump to Minnesota?"

"Oh, he lived here before, of course."

"How did he happen to come in the first place?" Isobel persisted.

Carney twinkled. "Just chose the nicest part of the U.S. to settle in."

"But he left it and went back to Paris," said Isobel, twinkling, too.

"And he's coming back, you notice."

"Not to Deep Valley."

"No. To St. Paul. But it's still Minnesota." And both girls laughed. They paused for breath, then Isobel continued, "Do they have money?" Isobel was always asking whether people had money.

"Yes. Mrs. Andrews' father made it in horseshoe nails. Bonnie and I used to howl about that." Carney smiled reminiscently. "Bonnie's awfully full of fun."

"You may find her very different."

"Paris won't change Bonnie."

"Paris changes anybody."

"It won't change Bonnie," Carney insisted stubbornly. And as soon as Bonnie had stepped off the train, Carney saw that she was right.

Of course, like the rest of them Bonnie was four years older. But she was still short and cozily round. Her dark red toque and traveling suit were made of rich materials but they had the old-fashioned look Bonnie's clothes always had . . . they didn't look a bit like Paris. Her blond hair was as smooth as always, her blue eyes as mirthful and as calm.

The Crowd—what was left of it—was at the depot. It was the first time Isobel had met them. Tom was there in his West Point uniform; slender, aristocratic Lloyd; jovial Dennie; likable Cab; Winona and blond Alice Morrison.

"How wonderful to see the old Crowd!" Bonnie cried, going from one to another.

"Bonnie, this is Isobel, my roommate from Vassar."

They shook hands, Isobel smiling, Bonnie beaming with friendliness.

Back at Broad Street, all the Sibleys were waiting on the porch. Bonnie kissed Mrs. Sibley.

"Do you still have the doughnut jar?"

"I certainly have. Especially filled for your arrival."

"And do you still make rarebits?" Bonnie smiled up at tall Mr. Sibley.

"I'll make one for you, Bonnie, while you're here."

The whole family, except Bobbie, remembered her with love. To him she was only another "bluing" prospect.

"Would you like a bottle of bluing, miss? I'm trying to earn a baseball suit."

"Bobbie!" said Carney, stamping her foot. He grinned, unabashed.

"Of course I want a bottle," said Bonnie, her laughter flowing.

Just as it always had, Bonnie's laughter flowed through every conversation. And her hands, Carney noticed at the table, were the same—small, plump and very soft, covered with rings.

There was a gala supper, and as they left the table, Isobel gave Carney a push.

"Now you and Bonnie go take a walk. I know you have a million things to talk about. Hunter will take care of me; won't you, Hunter?"

"Glad to," said Hunter, eyes sparkling.

"You're going to make Ellen aw—fully mad!" sang Carney. But she felt a surge of gratitude. It would be wonderful to have Bonnie to herself.

Arms entwined, they went out of the house and strolled down Broad Street. Although there was still pink sunset in the sky, it was growing dark under the trees. Men were watering shadowy lawns, and voices came out of dim, vine-covered porches.

"Is it nice to be back?"

"Wonderful! I wish you were coming to the U."

"Well, Betsy is going to be there."

"That will help. Tell me, has she seen the Humphreys?"

"Yes! Herbert's been giving her a terrific rush. Remember when he was in love with you?"

"It's one of my most treasured memories!" Bonnie gave her little rolling laugh. "Where's Tony Markham? You wrote me he had gone on the stage."

"He's in *The Chocolate Soldier*, on the road. Just a small part, but a good one."

"Where are Irma and Tib?"

"Vacationing."

"And the Kellys?"

"They've moved to Minneapolis. Katie's getting married this summer. And Tacy is engaged to that Harry Kerr I wrote you about."

"Engaged!" cried Bonnie. "One of our Crowd engaged!"

They were silent a moment.

"What does Betsy say about Larry?"

"She says he's nice. I wrote and asked her a lot of questions about him but she's been slow answering.

Bonnie, I wish I could see Larry."

"I know." Bonnie was sympathetic. "He's standing between you and . . . anyone you could get serious about. Is there anyone in particular, Carney?"

"No. Is there with you?"

"No," said Bonnie. "I'm in love but only with love. I want to get married, of course, have my home, start a family."

"Same with me," said Carney. "I don't want any career." She thought for a moment about her piano and what Herr Lang had said. But she didn't repeat it. It still rankled in a sore place in her heart.

The next day was Sunday. Mr. Sibley and his sons pressed their suits and shined their shoes, but Carney didn't feel embarrassed as she had expected to when Isobel observed the homely habit. Bonnie kept saying, with fond laughter, that they had always done it. At the breakfast table they discussed the Sunday School lesson and Bonnie—straight from Paris—entered into the discussion. She had studied the lesson, coming down on the train.

Afterward they assembled for church. Absentminded Jerry ran up and down stairs again and again before he was ready . . . first for his handkerchief, then for his dime, then for his lesson book, and then for his hat.

"He hasn't changed a bit," Bonnie remarked.

The family drove, but the three girls walked, dressed in their best and feeling formal. Carney wore her white serge suit and a white wastebasket hat, faced with brown shirred silk.

"Your hat is lovely," Bonnie observed.

"Winkie's mother helped me buy it in New York. It cost eight seventy-five."

"Heavens!" said Bonnie. "Mine only cost ten francs. That's about . . . two dollars."

She didn't say it as another girl might have said it, in a bragging way. Bonnie didn't drag in French phrases or references to Paris. She didn't need to, Carney thought, as they walked down Broad Street to the tall white stone church. Bonnie wasn't in the least conceited, but she had a calm unconscious confidence.

At Sunday School she was asked to speak, and she stood up and talked, not brilliantly, but effortlessly and sincerely. She remembered the names of parishioners, old and young, who clustered about her after church.

Isobel, Carney saw, was puzzled by her. She said she adored her, but that didn't, of course, mean that she did. However, Carney felt sure she would in time. You couldn't help loving Bonnie.

Again Sam Hutchinson dropped by in the Locomobile, still unshaven, bulky, in loose, careless clothes.

"Isn't he like a baby hippo?" Carney whispered to Bonnie. The three girls piled into the car along with Hunter and Lloyd and Tom who happened to be present.

On this ride the Locomobile sputtered, balked, and stopped. Hunter telephoned from a farm house and two mechanics arrived on bicycles. They tinkered while the party sang in the grass by the roadside. When the car started chugging again, Sam borrowed some silver from Lloyd. He pressed it into the mechanic's greasy hands and climbed behind the wheel.

"Charge it, Joe. Put it on the book."

The next day he bought Bonnie a box of candy. He took a fancy to a tie in a shop window and bought six. It was always the same. "Charge it, Joe. Put it on the book."

Carney was horrified. Naturally thrifty, she had been trained from childhood in a businesslike handling of money.

"It's wrong of you not to carry money."

"Not one of the Ten Commandments mentions carrying money."

"But why don't you?"

"I've told you. I hate to."

She looked at him scornfully. "I suppose you hate shaving, too."

"How did you guess it?"

She burst into laughter, and Sam looked at her triumphantly, rubbing the stubble on his cheeks and dimpled chin.

"Well," Carney said, "you'll have to start shaving soon. We're having a whole raft of parties. There's a masquerade at our house tomorrow night."

"A masquerade? I'll let my beard grow and come as a pirate."

"All you would need to do right now is tie on a red sash," Carney jeered.

She scolded him freely, but she liked him. She liked his kindness, his honesty, his hatred of form, his love of fun.

"That baby hippo is all right," she confided to Bonnie.

"He's going to add a lot to the house party," Bonnie agreed.

That began formally with a most informal masquerade.

7

The Masquerade

THE MASQUERADE HAD BEEN Mrs. Sibley's idea. She had almost insisted upon one.

"What's got into you?" Carney joked her. "It doesn't seem in character for you to want a masquerade."

"I don't see why not." Mrs. Sibley's eyes sparkled. "Don't you remember how I used to dress you children up for Hallowe'en? The sheets and pillow cases?

Tell your guests to wear masks," she added. "It will be fun to mystify Isobel."

Isobel was mystified in more ways than one. At masquerades in East Hampton, costumes were planned well in advance. They were elaborate and expensive. Here nothing was done until the morning of the party. No one could have been more forehanded than Carney, but part of the fun was extemporizing costumes. Accompanied by Hunter, Jerry, and Bobbie, the girls climbed to the attic.

The attic was hot, and smelled of sun-warmed timber, but it held ample material for disguise. Both grandmothers kept their treasures here because the third floor was so big. There were trunks full of ancient finery. Discarded clothing hung on hooks along one wall, with costumes Carney and her brothers had worn at school festivities.

"It's too bad Miss Salmon isn't here," Carney remarked to Isobel.

"Who is Miss Salmon?" Bonnie wanted to know.

"Our history teacher, the most stimulating person at Vassar. She's strong for local history," Isobel explained. "In one exam this spring we were asked to tell what historical records could be found in our own back yards."

"Well, you can certainly find the history of the Sibley and Hunter families in this attic. And it's pretty much the history of the Middle West," Carney said, looking around.

"Take that buffalo robe of Uncle Luke's. He wasn't our uncle, really. An old man with chin whiskers, awfully grim. He was sort of a missionary for the Presbyterian church and used to drive around in all kinds of weather, from forty below to a hundred above . . . in the early days, of course. He was retired when we knew him, and he died ages ago." She looked thoughtful. "I suppose he was typical of the men who started churches of all denominations."

Jerry spoke suddenly. "See that Civil War cap? It belonged to my Uncle Aaron. He fought with the First Minnesota. I suppose you know about that."

"I don't believe I do," Isobel replied.

"The charge of the First Minnesota at Gettysburg ought to be as famous as the charge of the British at Balaklava. General Hancock said there was no more gallant deed in history."

"Tell me about it," said Isobel. She had not heard Jerry talk so much since she arrived.

"Well," he began, "the Confederates were winning. If they hadn't been stopped they might have won the battle and the whole Civil War. Our troops were outnumbered. Reserves were coming up on the run but the Rebs had to be delayed five minutes.

"The First Minnesota was resting after a forced

march. General Hancock came at a gallop and ordered them to charge. They had to cross a field and go up a little hill in plain sight of the enemy. Everyone knew it was just a sacrifice . . . to gain five minutes . . . but they went forward like . . . like . . . lions. Out of two hundred and sixty-two, only forty-seven came back." He paused. "I learned those figures because I was proud of my Uncle Aaron being there."

"I should think you would be," Bonnie replied.

"My grandfather fought in the Civil War," said Isobel soberly.

"Gosh, Jerry, that's a swell story!" cried Hunter. Bobbie put on Uncle Aaron's cap. He stalked about the attic, looking stern.

Carney took down a faded parasol. "This belonged to Aunt Lily, who was stolen by the Indians during the Sioux Rebellion."

"Stolen by the Indians!" Isobel cried.

"Yes. She saw her parents killed before her eyes. She hid in a cornfield but the Indians found her and held her captive for months. She came back and married Uncle George."

Bonnie had found a faded paper. "'Reward of Merit,'" she chanted.

> *"By knowledge do we learn*
> *Ourselves to know*

And what to man
And what to God we owe."

"'This certifies that Laurenza Parke by diligence and good behavior merits the approbation of her friend and instructress. S. Burgess.'"

"That's from the Chester Academy back in Vermont," Carney said. "Laurenza is Grandmother Hunter. She and mother both went there. Deep Valley attics are full of things like that."

Isobel looked up from the trunk in which she was delving. "I'm surprised to find such elegant things here. There are beautiful shawls, and fans, and satin shoes."

"Why," said Carney, "the pioneer women came from civilized towns in the East. They brought their best and wore it, too, although they nearly froze in unheated homes and churches."

"But I thought they milked cows."

"Some of them did, and made soap and wove cloth and washed and ironed and baked. But some of them taught school and gave music lessons and started singing schools and lyceums." She laughed. "What a topic! Wouldn't Miss Salmon be proud of me?"

Turning to the trunk she lifted out a dress of changeable green taffeta.

"I know this!" she cried. "It's Grandmother

Hunter's wedding dress. There's a picture of her wearing it. She wore it over hoops with a black lace shawl, and the cameo brooch and earrings she wears all the time."

"There's your costume for the masquerade, Carney," Isobel said.

"I believe it is!" Carney jumped up. "I'll copy the picture."

Isobel chose a pink satin covered with cobwebby lace. She would go as the Pink Lady, she said. She and Carney had seen the light opera in New York. Bonnie decided on a costume Carney had once worn to a school entertainment. She would be a Sunbonnet Baby.

Jerry took no interest in the party; he just liked to rummage. But Bobbie wouldn't let go of Uncle Aaron's cap; he declared he would go as a soldier. Hunter settled on a cowboy outfit. He grinned with pleasure while Isobel knotted a red bandana around his throat.

She stepped back to survey the effect. "Good looking!" she exclaimed.

"Ellen will be crazy about you," cried Carney.

But Hunter didn't seem to like the reference to Ellen.

Downstairs they all tried on what they had chosen. Then they started ripping and sewing, mending and pressing, dashing off now and then to Front Street for ribbons or buttons.

"It's really more fun than the kind of masquerade where the costumer does all the work," Isobel said.

After supper the rooms were cleared for dancing. The girls went upstairs and hurried into their costumes. They tinted one another's cheeks and lips, darkened their eyebrows and lashes.

"Isobel, you look lovely!"

"Is my sunbonnet straight?"

"Grandmother Hunter loaned me the brooch and earrings," Carney said. She had loaned the black shawl, too, and Carney had found hoop skirts in the attic. They made her waist look flower slim.

They were adjusting their masks when music rose from the parlor. The aunt who had promised to play the piano was trying to catch the rhythm of "Alexander's Ragtime Band."

"Come on and hear, come on and hear . . ." the girls hummed as they started down the stairs. Carney's hoop skirt swung from side to side in time to the music.

They were none too early. A gypsy was just coming in the door, closely followed by a blond-haired flower girl and Uncle Sam with bunting twisted around his stove-pipe hat. Presently Carney recognized Winona, who always wore the same Scottish kilts to masquerades. She could always be recognized anyway, being taller than the other girls.

Very few people could deceive anyone long. They knew each other too well. Moving with dignity in her hoop skirt now, Carney went up to a burly unshaved Pirate.

"Howdy, Sam!"

"G-r-r-r! Don't you know I eat little girls?"

"Not grandmothers," said Carney. She revolved delightedly. "This is my grandmother's wedding dress."

"Looks nice on you," Sam said.

"Have you guessed anyone?"

"Isobel's the Pink Lady."

"And pink's your favorite color."

He turned to look at her. "It was you I told that to," he said. He took hold of her arm. "Now sit down and tell me who everyone is."

"It isn't fair," said Carney. "But everyone else knows, and I want to get my mask off. Don't you? Tom is the Indian Chief. Lloyd is Uncle Sam and Dennie is the Irishman."

"And Cab is Buster Brown?"

"Yes. And Alice is the Flower Girl. Doesn't she look pretty tonight? The Gypsy is Ellen, Hunter's girl."

"Who's the Valentine?"

"The Valentine? Why . . . who can it be?" Carney stared, puzzled, at a tall slender girl whose white dress and wide hat were covered with Valentines, old and new, bright and faded, comic and sentimental. "Mother must have invited one of my cousins, but I don't remember a cousin who looks like that."

"Let's go up and talk with her. How do you talk to a Valentine, anyway? Let's see! 'If you love me, as I love you,'" he chanted.

Carney chuckled gleefully. "Roses are red, violets are blue . . ."

But the Valentine didn't reply.

"This Valentine is as dumb as an oyster," said Buster Brown.

"We've all been trying to make her talk," said the Gypsy.

"Please speak to us, Valentine . . . just say anything," they urged.

There was a faint squeak. "Won't you be my Valentine?"

"Oh, come now," said Sam. "You'll have to speak up a little."

"I don't know you," squeaked the Valentine.

"You don't know *me*?"

"A clue! She doesn't know Sam Hutchinson. That means she hasn't been around lately."

The Valentine seemed disturbed by this. She hurried away but they pursued her.

"Do you know me?" demanded Carney.

"Certainly," came the squeak.

"Do you know me? . . . And me? . . . And me?"

"All too well, all too well."

"See here!" said Carney. "I wrote all the invitations myself. I know everyone on the list and you're not on it."

The Valentine squeaked indignantly. "What an insult! I'm a member of your house party!"

"What!" Carney cried. "Mother, I can't stand this suspense. When do we unmask?"

"At midnight," said Mrs. Sibley, smiling from the doorway.

"But these masks are hot, and everyone knows everyone else except for this Valentine who will probably turn out to be Grandmother Hunter or one of the boys."

"I'm not a grandmother and I'm not a boy," came the voice like a squeaky pencil.

"Give us some clues then. What are you like?"

"Oh, I'm beautiful . . . and very bright." A smile she could not repress curved the Valentine's mouth beneath her mask. Her teeth were parted in the middle.

"Betsy! Betsy Ray!" There was a volley of shouts. There was a flying barrage of hands trying to tear off the mask. It fell to the floor, and all the masks went whirling in every direction. The Valentine *was* Betsy Ray.

The girls in the Crowd fell upon her with kisses, and so did some of the boys. Her dark hair shook loose about a smiling face lighted by hazel eyes. She was breathless with laughter.

"When did you get back?"

"To Minneapolis? Last week."

"How do you happen to be here?"

"Mrs. Sibley invited me."

Mrs. Sibley stood very straight as though to atone by the dignity of her erect carriage for the dancing of her eyes.

"Mr. Root told me that Betsy was home."

"Then you knew, Winona!" Carney cried.

"Yep," said Winona. "Power of the press. The distinguished ex-Californian and near-author arrived this morning. We've been sewing on those darn Valentines all afternoon. A good thing I didn't have to worry about my own costume."

"And I'm really invited to your house party!" cried Betsy. "You'd just better want me."

She and Carney hugged. Then she held Carney at arm's length.

"Turn around. Let me see your air of academic distinction."

"I represent Vassar on every occasion," said Carney, whirling.

"And Bonnie!" Betsy flew to her arms. "You haven't changed a bit."

"Betsy, I want you to meet Isobel. And this is Sam Hutchinson . . ."

But the piano-playing aunt cut in. "You really must get to dancing." She started to play "Chinatown," and everyone found partners.

Betsy Ray was dancing with Cab. They had been next-door neighbors when the Rays lived in Deep Valley. Isobel was dancing with Hunter whose handsome face glowed with admiration. Little Ellen didn't like it too well, although Lloyd whirled her in his very best manner. Carney watched them as she two-stepped with Sam. He was surprisingly light and deft.

They danced in the front and back parlors and out on the porch, in sight of the warm summer stars. They danced the two-step and the waltz, the barn dance and the graceful Boston, the new Cubanola Glide.

They sang as they danced, "Call Me Up Some Rainy Afternoon," and "Come, Josephine, in My Flying Machine," and "Down by the Old Mill Stream." They sang that one in parts.

"Not much like a Vassar dance," Carney whispered to Isobel.

At midnight there were no masks to remove but Mrs. Sibley served ice cream and cake.

Carney and Betsy slept in Carney's room. Carney had said frankly that she wanted to talk. After they were undressed and ready for bed, she asked briskly, "Did you see any more of Larry?"

"Yes," said Betsy. "He was at home for spring vacation and again after college closed in June. He's very . . . personable. Not exactly handsome, but fascinating."

She burst out laughing. "He was cautious even with me. He acted as though we had just been introduced, talked about the climate and his school and things like that. *I* didn't have designs on the boy. *I* didn't have a marriage license in my pocket, but he wasn't taking any chances."

Carney whooped with laughter. "Didn't he know about Joe?" she asked. Betsy Ray went with Joe Willard, who attended the University and worked part time as a reporter on the *Minneapolis Tribune*.

"I told Herbert about Joe. But I didn't confide in Larry and he didn't confide in me. His mother did, though."

"His mother?" Carney asked quickly.

"I had quite a heart-to-heart talk with Mrs. Humphreys. She's my godmother, you know. She gave a party for me when the boys were home for spring vacation, so I met their crowd. And the general impression—both with Mrs. Humphreys and the crowd—seems to be that you and Larry have been as true as steel and that you're both pining for the day when your hearts can be reunited."

"Betsy!" said Carney. "You're just being silly!"

"No, I'm not," said Betsy. "Larry scorned every girl in San Diego High School, and he's doing the same at Leland Stanford, and they all lay the blame on your shoulders.

"His mother is really anxious for Larry to make a visit here. She thinks it would be better for him . . . and for you, too . . . to see each other again. Then, if you don't like each other, you can find it out. And if you do . . ." Betsy paused.

"When do you think he will come?" Carney asked.

"I don't know," said Betsy. "I know he's working in the post office this summer to save money for the trip. Hasn't he told you that?"

"I knew he was working."

"Well, now you know why," Betsy said.

"How is Joe?"

"He's wonderful! He's nicer than ever! Don't get me started on Joe or we'll never get to sleep."

"We'd better get to sleep," said Carney, "for we're going out to Murmuring Lake tomorrow. That Sam Hutchinson has invited the house party and some boys out for the day. They bought the old Dwyer place, you know."

"Is he one of *the* Hutchinsons?" asked Betsy. "The New Town Hutchinsons?"

"That's right."

"What's he like?"

"Nice, but isn't he a baby hippo?"

And Carney got up and turned out the gas. The windows were open and darkness flooded the bedroom. Presently Betsy fell asleep, but Carney lay awake thinking about what Betsy had told her.

"If he's coming, I wish he would come," she thought. "Well, wishing can't bring him!" She turned over determinedly, tucking her pillow underneath her cheek.

"As true as steel . . . scorned every girl in San Diego High School . . . doing the same at Leland Stanford, and they all lay the blame on your shoulders . . ."

Although the darkness hid it, the dimple flickered in Carney's cheek.

8

Purple and Dove Gray

THE HOUSE PARTY WAS still at breakfast, gossiping over pancakes, while Olga, in the kitchen, stood by her griddle and Bobbie pushed through the swinging door delivering fragrant, steaming, golden-brown stacks.

The girls were dressed in the middies and sailor

suits they would wear to the lake. Their bags were packed with bathing suits, for Sam had invited them to stay all day.

"Come for lunch," he had said, and Isobel had smiled slyly at Carney. The girls teased one another about dinner-and-supper versus lunch-and-dinner.

"Sam Hutchinson!" Carney had cried. "How can I educate Isobel in Middle Westania if you bring in effete eastern customs like lunch in the middle of the day?"

"Gosh, I apologize! That was a bad slip," he grinned.

"Who's coming?"

"Well, most of the fellows are working, but Lloyd and Tom can come, and Hunter . . . enough to protect me from you girls."

"Until you shave," Carney had bubbled with laughter, "you won't need any protection against *me*."

"Isobel, does she nag all the time?"

"A common scold! In New England we'd put her in the stocks."

"I'm glad I won't be in the stocks tomorrow," Carney had said. "Jinks, Sam! It sounds like a wonderful day."

She thought it again, looking around the chattering table, and when the doorbell rang she ran eagerly to answer it. But for a moment the immaculate figure on the threshold seemed completely strange. Then she found something familiar in it.

"Sam Hutchinson!" she cried.

It was Sam, and he was shaved. His cheeks were pink from the recent scraping of a razor, and below his firm smiling mouth she saw clearly that dimple in his chin. His soft brown hair was brushed back into a shining pompadour. He was wearing sailing blues, and his white canvas shoes were as spotless as her own.

Carney burst into laughter. "Why, you're very good-looking!"

"Of course," answered Sam.

"Come in! Turn around!"

"Why all the fuss? I clean up sometimes. Just a whim I get now and then. Nothing to do with the impertinent remarks of impertinent little girls."

But he smiled at her, his blue eyes crinkling.

"You look nice yourself," he said, and inspected the red ribbon binding her hair, the snowy middy. "You always look so clean . . . as though you'd just come from that Spotless Town in the Sapolio ads."

"What a compliment! Come on into the dining room. I can't wait for Isobel to see you. Besides, there are pancakes, and Mother gets the maple syrup from Vermont."

She watched Isobel's face as they entered. A look of

astonishment was quickly concealed as Sam drew up a chair beside her.

"Why don't you speak up and praise me, the way Carney does?" he asked.

"I don't object so violently to your beard."

"You look lovely," Bonnie giggled.

"I wish," Betsy Ray said plaintively, "that someone would tell me the joke."

"Bobbie," called Carney as her brother peeped through the swinging door. "Pancakes for Sam!" And presently Bobbie came in, walking slowly and proudly with his burden. His straight hair fell into his face; his lower lip was gripped in concentration by two king-sized front teeth. Those teeth had outgrown all their companions.

The pancakes delivered, he inspected the table with a calculating eye. Then he went over to Betsy.

"Want to buy some bluing?"

"Why, yes. Are you in the grocery business, Bobbie?"

"If I sell enough bluing I can win a baseball suit."

"I have my pocketbook right here."

The transaction completed, Bobbie proceeded to Sam. "Want to buy some bluing?"

"Sure," answered Sam. "I've just been needing some."

Bobbie looked ingratiating. "How many bottles?"

"I'll take a dozen."

"Boy!" Bobbie let out a whoop. "Sis!" he shouted, running to Carney. "I can send for the baseball suit!" He raced to the library and returned with a pile of bottles. "That will be a dollar and twenty cents," he said, forcing a businesslike tone. "It's very good bluing. Your mother will like it."

"A dollar and twenty cents. Ch . . ." as the familiar word formed on his lips, Sam caught Carney's twinkling eyes and stopped. He put his hand in his pocket and left it there. Bobbie was watching him radiantly.

"I started to say 'charge it,'" Sam said to gain time. "But I'm sure you wouldn't do that."

"I should say not," said Bobbie. "My terms are strictly cash." He waited a little anxiously for Sam's hand to emerge from his pocket.

Carney's gaze was triumphant. Sam scowled at her and spoke in an undertone. "There's one person I won't borrow from, and that's you!" he said.

"Our Dad doesn't approve of borrowing; does he, Bobbie?" Carney asked.

"I should say not. That's the way to the poor house, he says. Gee!" added Bobbie, his face dimming a little. "Maybe you can't afford to buy twelve bottles?"

"Yes I can," answered Sam. "My mother would never forgive me if I passed up a bargain like this."

Betsy Ray had reached for her purse again but Sam's eyes went to Isobel who smiled understandingly.

"I have my pocketbook right here, Sam, in case . . ." she glanced at Bobbie . . . "in case your wallet is out in the auto."

"Why, thanks," he answered in a tone which breathed relief. "Just a couple of dollars."

Walking out to the Locomobile Carney danced up to Sam. "Maybe *that* will teach you to carry money!"

"It was a close shave, all right," he answered, smiling. He was really remarkably good-looking. And not even very fat, she thought, marveling. In proper clothes, he was just stocky and strong.

Lloyd and Tom had arrived in Lloyd's auto. Tom had laid aside his uniform, but he was so straight that he looked military even in civilian clothes. He was a large, dark-skinned, heavy-featured boy, not handsome, but with an arresting white-toothed smile. He was obviously affected by Isobel's charm.

"I've made a momentous decision. You're coming in our car," he told her, taking her arm.

That was hard on Sam and Hunter, Carney thought, but it couldn't be helped. Isobel and Betsy went with Tom and Lloyd, while Bonnie, Carney and Hunter climbed into the Locomobile. Although the day was warm there was a breeze rippling through the grain fields.

"A good day for sailing," Sam said with satisfaction. "Know anything about it?"

"Not much, but Isobel does."

"I like rowboats better," said Bonnie.

"I like canoes," said Carney.

"Do you paddle, or just sit and look beautiful?"

"I paddle. I'll race you to The Point."

He looked at her thoughtfully. "I think I'd rather be in the same canoe," he said. Now why did he say things like that, Carney wondered irritably, when he was so obviously in Isobel's train?

"Bonnie," she said, to squelch him, "remember the races we used to have with Larry and Herbert?"

"Who are Larry and Herbert?"

"Who are Larry and . . ." The girls laughed.

"They're important people," Bonnie said. "At least, Larry is."

Before she could say any more the big Locomobile, followed closely by Lloyd's Buick, swept through the gateway of the Hutchinson place, and up the ascending driveway to the big white clapboard house. Sam halted in the porte-cochere.

"We'll leave your bags," he said. "And I'd like you to meet Mother."

The entrance hall was stately, with a fireplace, and

on the newel post at the foot of the wide stairs stood a bronze lady holding lights. As they passed from room to room Carney looked with admiration at the lofty hand-painted ceilings, the dark paneled walls and richly carved furniture. Velvet draperies covered with gold embroidery hung in the doorways.

Only the music room was light. This was in white, and a mirror which covered one wall doubled its whiteness. The carpet was sprinkled with roses. A Steinway grand piano stood invitingly open.

"I'll try to slip in and play on it, before I go," she thought.

"Mother!" Sam called, entering the library. Carney saw Betsy gazing up at the books which were in cases five shelves high with cloisonné jars at the top. The chairs here were deep and soft. A Persian carpet spread color on the floor.

Open doors beyond showed a massive four-post bed, bedroom chests, and bureaus. Carney remembered having heard that Mrs. Hutchinson was a semi-invalid. Probably she slept downstairs.

"We live in this library except in the summertime. Then we move on to the north porch," Sam said, leading the way.

They heard a chime of voices, and when he opened the door they looked through green vines, down sunshine-flooded lawns to the silvery lake. The wide screened porch was furnished in wicker with a swing hung from the ceiling, and it was sociably crowded.

Mrs. Hutchinson lay on a chaise lounge with *Queed* in her lap. She was small and fragile in a silken tea gown. Her welcoming hand flashed with rings. A little girl on a stool beside her was leafing through a copy of *Puck*. An elderly lady was knitting. Two youngish women shared the swing.

"We always have relatives around," Sam observed to Carney.

"So do we," she replied. But the effect, she thought, was different in her home. In the course of brief introductions, Sam had kissed his mother, his little sister, and his grandmother, and hugged two cousins. In her home such demonstrations were reserved for important meetings and partings.

Sam and his guests didn't sit down, although they were urged to do so.

"We want to get to sailing while there's still a breeze," he said.

"But you're coming back for lunch?"

"Oh, sure! See that there's plenty to eat."

A smiling maid took the bags. She wore a cap and a ruffled white apron like maids at East Hampton, not just a clean kitchen apron over gingham as Olga did. The house party and its attendant cavaliers ran down to the beach.

Green white-capped waves came racing to meet them, and the new boat was a shining beauty.

"How many can you carry?"

"Four in a pinch," Sam said. But he soon announced that he would keep his load to three. It was clear that Isobel was the only girl present who knew anything at all about sailing. The others were slow about scrambling up the sloping deck when the sailboat heeled over, and even slower about ducking when he tacked and the boom swung. Pretty dunderheads, Sam called them.

Isobel, however, was magnificent. Her years at East Hampton had made her familiar with all the maneuvers of small craft. She scrambled expertly to provide balance; she ducked even more expertly to avoid the swinging boom. Alone of all the girls, Sam remarked, she had had sense enough to put on nonskid shoes.

When he suggested that she sail the boat for a while, she accepted with delight.

"She sails it like a clipper captain," he shouted as they set off. Isobel was radiant, quite undisturbed by wet skirts and windblown hair. The spray caused her hair to curl in tendrils about her face.

Carney and Lloyd were already in a canoe. Fred, the man-of-all-work, was bringing oars for a rowboat, for Betsy and Bonnie proposed to row to Pleasant Park, Betsy's mother's girlhood home.

So with Isobel and Tom, or Isobel and Hunter, but always with Isobel, Sam sailed to the Inn Point, to Babcock's Bay, and other beauty spots. Paddling leisurely, Carney glanced now and then toward their adventurous sail. She heard Sam's big laugh and Isobel's soft one, and she felt a little twinge of loneliness for Larry. It was really too bad to have your best beau half a continent away!

A bell ringing from the big white house called them to luncheon.

"We're perfect frights," Carney remarked.

"You look swell," said Sam. But in spite of this reassurance the girls were relieved when Rose, the pretty maid, led them upstairs, past the lady on the newel post, to a large high-ceilinged bedroom with satin draperies and mahogany furniture and an enormous bed covered with a satin spread. A bathroom adjoined.

"Isn't it the most gorgeous house?" Betsy asked. "I feel as though I were in one of my own stories."

"Yes, it's gorgeous, and homelike, too."

"Your baby hippo has turned into a very handsome young man."

"Tell that to Isobel."

"Long Island's fairest daughter," Betsy joked.

Isobel laughed her soft, lazy laugh. "He's a perfect darling," she said.

Luncheon was served on the north porch. There was a window near the table opening off a pantry, and the cook passed things through to Rose. The table was set with place mats. Carney had seen them used at Professor Bracq's at Vassar, and resolved now to give her mother a set for her birthday. The effect of the partially bare, polished table, reflecting a bouquet of daisies and delphiniums, was very attractive.

Mr. Hutchinson sat at the head of the table. He dominated it, and not only because he was handsome. He was like a large warm sun sending out rays. He was expansively pleased, Carney could see, to be surrounded by family, relatives, and friends, lavishing them with everything good.

The food was richer and heavier than Carney was accustomed to at home. There was thick spiced gravy on the meat, highly seasoned dressing on the salad; the vegetables were drowned in butter; great squares of butter accompanied the hot biscuits; and the dessert—mousse, they called it—was made from frozen cream.

Talk was easy and merry. Everyone was relaxed to an extent unusual in family parties as Carney had observed them. Until she went to college she had always taken her family for granted. But since coming back to them from the outside world, she sometimes tried to evaluate and classify the Sibleys. Now she found herself comparing this opulent family life with her own.

Somewhat to her surprise . . . not being used to fanciful ideas . . . she compared them in terms of color. Sam's home, with its lavishness, its warmth, its indulgent extravagant affection, was like a rich deep purple. Her own, she decided, was dove gray. Dove gray seemed to express disciplined affection, reticence, order, thrift, justice, and kindness.

She had never, she thought suddenly, heard her father or mother say an unkind word about anyone. But they didn't laugh and play like this.

"We have fun, though," she thought. "We pop corn on Sunday nights. Dad makes rarebits for company. We get maple sugar from Vermont and 'sugar off,' when there's new snow, like Mother used to do when she was a girl."

She felt suddenly a little uneasy.

"I don't know how I'd get along in a family like this. I hope Larry is sort of . . . dove grayish."

And then she felt really confused, for her thought was a tacit admission that in her heart she expected to marry Larry.

Mr. Hutchinson was beaming at her down the table.

"And what about you, Miss Caroline?" he asked. "Are you for or against?"

Carney was dismayed. She hadn't been listening to the conversation. She had no idea what they were talking about.

"I believe," said Isobel, "that she agrees with Miss Milholland."

That explained it. Isobel had been telling about Inez Milholland, the Vassarite who, forbidden to lecture on Woman's Suffrage on the campus, had addressed her fellow students from a graveyard just over the boundary line.

"Yes, I'm for it," Carney said.

"I'm surprised," said Mr. Hutchinson. "I'm surprised and disappointed. You're too pretty to be a Suffragette."

Now *her* father, Carney thought, favored Woman's Suffrage. He believed it would be an influence for good.

She was still woolgathering while everyone looked at her expectantly, but Betsy Ray came to her rescue.

"You promise not to throw rocks through the Hutchinsons' windows, don't you, Carney?"

"Yes, I promise that," said Carney, smiling at the Sun God who relented and asked Rose to bring her some more mousse.

9

Carney's Future in a Handbasket

THEY COULDN'T SWIM, of course, until two hours had elapsed, so after lunch they spread blankets on the lawn. The wind had died down, and it was growing hot. The air smelled of red clover; and hollyhocks in a hedge along the kitchen garden glowed in the sunshine like a stage set.

Isobel looked up at the sky where thick white clouds were piled against the blue. She said with a glance at Sam that they looked like sails. Tom said they looked like continents and Betsy said they looked like white of egg pricked out by a fork.

"They're like nice clean clothes hung to dry," Carney declared.

She and Bonnie brought out sewing bags which they had packed along with their bathing suits.

"Such industry!" cried Betsy, piling cushions for her head.

"We're embroidering center pieces, just alike."

"Do you girls have hope chests?" Lloyd asked.

"We certainly do."

"I don't," said Betsy. "My husband and I are going to use paper plates and napkins."

"Poor Joe!"

"Lucky Larry!"

"Who is this Larry you're always talking about?" asked Sam with a meaningful glance toward Bonnie. His misapprehension brought delighted smiles.

While Carney and Bonnie sewed, and Betsy did nothing, Sam and Hunter played mumble-the-peg. Lloyd, who had brought his camera, got a shot of a mother bluebird feeding her babies. Tom strolled to the car and returned with a box of chocolates. In spite of the enormous luncheon so recently consumed, this was greeted by approving shouts.

"You used to bring fudge when you came down to see me at West Point," he said to Carney, offering the box.

"Wasn't I a good 'drag'?"

"Swell!"

"This year you have to come to Vassar to a dance."

Carney and Isobel began to tell about dances at Vassar.

"They start at four o'clock sharp."

"Four in the *afternoon?*" demanded Sam.

"Of course. Broad daylight. And you have to come in full dress, white tie and all. It's so every male menace can be off the campus by eleven."

"Isn't it," Sam asked solicitously, "just a little hard to round up men for your dances?"

"A little," Isobel admitted.

"But our crowd is lucky," Carney put in. "Win, one of our Tower girls, lives in a boys' school. Her father is head master there. She rounds up boys enough for all of us."

"And next year," added Isobel sweetly, "Tom is going to come. Aren't you, Tom?"

"Yes," said Tom. "I'm a bold fellow. Are the dances fun after they start?"

The girls looked at each other, and Isobel's laugh rippled.

"Well," she admitted, "bunny hugs and turkey

trots aren't allowed. I lost my privileges for six weeks last spring because I tried one innocent little turkey trot."

"I was put off the dance floor because my psyche knot fell down," chuckled Carney. "The walls are lined with chaperons, watching out for unladylike behavior. They even pass on the music we choose. Last year they struck 'Too Much Mustard' off the program. Now what under the sun is wrong with 'Too Much Mustard'?"

"Bonnie!" cried Betsy. "Aren't we glad we're going to the U?"

"Oh, but Vassar is wonderful!" Carney insisted. "Men aren't everything. Are they, Isobel?"

"Certainly not. Besides when we girls dance in J parlor, Carney dresses up in her father's dress suit. She's as handsome as Jack Barrymore."

Carney burst into a laugh. "One night we stuffed that dress suit with pillows and put it out in the hall. We scared the night watchman into fits."

Inspired by these happy memories they broke into song:

> *"We are from Vassar,*
> *Vassar are we*
> *Singing for gladness*
> *Right merrily . . ."*

Betsy and Bonnie, Lloyd and Sam tried to drown them out with, "Minnesota, Hail to Thee." (Bonnie didn't know it very well, but she did her best.)

Tom burst in, too.

> *"On, brave old army team,*
> *On to the fray,*
> *Fight on to victory*
> *For that's the famous army way . . ."*

And Hunter, who was registered at Carleton, shouted, at the top of his voice:

> *"Carleton, our Alma Mater,*
> *We hail the maize and blue!"*

Sam cupped his mouth in his hands.

"Four o'clock!" he yelled. "Who's for a swim?"

Everybody was.

Back in the house, the girls went upstairs again. They changed into bathing suits, tying bandana handkerchiefs around their heads and putting on stockings and bathing slippers. Fred greeted them like an old friend, and when Carney and Isobel set off with the boys to swim to the diving tower, he offered to take Betsy and Bonnie along in a rowboat.

Both Carney and Isobel were excellent swimmers.

Again and again Carney climbed to the tower and dove. She loved the cold shocking plunge, the vigorous push through cool greenness up into sunshine and the wonder of blue arching sky.

"Race me to the raft?" called Sam who stood behind her on the diving board. "That is, if you think you can make it."

"If I think I can make it!" repeated Carney scornfully, and dove.

Just two strokes behind him, breathless and laughing, she pulled up on the raft which was moored in front of a neighboring estate. Around them the lake glittered and twinkled. She wrung the water out of her heavy skirt and wished she could take off her shoes and stockings as she did when swimming alone with her brothers.

"Gee, it's fun out here!" she said.

"I want to have your whole Crowd out. We'll have to make it on a Saturday, though, so many of the boys are working."

"How does it happen you're not working?"

"I'm on vacation."

"I have an idea," she said mischievously, "that you're on vacation all the time."

"The heck I am! I fire the boiler at the mill."

"But for your father! It isn't the same thing."

Sam looked at her in exasperation. "What are you

like when you aren't scolding?" he asked.

Carney showed her dimple. "I embroider center pieces. And sometimes I play the piano. By the way, I'd like to play your Steinway. Would anybody mind?"

His face warmed. "We'd love it. Mother especially. She's very fond of music and she doesn't get out much."

"I'd like to play for her," Carney said quickly.

After the swim, while the other girls bathed luxuriously in the big tub and took their time dressing, Carney twisted up her still damp hair and hurried into her skirt and middy.

She ran downstairs and into the music room, leaving the door ajar. She struck a few chords, listening with pleasure to the resonant tone, and began Mac-Dowell's playful *Brer Rabbit*. She heard Sam come in and presently saw him in the mirror listening with attention.

She passed from MacDowell to Weber's *Perpetual Motion*. She was rather proud of the way she played that. Then she played a Chopin prelude and the *Nocturne*, Opus Nine, No. 2, and Grieg's *Witches Dance*, which was one of her favorites. It pleased her to think of Mrs. Hutchinson, who was never able to go to a concert, listening from her chaise lounge.

When she jumped up at last Sam rose and came toward her.

"You play very well," he said, sounding surprised.

"Do you like music?"

"Very much."

"Do you play the piano yourself?"

"No, but I fool around with a saxophone."

"Won't you show it to me? I never saw one."

"Sure," he answered. "It's up on the third floor."

The third floor was filled by one large room. It held a billiard table and cases full of the mementos of travels. A birch bark canoe hung from the ceiling. There was a phonograph with a pile of records.

Sam took his saxophone out of its case and Carney sat down in a window seat beneath tall uncurtained windows. Across the lake the sun was sending up showy fountains of color.

He licked the reed energetically. "I have to do that to get it going. I warn you I make horrible squawks at first." He did, but when he started running up and down the scale, his instrument sounded like a cello.

"I just play by ear," he said and began a song she knew.

"Pale hands I love,
Beside the Shalimar . . ."

After one song he put the saxophone aside.

"Did you hear much music in New York?" he

asked, sitting down beside her.

"I went to the Metropolitan Opera," she replied. "We heard *La Boheme*. I liked the music but it seemed a little silly . . . a fat prima donna dying of consumption, people shouting their hearts' secrets all over that big auditorium."

"How about orchestra concerts?"

"I liked them. Have you heard Tschaikovsky's Fifth?" she asked eagerly.

"Yes."

"That's my favorite. I wish I knew how to follow a symphony properly. Can you pick out the themes?"

"I'm learning to."

"And I wish I understood the set-up of a big orchestra." She frowned. "I don't know what the different instruments do."

"It's fascinating how they work it out," said Sam. "One instrument takes a cue from another, repeating the same melody. I wish we could go to a concert together sometime. I would show you what little I know. Who's your teacher in piano?"

"Kate Chittenden."

"She's good."

"She's very good, and she's been very kind to me. She took me to New York to play for Matthew Lang." After a pause Carney said abruptly, unsmiling, "He said my Scarlatti sounded silly."

"Maybe you were frightened," suggested Sam.

"I was, and Miss Chittenden said so, and Mr. Lang said, 'By their works shall ye know them.'"

"He sounds like a pleasant character."

"He's a very fine pianist."

"Of course. What else did you play for him?"

"Some Chopin. And do you know what he said to that? 'You play those notes beautifully, but you don't know what they mean.'"

"Anything else?" asked Sam, for it was obvious from Carney's painful swallowing that she hadn't yet got it all out.

"He said, 'You ought to lose your money, or have a sorrow, or fall in love.'"

After a thoughtful pause Sam asked, "You don't want to play professionally, do you?"

"No. I wouldn't for the world. And I know I'm not good enough. Still . . . I was humiliated at his saying that."

"Why?"

"It made me sound so shallow."

"Not shallow, just young." Sam's voice, which was always soft, grew very gentle. "Probably," he went on, "you *will* play better after you fall in love. But the joke on Mr. Lang is that it won't seem important to you then. Those musicians think music is everything. Writers are the same about writing, and artists about painting. They live in a different world from the rest of us. No telling whether it's better or worse than ours.

"Myself, I like the world ordinary people live in. I just want the Loco, lots of fishing, poker at low stakes, my sax . . . a home and kids sometime, of course. A girl like you, I think, would like a home and kids, with music just for the frosting on the cake.

"You'll keep on playing the piano. Probably your husband will hound you to play for him every night after supper. But as the kids grow older you'll play less and less. And you won't feel bad about that, for one of the kids will be musical, maybe . . . all your technical skill and talent plus a little from his dad. Say, that would be swell!"

"Wouldn't it!" They glowed at each other.

There was a shout from downstairs. "Carney! Sam! Where are you?"

Carney jumped up and she saw that the third floor room had grown quite dim. Beyond the tall windows the western sky was a sheet of flaming color.

"Heavens!" she cried. "It's time to go home."

Sam put his hand over hers. He gave it a warm squeeze.

"There's your future in a handbasket," he said.

During the farewells, while Mrs. Hutchinson thanked her for the music and Mr. Hutchinson urged them all to come again, Carney kept thinking about the strange conversation. The ride home was hilarious. Isobel rode with Carney, Sam, and Hunter in the Loco, and she taught the boys Vassar songs ... about the Female blowing off the college, about Matthew Vassar's ale.

> *"The ale he brewed was excellent,*
> *His neighbors liked it well,*
> *And Matthew was a miracle of thrift ..."*

The boys shouted it enthusiastically and Carney could hardly sing for laughing. Yet underneath she kept thinking about the talk. The memory of it warmed her.

She had always known what she wanted to do—get married and have children. There had never been a moment's doubt, no other possible choice. And yet Sam Hutchinson seemed to have molded her future.

He had decided that her oldest child was a boy—and musical. Carney could almost see him. He had thick dark hair and a crooked smile.

10

The Little Colonel's House Party

"GIRLS!" CRIED BETSY RAY, on the sleeping porch that night. "Do you know what this is?"

"It's a house party."

"It's The Little Colonel's House Party!" *The Little Colonel* books for girls had been the rage during their childhood.

"Hurray!" said Carney. "Then I'm The Little Colonel."

"You always did remind me of her," Betsy replied. "I'm the gal named Betty because she was a writer. And Bonnie is Joyce, the artist."

"I'm not an artist."

"No. But you've been in France, and so had Joyce. And Isobel is Eugenia, the rich eastern snob."

"Well, I like that!" cried Isobel.

"Oh, you have a heart of gold! Don't you remember?"

"I never read the things."

"You take us all abroad," chirruped Bonnie, "and support us the rest of our lives."

They were all acting silly. The day at Murmuring Lake, the gay ride home had welded them together. They were beginning to feel like a house party, Carney thought with satisfaction, climbing into bed beside Isobel. Betsy and Bonnie were giggling in the adjoining bed.

There was room for all four girls on the sleeping porch now, for Hunter and Jerry had obligingly moved inside. Only Bobbie still slept behind a curtain in the corner.

The giggling stopped at last but Carney lay awake, looking up at the dark lacy treetops. She was thinking about the singular conversation with Sam. When she fell asleep at last, it was only to come suddenly awake, knowing instinctively that her nap had been short.

Isobel was sleeping peacefully but as Carney's eyes grew accustomed to the darkness she saw that the bed where Betsy and Bonnie slept was empty.

"They must have gone downstairs for a snack," she thought. "Well, I could eat!"

Slipping out of bed, she stepped through the window into the boys' closet. The hall was dimly lighted by a gas flame turned low. The door admitting to the back stairs was open and as Carney tiptoed toward it she saw two ghostly figures.

Betsy and Bonnie were ascending with a fearful caution, carrying between them a large awkward object. When they reached the top step Carney saw what it was.

"You demons!" she hissed.

Her appearance was so unexpected, her whisper so violent, that they dropped Snow White's cage. The door flew open and white mice raced in all directions.

"Oh! Oh! Oh!" Clutching at their long night gowns Betsy and Bonnie ran toward the sleeping porch. They leaped through the closet window to the nearest bed, where Isobel was sleeping. Carney leaped after them, and Isobel sprang up.

"What's wrong? What's the matter?"

"Plenty! Those fiends were going to put mice in our bed."

"We weren't!" wailed Betsy and Bonnie, but unconvincingly.

"They dropped the cage and the mice got out. Goodness knows where they are by this time! Ssh!" Carney cautioned as laughter shook the bed. "You'll wake the folks."

"Could mice jump over a closet window?" Isobel shuddered, sitting on her feet.

"Of course not," said Carney, but she whisked her feet under her, too. So did Betsy and Bonnie.

"They're sure to go into our bedroom. They'll climb into our shoes."

"They'll climb up the curtains."

"They'll be looking in our mirror polishing their whiskers."

Again the bed shook with giggles.

Carney "Sshed!" again. "It won't be so funny," she declared, "if they get into father's and mother's room. Somebody has to catch them."

"That's obvious," said Isobel. "And it's obvious, too, who the somebody is."

"Perfectly obvious," said Carney, and she and Isobel began pushing and prodding their companions who clung to one another with muffled shrieks as they slid slowly and inexorably toward the floor.

"Wait a minute! I have an idea!" Betsy grabbed at Bonnie and the bed clothes.

"Bobbie!" she called softly. "Bobbie!"

"You'll never wake him by calling," Carney jeered. "You'll have to go over and shake him."

"But I wouldn't get out of this bed for a farm."

"Neither would I," Bonnie squealed.

"Bobb-ee!" They called together, "Bobb-ee!"

Their whispers had the force of desperation.

"What is it?" he answered sleepily.

"Wake up, Bobbie. Come here, please, Bobbie," they wheedled.

He came around the curtain, rubbing his eyes.

"Bobbie," said Betsy dramatically, "Snow White's babies came upstairs looking for a cool place to sleep. Snow White came after them, and now they're running all over. Would you catch them for us?"

"How did they get out?" asked Bobbie. "I shut the cage myself."

"Did you carry it upstairs?"

"No, I left it in the basement."

"Well, it's upstairs now. It's out in the hall." Betsy lowered her voice mysteriously. "Sometimes," she said, "I think there's lots we don't understand about Snow White. She can do things that ordinary mice can't do."

Bobbie was puzzled, but the Sibleys weren't easily taken in.

"Aw, shucks!" he said, and turned to go back to bed.

Bonnie tried a more realistic approach.

"If you'll catch them," she promised, "I'll buy you a bat to go with your baseball suit."

"And I'll buy you a mitt," said Betsy.

"You will?" Bobbie was alert at once. "All right," he added, heading for the window.

"Be careful not to wake Dad and Mother. At least," Carney said, with a giggle, "be careful not to wake Dad."

"'Nuff said," answered Bobbie and climbed through.

Snow White and her babies were found and returned to the basement. Bobbie went back to bed, but still waves of laughter swept the sleeping porch. Next morning there was tacked to the bedroom door a sheet of foolscap headed, "Rules For The Little Colonel's House Party."

It was decorated with mice, jaunty fellows with long curling whiskers and tails. The first rule announced that mice in bed were strictly forbidden.

Wearing boudoir caps to breakfast was forbidden also. (Carney had already warned them that her father detested the habit.)

Flirting was forbidden. Isobel was enjoined to consider Ellen and leave Hunter alone.

Betsy was asked to throw away her Kosmeo, her

Pompeian Massage Cream, and her pink face powder. (She adored such items.)

Carney was warned that she represented Vassar on every occasion.

Bonnie was reminded that she was a preacher's daughter.

Betsy was told not to write so many letters to Joe. Carney was told not to write so many letters to Larry. Isobel was told not to write so many letters to whomever it was she wrote them to. "Is it Howard Sedgwick???" demanded the Rules.

"I write to my parents, of course," said Isobel.

"Such daughterly devotion!"

"Oh, I have friends, too."

"Friends who write you every day in the same sprawling handwriting?"

"It's not sprawling!"

"It isn't so handsome as Joe's," sang Betsy.

Yes, the house party was beginning to feel just as a house party should.

Betsy was partly responsible, Carney thought as the days went by. She loved fun and was very inventive. If the girls didn't react to one idea, she offered another, but if someone else had a better one she accepted that—anything for fun! Bonnie's laughter, flowing in appreciation of everyone's jokes, helped, too, and so did Isobel's good nature.

To Carney's relief both Betsy and Bonnie liked Isobel. The town girls at first were a little guarded with her. She had been abroad, she had attended private schools, she had an Eastern accent, and her clothes were exquisite. But as party followed party, her tact and charm won them.

There were parties almost every day. The opening affair was a luncheon given by some favorite second cousins, school teachers from Vermont. It was a rose luncheon, very elegant, with pink streamers from the chandelier to each place, pink baskets filled with candy, and a fresh rose, with the name of a girl attached, pinned to each napkin.

Grandmother Sibley gave her thimble bee, using the heaviest Sibley silver, and the thinnest Sibley china, and the lace cloth and napkins from Brussels. Tall and stately with her halo of white hair, she sat down graciously to pour.

Isobel's appraising glance turned to admiration.

"Your grandmother looks like a duchess," she told Carney.

Grandmother Hunter didn't look like a duchess, but Carney loved the way she looked. Although her gray hair was carefully crimped, scolding locks fell over her collar. A white apron was tied about her soft uncorseted waist. A long black skirt sprang out with unfashionable fullness. In honor of her party she wore the brooch and earrings that Carney had worn for the masquerade.

She was a good cook and knew it. Her eyes twinkled when the girls exclaimed over her feathery popovers. These were served with strawberry jam and ham and eggs and fried potatoes and a pitcher of milk and a pot of fragrant coffee. She brought out sugar cookies too.

After breakfast the girls showed Isobel the kaleidoscope. You put it to your eye like a telescope and, as you turned it, pieces of colored glass in its mirrored insides fell into magical patterns.

"I remember looking in this when I was a little girl," Bonnie cried.

Laurenza Hunter looked on with pleasure, holding her lips tightly while her eyes brimmed with fun.

"I hope," Carney thought, "that when I'm a grandmother I'll be just like Grandmother Hunter."

Alice gave a porch party. Her home was on a hillside with a view. The vine-hung porch was furnished with chairs and pillows and a table which held magazines and a pitcher of lemonade.

All the girls except Betsy had brought hand work—sewing, or tatting, or Irish crochet.

"Perhaps your conscience would hurt you less, Miss Ray, if you read out loud to us," someone suggested.

"I won't admit to a single pang of conscience, but I'd love to read." Betsy picked up the new *Ladies' Home Journal*. "Here's just what we want, an article on women's colleges."

It was written by a parent, and he didn't like women's colleges any too well. "'Our daughter has come back to us mentally broadened, but somehow we feel a loss in emotional qualities. The head of the girl has been trained without the heart.'"

"What nonsense!" Carney interrupted. "You don't go to college to get your heart trained."

"Maybe if you went to the U you'd have emotional qualities like Bonnie and me," said Betsy. "We're frightfully emotional, aren't we, Bonnie?"

"I just palpitate," said Bonnie. "Or I will. I can feel it coming on."

"I like Teachers College," put in Alice. "It doesn't take four years, and I'm anxious to get out into the world."

"I like it, too," said Winona. "It's near Dennie." Winona and Dennie were going together.

Perhaps because of Dennie, Winona was giving an evening party with men.

In spite of all the daytime parties, men hadn't been exactly absent from their lives. Every evening after work they descended on the Sibley household. Sam drove in from the lake, unshaven again, nonchalantly untidy. The Crowd, Carney noticed, had already taken him in. His wealth was easily forgotten, in spite of his extravagant ways, for he never brought his father's money into a conversation. And he seemed to like the Crowd.

They piled into his auto, or the Sibley's, or Lloyd's, and took the Seven Mile drive, three and a half miles out and three and a half miles back on the Fletcher Road. They sang loudly about Josephine and the flying machine, or "Let Me Call You Sweetheart," or "Down by the Old Mill Stream."

Carney felt that she belonged again. Had she ever found Deep Valley melancholy?

The famous Minnesota heat arrived, pressing down over the valley like a smothering blanket. Almost every evening an electric storm cleared the air. Thunder crashed and rolled; lightning wrote its jagged fiery messages. For an hour or so it was blessedly cool. But the next day would be as hot as before.

The girls didn't mind. The sleeping porch was a boon, and they made a beauty parlor down in the basement, between the furnace and the laundry tubs. There they dressed one another's hair in elaborate coiffures.

Every morning Mrs. Sibley closed the windows and drew the shades for coolness, and, between engagements, the house party stayed in this semitwilight playing five hundred or social solitaire, reading, writing letters, playing the piano. Sometimes in the late afternoon they opened their parasols and walked down to Heinz's for a soda.

On the Tuesday of Winona's party Carney and Betsy went to Heinz's, and they fell to talking, as they often did, about California. Carney liked the subject because of Larry, and it was easy to get Betsy started.

Betsy described her grandmother's cottage.

"She has a palm tree and a guava tree on her front lawn, and an arbor covered with bougainvillea in the back. She had a garden all winter long."

"Doesn't it rain all winter?"

"Just in the mornings, usually. We had a little fire for breakfast. Then I always went at my writing. I certainly led a lively bunch of heroines to the altar.

"By noon it would have cleared, and I'd go for a walk. The pepper trees would still be shiny with rain, and the world would be so hot and bright, smelling of roses . . ." Betsy stopped, smiling.

"Weren't you lonesome," Carney asked, "when Larry and Herbert were away at college?"

"No," Betsy answered. "Not a bit. I must be cut out for the quiet life. I got acquainted with a few kids, of course, but what I liked best was just being with my grandmother.

"She told me stories about her childhood, and her married life with my real grandfather who went to the Civil War, and about when Mamma was a little girl. And, of course, Uncle Keith was there."

"Your uncle who is an actor?"

"Yes. After my step-grandfather died, Uncle Keith bought a little ranch up in the mountains near Grandma. He drove down to see her every week-end and that was wonderful for me because . . . Uncle Keith likes to write, too, and he took such an interest in my work. He thought my stories would be more apt to sell if they were typewritten. And he gave me a typewriter."

"Have you sold any yet?" Carney asked.

"Yes. It was partly the typewriter and partly . . ." Betsy paused.

"Partly what?"

After a moment Betsy pushed aside her chocolate nut sundae. She was wearing a Dutch collar with a Paisley tie, the green-brown color of her eyes, but it wasn't just the tie which made her eyes so bright. Her cheeks were growing pink as they did when she got excited.

"Near San Diego," she said, "is Ramona's marriage place . . . out of the novel. And there's a wishing well with this sign on it." She began to recite in a deepened voice.

"Quaff ye the waters of Ramona's well,
Good luck they bring and secrets tell,
Blest were they by sandaled Friar,
So drink and wish for thy desire."

"I wished I would sell a story, and I did," she said, resuming the chocolate nut sundae.

"Betsy!" cried Carney. "You don't believe in wishing wells!"

"Don't I?" Betsy asked.

"Besides, if you did, what a silly thing to wish for. I should think you'd have wished something about Joe."

Betsy's eyes grew wide. "Why, when I sold my story Joe was as happy as I was. I telegraphed him and he telegraphed back. We nearly died with joy."

Carney's thoughts returned to what Sam Hutchinson had said. "Those musicians think music is everything. Writers are the same about writing . . ."

"I don't believe in wishing wells," Carney thought. "But if I *could* make a wish, I'd wish for Larry to come."

As they neared the Sibley house Bobbie came running to meet them.

"Sis! Sis! You've got a telegram."

Carney was astonished. "Who in the world could be telegraphing me? Everyone I know is here."

"Except Larry," Betsy replied.

Carney turned and looked at her. Larry! His letter was overdue.

She ran up the steps and into the hall to a slender-legged table where mail was always placed. A yellow envelope was lying there.

"Carney," said her mother, coming out of the parlor, "there's a telegram for you."

"There's a telegram for you, Carney," Bonnie and Isobel called down the stairs.

Carney opened the envelope and unfolded the yellow paper. She read it and swallowed hard.

"Larry is coming."

"What?"

"Larry is coming. Friday. He's staying with Tom."

"What is he coming for?" asked Mrs. Sibley.

"He doesn't say," answered Carney. He didn't need to, of course. She felt a tightening at her heart.

"Right in the midst of the house party!" said Mrs. Sibley, sounding not too pleased. "And in all this heat!"

Carney's firm lips belied her sparkling eyes. She looked like Grandmother Hunter.

"Oh, well, if he's coming, let him come," she said.

11

Young Lochinvar

WINONA'S PARTY RANG WITH the news that Larry Humphreys was coming.

"Have you heard . . . Have you heard . . ." everyone asked everyone else, "Larry is coming back from California to see Carney."

When someone said it to Sam Hutchinson he was

startled. "A man at the house party?" he asked.

The circle around the piano laughed. "Oh, no, not that! He's staying with Tom."

"Then why do you say he's coming to see Carney?"

The circle laughed even more heartily, and Winona explained, "Larry and Carney used to go together."

"Larry and Carney! I thought it was Larry and Bonnie."

"That's a good one!" Alice cried.

"Heck, no! Larry and Carney. They were practically Romeo and Juliet," Cab said.

Sam grinned amiably at his mistake. He was shaved tonight. He was wearing a white coat and navy blue trousers, looking, Winona had told him, suave.

"But weren't they just kids when the Humphreys went away?" he asked. "I can't see what's so important about this."

"It's important, all right," Winona answered. "They've corresponded for four years and haven't missed a week. Lots of boys have rushed Carney . . . Al, Dave . . . but no one ever got anywhere. We all think Larry's coming back to get engaged."

"Young Lochinvar in person," said Sam, and he sought out Carney.

She was all in white and looked sparkling and triumphant. Sam began to chant as he drew near:

"Oh, young Lochinvar is come out of the west;
   Through all the wide border, his steed was the
       best . . ."

"Don't be silly," Carney said.

"Silly, is it? I understand that you're practically at the altar."

"Well, I'm not."

The others took their cue from Sam.

"'So faithful in love,'" Betsy said.

"'And so dauntless in war,'" Tom added.

"'There never was knight like the young Lochinvar.'"

"Oh, stop it!" Carney cried. But she was too happy to mind. Larry was coming half way across the continent to see her. He was on his way this minute.

It was a jolly party. Winona's parties were just like Winona, full of careless gaiety. There were tables for cards but no one played much five hundred. They sang around the piano to Winona's dashing accompaniment. They played wild games, and raced up and down stairs and in and out of doors.

Winona loved races, fights, and scuffles. She would be a teacher soon. She had learned how to assume an expression of gentle sweetness. But tonight her black eyes flashed and her white teeth gleamed. Dennie of the curly topknot and deceptively cherubic face, was never far away.

Carney's thoughts kept racing ahead to the parties they would have when Larry came. He could stay two weeks, Tom had said when she telephoned him after receiving the wire. Now he radiated pride at having kept Larry's secret.

"How long have you known it?" she asked.

"Two days."

"How did it happen? Did you write and invite him?"

"Oh, I've invited him at intervals ever since they went away. And I've known for a long time that he was saving money for a trip. But this wire came out of a perfectly clear sky."

He must have wired on receiving her last letter. She had written him after the day at Sam's. Carney felt that he had been drawn by her own urgent wish.

Sam strolled up again.

> "Oh come ye in peace here, or come ye in war,
>   Or to dance at our bridal, young Lord
>   Lochinvar?"

Carney tried to box his ears.

Sam had given the house party ammunition which it used freely between Tuesday and Friday. From morning until night, all over the house, on walks downtown, on automobile rides, at parties, someone always picked up the chant.

> *"He stayed not for break, and he stopped not*
> *for stone . . ."*

or

> *"So stately his form, and so lovely her face . . ."*

"Stop it!" Carney would beg.

Only Bonnie was merciful. "I won't let them do it when he comes, Carney," she promised. "You won't hear a word out of them then."

Carney took the teasing good-naturedly, but as Friday drew near her smile became a little fixed.

"You kids may not know it, but I'm fussed," she said.

She tried not to be. She tried to drive her nervousness away by keeping busy: she washed her hair and pressed her pink sprigged dimity. But inside she felt a growing excitement. Sometimes it pushed up into her throat and almost choked her. Larry had been important to her for so long!

She asked Bonnie to walk down to Front Street for a soda. Maternal little Bonnie, warm and loving, was an ideal confidante. Isobel seemed amused by the California invasion. Betsy was most sympathetic but she dramatized the visit so much that she made Carney fidgety. She grumbled to Bonnie, "Betsy makes me feel like the star of a play. I don't know how to act like Sarah Bernhardt."

"Larry won't want you to. He likes you because you're the way you are, always natural, never putting on."

"He used to like me, but do you suppose he still will?"

"Of course. Everyone does. This is a good time for him to come," Bonnie added. "There's so much going on."

"I'm glad," answered Carney, "that there'll always be a lot of people around."

She had advanced so far in her thoughts that now she was withdrawing a little. But she still felt sure that she and Larry would reach an understanding.

"I don't suppose Dad would like an engagement until I'm through college," she thought. "But we'll know whether there's ever going to *be* an engagement."

Wednesday passed, and Thursday. On Friday the heat simmered over the green lawn. It simmered over Mrs. Sibley's bed of pink and white cosmos, and in the house behind the close-drawn shades.

The girls were dressed in their thinnest clothes, playing cards, reading, doing fancy work as usual.

Even the boys preferred to stay inside. Jerry was reading in his father's big chair. Bobbie had brought up Snow White's cage and was playing with the mice. He opened the door and let them run a little; the girls didn't mind any more.

The girls wanted Carney to play for them, but for once she refused. She would have been happier working but due to her unfortunate forehandedness—and her mother's—there seemed to be nothing to do. She went out to the kitchen and made a pitcher of lemonade.

Tom had not been able to tell her when Larry would arrive.

"He didn't mention a train," Tom had said. "I suppose he'll come up from Omaha but it could be down from Minneapolis. Depends on his route."

This increased the suspense.

At first, whenever the telephone rang, Carney jumped. Once she dropped a winning five hundred hand all over the floor. But the rings were always false alarms. Ellen was calling for Hunter, or a grandmother for Mrs. Sibley, who was out, or Lloyd or Cab for one of the girls. At last the telephone lost its power to agitate. Carney answered without even thinking that it might be Larry, and she heard a deep voice.

"Hello. May I speak to Carney, please?"

The speech was slow, leisurely. Larry had always spoken so. Carney swallowed for her throat felt dry. Her heart seemed to race around like one of Snow White's babies.

"This is Carney," she replied.

"Well . . ." and he gave a little laugh. "Here's your bad penny."

"I'm glad you're here."

"Four years is a long time," he remarked.

"Yes, it is."

"May we come right up?"

"Of course."

The girls were listening undecidedly. Carney's replies might indicate Larry, but her matter-of-fact tone certainly didn't. She shut down the receiver.

"He's here. He and Tom are coming right up."

There was a scream in which she didn't join, although she was smiling.

"Is there time to change your dress?" asked Isobel.

"I'm not going to change my dress."

"But you pressed the dimity."

"Just to have something to do."

Betsy was astonished. "Aren't you even going to powder your nose?"

"Of course not," answered Carney. "You know I never use that stuff. Maybe I'll wash my face," she added trying to joke.

Bonnie took charge. "Pick up those cards, Isobel," she said. "And Betsy, you put the table away. Take Snow White back to the basement, Bobbie. Come on upstairs now. We're going to let Carney meet him alone."

"I'm not sure I want to," Carney said

"See?" cried Isobel sinking back into a chair. "She really wants us around."

"It would be wonderful for a lady author," Betsy pleaded, "to see a reunion like this. I'd know how to describe one in a novel some day."

But Bonnie was inexorable. "No," she said firmly. "Upstairs with you. I'll follow."

"Bonnie," said Carney, "you stay! I'd rather you did. Mother would like it better, too."

"All right," Bonnie replied. "If you want me to. Shoo, now!" She clapped her hands, and Betsy and Isobel rushed up the stairs.

"'The Little Colonel's Knight Comes Riding,'" they chanted as they headed not for Carney's room, which was headquarters for the house party, but for Mrs. Sibley's room which looked down to the street.

Carney went to the mirror in the hall. Her blue lawn dress was fresh. Her pompadour was smooth. She looked just as usual except that her brown eyes had little snapping points in them.

"It's just Larry coming," she told herself firmly. "Just Larry. He's been to this house a thousand times."

Bonnie ran her arm through Carney's and they went out to the porch.

"Will you keep them for supper?" Bonnie asked.

"I don't know. I forgot to ask Mother. Do you think we should?"

"It would be a nice thing to do unless Mrs. Slade is expecting them back. What are we having?"

"Everything cold . . . except green corn. But I could bake muffins."

The commonplace housewifely conversation helped.

At last Tom and a companion could be seen walking up Broad Street.

"He's tall," Carney said.

"He looks nice," said Bonnie and squeezed Carney's arm. But Carney didn't return the squeeze. She waited stiffly.

The pair turned in at the Sibley walk, and Tom suddenly became invisible. Carney saw only a tall, strapping, broad-shouldered young man in a handsome light-colored suit, wearing a bow tie and a straw hat set at a jaunty slant.

She ran down the steps and put out one of her hands. He took both of them. For quite a long moment he looked into her face. Then she gave her mirthful, explosive little chuckle.

"Do you feel as fussed as I do?" she asked.

"I do," he answered. And she saw the crooked smile she remembered. They both laughed.

Bonnie and Tom, who had been looking the other way, came up when they heard the laugh. Bonnie, beaming, shook Larry's hand. The Sibley car stopped in front of the house. Hunter was bringing his mother home from the Ladies' Aid. Mrs. Sibley got out and walked toward Larry, her slight figure impressively erect.

He said just what Bonnie had said.

"Any doughnuts in the doughnut jar?"

"Plenty," Mrs. Sibley answered, and some of her frosty doubts must have melted for her eyes began to sparkle in the Hunter family way. "Unless the house party has eaten them all up. Can't you and Tom stay for supper and find out?"

Carney called the girls, and during the ensuing melee of greetings she watched Larry. Without being exactly handsome, he was even more attractive than he had been as a boy. That crooked teasing smile was full of charm. He seemed, as Betsy had said, to be laughing at you, but he was also laughing at himself.

He was immaculately groomed. His thick dark hair was parted on one side and smoothly combed. His suit was a light oatmeal mixture, very well tailored; his shirt was white, his bow tie exact. Carney thought suddenly of Sam, unshaven and unkempt.

To her delight she didn't feel nervous any more. She just felt happy as she had the first night she knew he was coming. Betsy asked about Herbert. Mr. Sibley came in and asked about his parents. Jerry and Bobbie came up from the basement.

"Play baseball?" asked Bobbie. "I'm going to get a baseball suit."

Through all the excitement, Larry was completely poised. Nothing hurried his slow speech or deliberate manner. Now and then his smiling gaze went to Carney.

"He's very nice," she thought.

Bonnie carried her off upstairs to change for supper. Carney put on her pink sprigged dimity dress with black velvet ribbon run in the neck and sleeves, and the abalone shell pendant Larry had sent her.

"How do you like him?" Bonnie asked.

"Why, he's just the same. And that's what I'd been hoping."

Bonnie hugged her.

After supper Sam dropped in, himself shaved and immaculate.

"How about it?" he asked, when Carney answered the door. "Has Young Lochinvar shown up?"

"Out of the west," responded Carney, smiling. She didn't feel embarrassed by his teasing now.

"'There never was knight like the young Lochinvar,'" quoted Sam. He too was smiling brightly.

He smiled when he was introduced to Larry. They shook hands firmly. But as the evening wore on Sam grew restless. Winona and Dennie, Alice and Cab dropped in. Talk was given over to the old days, the old Crowd. Sam stalked about, examining the articles on the "what-in-ell," staring up at Grandfather Sibley's portrait, smoking cigarettes. At last he went over to Isobel.

"How about you and me going out for a spin?"

"I'd love it. The East doesn't belong in this gathering."

Isobel kissed fingertips, and they departed.

Carney waved good-by happily. "I wish Isobel would hook Sam Hutchinson," she thought. "Maybe she's planning to. Maybe she came to the Middle West looking for money."

Larry didn't have money but he was very, very nice.

They began to make plans like busy spiders weaving webs. Tomorrow was Saturday; it would be a good day for a picnic.

"Let's go see the new dam at Orono," Cab suggested. This engineering marvel was new and exciting.

"I'd rather go to Two Falls Park," Carney replied. The Crowd had often gone to the Two Falls in the old days. She and Larry had gone there together.

He remembered. She could tell from the half-teasing smile he turned upon her.

"Yes, let's go to Two Falls," he said. "Let's save Orono for some special occasion."

12

Baseball for Bobbie

THE NEXT MORNING Carney woke so early that there was still color in the east. Slipping out of bed she tiptoed to the railing. A dewy freshness lay on lawn and garden. The flowers were standing straight and eager. Everything was still except for a gray cat down in the shrubbery going off on an adventure of his own.

Larry had come, and he was everything she wanted

him to be. He was so manly and well-mannered, so full of fun. They were already good friends.

"And that's the way to begin," Carney thought. She felt happy from her head to her toes, and she looked up at the sky with a feeling of gratitude that was almost like a prayer. Then she began to plan about the picnic.

During the morning she and Bonnie helped Olga prepare the lunch. Bonnie stuffed eggs while Carney baked a chocolate cake. She remembered from the old days that Larry liked chocolate cake; and she made good ones.

Isobel and Betsy had accepted with alacrity Carney's assurance that they didn't need to help. They were writing letters which they wanted to give to the postman. They were always writing letters, Carney remarked.

"It isn't so strange about Betsy," she said, watching syrup drip from a fork. "She and Joe are practically engaged. But I can't make Isobel out. I don't believe she cares a thing for this Howard Sedgwick."

"Neither do I," Bonnie replied. "She's having too much fun with the boys around here. Those looks she gives Sam Hutchinson!"

"They're as sweet as this frosting."

"And she looks the same way at Tom, almost."

"And if Tom isn't around she looks that way at

Hunter. Poor Hunter has it awfully bad!" Carney's smile was rueful. Hunter's crush was hard on him, she thought, and hard on Ellen too.

Her boiling sugar spun a thread, and she poured it slowly over beaten white of egg. Bonnie glanced out the side kitchen window.

"Here comes the postman!" she called lifting her voice. "Have you finished those letters?" She looked out the window again. "There's time for one post-script. He's stopped to talk to Bobbie. No, here comes Bobbie now, running like mad, with a package!"

"Maybe it's the baseball suit," said Carney.

It was! And Larry's arrival the day before had been as nothing compared to the arrival of the baseball suit. Bobbie burst in with his face shining, threw the package on the back parlor floor and began to tear off papers frantically.

"It's my baseball suit!" he shouted. "It's my prize!"

The ecstasy in his voice brought his mother from the second floor, Isobel and Betsy from the library, Carney, Bonnie and Olga from the kitchen, even Jerry from the porch and Hunter from the garage.

"It's my baseball suit! It's my prize!" Perspiring, Bobbie wrenched and pulled at a bundle of flannel.

The shirt and bloomers were gray, with narrow red stripes. There were two big red letter B's lying loose in the box.

"They stand for Baseball," Bobbie chattered. "Will you sew them on for me, Mother?"

"I certainly will, right on the front. Run get my sewing basket."

When he was gone she lifted the sleazy suit. "Isn't this disgraceful?"

"It'll tear to pieces the first time he slides into first base," Carney said.

"But I'll go over these buttonholes," said Mrs. Sibley, "and tighten the buttons. Don't say a word. He's so happy."

He was beside himself with joy. He waited radiantly while his mother sewed on the B's. But when she began on the buttons and buttonholes he shifted from foot to foot.

"Hurry up, Mother! Those are all right!"

"I'm hurrying. I'll be done in a minute."

Betsy and Bonnie brought out the baseball bat and mitt which they had purchased earlier. These were greeted with shouts. Hunter contributed an old cap with a visor and Jerry offered some heavy, ribbed, red stockings.

Bobbie seized the loot and as soon as the suit was ready clattered upstairs. When he reappeared, his big front teeth were shining, and his hair seemed to be standing on end with delight. The elastic in one bloomer leg had already given out. No matter how often he pulled it up, it kept sliding down. But he wouldn't wait for his mother to put in new elastic. He rushed out to show his glory to the neighborhood boys.

That afternoon he showed it to the Crowd gathering for the picnic.

"How do you like it, Sam?" he called before Sam was out of the Locomobile. He planted his feet wide apart, spat vigorously, swung with his bat at an imaginary ball.

"Say!" said Sam. "It's swell!"

"Pretty flossy!" said Bobbie and dropped his bat to pull up the sagging bloomer leg, picked up the bat again, and swung with unabated joy.

"When are we going to have a game?" asked Sam. "Why don't you and Jerry come along on this picnic? There's a diamond out at Two Falls Park."

"Can we? Can we?" Bobbie rushed off in search of his mother. Jerry stood where he was, but a smile broke over his calm face.

Carney smiled at Sam. "Go tell Mother there's plenty of lunch for you," she said to Jerry. She thought to herself, "Sam certainly likes those boys!"

Three cars were soon full to overflowing. Carney and Larry were somewhat pointedly assigned seats together. Larry looked as well by morning light as he had the night before; his thick hair was as glossy, his bow tie as neat. He had taken off his coat and his shirt was like snow.

Sam, of course, was thoroughly unshaven and untidy.

"I thought this was a *picnic*," he said in mock scorn, slapping Larry on the back. He swung his arms around the shoulders of Lloyd and Tom, pushing them about as though to rumple them.

"It *is* a picnic!" Carney cried. "Wait till you see my chocolate cake!"

"Did you make a chocolate cake?" asked Larry. "That's my favorite kind."

She couldn't pretend she hadn't known it. Her eyes and dimple twinkled.

"Such devotion! It's touching!" Sam remarked to Isobel who gave him a lingering smile.

Larry seemed to enjoy the ride which took them out of Deep Valley to the west, over the slough, across the red iron Cutbank River bridge. The Cutbank, which joined the Minnesota shortly, curved through a deep green valley. That green looked beautiful, Larry said, after California where grass must be irrigated. But he loved California, just as Betsy did.

"You would, too," he said, turning to Carney.

Beyond the Cutbank the road ran along a serried hilltop which now and then rose high enough to give a glimpse of the distant Minnesota curling through its spacious valley.

They passed a cluster of crumbling stone buildings. Tiger lilies glowed in ancient house foundations.

"There used to be a town here," Carney explained. "There was even a three-story hotel. Then the railroad went to Deep Valley and it all fell into ruins."

"Ruins in the young Middle West!" Isobel cried.

At last a line of cottonwoods and willows showed them Two Falls Creek. Inside the park they ran at once to the falls. First the creek took a downward jump of about the height of a man. Then, as though it had gained courage, it took a truly heroic leap, fifty feet or more, through a wild gorge. Trees and bushes leaned out dangerously from rocky slopes to watch.

Lloyd had brought his Kodak, of course. The party took snapshots of one another at the little falls and at the big ones and on the rustic bridge between. Larry and Carney were snapped together, smiling.

They went down under the big falls braving the noise and the spray.

"We used to do this when we were kids," Larry said, and Carney remembered. She used to be afraid, and glad of his protecting presence.

In the picnic grove tall trees provided green-gold shade. The party dropped their baskets on a table and ran for the swings. Carney and Larry "pumped up" together as they used to do when they were children. They had a "pumping up" match with Betsy and Cab.

Bobbie went out to inspect the baseball diamond and he came back howling for a game. Hunter had found a crowd of high school boys, more than ready to oblige.

"There are plenty to make up two nines if you really want to play," he said.

"Of course we want to play." Sam dropped his hand to Bobbie's shoulder. "What position would you like, Larry?"

"Why, I don't care. I pitch a little with the Stanford team."

Tom guffawed. "Pitch a little! A little! The last week of school he pitched a three-hit shutout, got three hits out of five times at bat and won his own game with a triple."

"That settles it," said Sam. "Larry pitches on the Lochinvar Nine. Bobbie and I are going to play center field on the World's Best Bluing Nine. Bobbie is assistant center fielder."

"What's assistant center fielder?" Bobbie wanted to know.

"You'll see. It's important."

Two teams were quickly organized. Winona said hopefully that if they were short a player she was good at almost any spot.

"You sit in the shade and cheer for me," said Dennie.

"I don't see why I can't play if Bobbie can."

"Have *you* got a baseball suit?"

Winona took her place with the girls in a grove of poplars near the diamond. Carney leaned back against a tree trunk and brought out her tatting.

"Don't you ever move without tatting?" asked Betsy, who was stretched on the grass.

"Bonnie's got crochet work, and so has Alice."

"So have I," said demure little Ellen, opening a sewing bag.

Betsy groaned. "I wish Tacy were here."

"Do you know," said Bonnie, "it seems strange to see you around without Tacy."

"She's engaged," said Betsy. "She's going to get married. But she'll never tat, and neither will I."

Alice poked her with a reproving foot. "You're just plain lazy."

"My mind is working," Betsy explained. "Maybe I'm making up a story that I'll sell for ten dollars . . . maybe. This is an awfully romantic situation, Larry coming back."

Carney snorted.

She tatted busily but she watched the diamond, too. She watched Larry's tall, lean, muscular figure on the mound. When he wound up and threw the ball, he was the personification of athletic grace and strength.

"He ought to make Sam want to lose a few pounds," she thought, and looked around to see whether Sam was impressed. But he was fooling with Jerry and Bobbie.

To the girls' amusement Sam was as good as his word and took Bobbie with him out in center field. Every time Sam caught a fly ball and there was no opposing runner on base threatening to advance, he would throw the ball to Bobbie who was stationed about ten yards nearer to second base. Bobbie would throw it as far toward second as he could manage, and then, happily hitching up the slipping bloomer leg, he would run and recover it and throw it farther.

Carney laughed until tears came to her eyes.

"Sam's team is putting up with a lot," she said to Bonnie.

"Everyone likes Sam," Bonnie replied. "And it isn't just that he shares those charge accounts at ice cream parlors all over the county. He really is a dear."

"Well, it's awfully good-natured of all the boys," said Carney. The rest of them were playing a serious game. And Larry's skill became more and more evident.

Once an opposing batter hit one of Larry's pitches sharply and lined it straight back at the pitcher's box. Larry caught the ball as easily and casually, Carney thought, as Sam would have picked up a bat.

At bat, too, Larry was grace and strength personified. Watching him it was easy to believe that he had got three hits including a triple in the Stanford game.

At Two Falls Park he met the ball fairly every time he came to bat. Once he slashed a two-base ground ball between first and second. Once he drove a line single into right field; and once, meeting the ball squarely and with every ounce of his strength, he electrified his audience by hitting a genuine, dyed-in-the-wool home run. Even Sam's assistant center fielder swallowed chagrin and cheered as the triumphant ball soared overhead.

Sam was only a fair player. He caught without a fumble the fly balls hit to him in distant center field, but he ran ponderously and with none of Larry's grace. Nor was he any great shakes at bat. Once he struck out; once he popped a feeble little fly to the third baseman, and only once did he get a solid hit. But he got that with the bases full, and it was a double which brought in three scores, momentarily tying the game.

He was thoroughly enjoying himself, Carney observed. And he was a good loser. He grinned cheerfully at Larry when the Lochinvar Nine won, 8 to 6.

Larry brushed off compliments. "Football's my game."

"Tell us about the Stanford team," said Tom. They

had returned to the picnic grove where long rays now slanted through the trees gilding the grass. Jerry and Bobbie had brought water. The boys had made a fire and Carney had put the coffee to boil. The girls were spreading a long rustic table with a cloth and dishes, knives, forks, and spoons.

But Larry was genuinely modest. He wouldn't be drawn out on the subject of his football prowess. He gave some amusing accounts of gridiron battles but omitted his own exploits.

Sam listened attentively. In his one year at the University he hadn't gone in for athletics, but he loved sports just as he loved tinkering with a car or playing low-stakes poker.

How endlessly men could talk about sports, Carney thought, as they passed from a discussion of football and baseball teams to wrestlers and championship matches. And what a bond it was between them! She knew instinctively that Sam didn't like Larry and she suspected that Larry didn't like Sam, but personalities were forgotten in their earnest consideration of Jack Johnson's murderous skill. Jerry and Bobbie hung on every word.

They picnicked . . . abundantly. Potato salad, baked beans, sliced veal loaf, Bonnie's deviled eggs, sandwiches, watermelon pickles, coffee, lemonade, and Carney's magnificent cake. After supper some of the boys smoked while the girls cleared and repacked the baskets. Jerry and Bobbie threw horse shoes.

Dennie and Winona wandered off alone to investigate the creek. After making its two leaps it proceeded peacefully toward the Minnesota. Dennie and Winona threw sticks and watched them sail away; they threw again, and this time they followed the sticks and disappeared.

It would have been natural, Carney thought, for her and Larry to go off by themselves. But they didn't. Neither of them seemed to have any wish to do so.

There was a gorgeous sunset which covered half the sky. The Crowd went back to the baseball diamond to find an open view. The boys spread blankets—Larry sat down next to Carney—and they watched the afterglow fade and the stars come out.

They sang, of course.

> *"Come Josephine in my flying machine,*
> *Going up she goes, up she goes,*
> *Balance yourself like a bird on a beam,*
> *In the air she goes, up she goes . . ."*

"I've seen an aeroplane," Betsy announced at the end. "I saw one in California."

Tom had seen them, too, and so had Larry.

"I'd like to fly in one," he said.

"So would I," said Winona. "I'd like to fly over the ocean."

"Someone will some day, I suppose."

"Someone will fly around the world."

"You can get around the world now in forty-one days and eight hours," Jerry announced.

"That ought to be fast enough for anyone," Bonnie declared.

They sang "Down by the Old Mill Stream" and "I'd Like to Live in Loveland." They sang songs of the University, of Carleton, of Stanford, of Vassar. The boys were very proficient now in the one about Matthew Vassar's ale.

It will be nice, Carney thought, to sing these songs at Vassar and remember the Crowd singing them here.

Maybe Isobel's visit had been a good idea. The house party had tied the East and Middle West together. Come to think of it, Larry tied in the West, too.

He sat next to Carney on the blanket, singing heartily.

13
Rarebit for Bonnie

BRISK AS THE PACE OF life was, it quickened after
Larry came. He would be in Deep Valley for only two
weeks and a day. And at the end of his visit, the house
party, too, would end. Bonnie and Betsy would return
to the Twin Cities. Isobel would go on to another
house party in Swampscott, Massachusetts.

Sam had spoken for the final evening.

"We want you out to Murmuring Lake for a dance. It will be on Saturday so the whole Crowd can come. Maybe," he added, addressing Betsy, "that Willard guy would come?"

"Sam!" cried Betsy. She stood very still while color rushed up into her face.

"That settles it! He'll come," said Sam. He turned to Carney. "She likes the guy."

Carney was very pleased, although the radiance on Betsy's face almost embarrassed her. It would be grand to have Joe Willard come down from Minneapolis for the dance. And a dance in the fabulous Hutchinson house would be a perfect finale not only for the house party but for Larry's visit.

In the meantime there was a rage for sightseeing. Isobel seemed to have a passion for everything midwestern. They drove her to the site of the valley's first white settlement, to the abandoned Indian Reservation, to colleges and churches, flour mills and quarries.

Larry and Bonnie wanted to see all the places they remembered. Betsy did, too. Living in Minneapolis now, she was sentimental about Deep Valley. She made the girls take a picnic up on the hill where she and Tacy had played as children—the Big Hill, she called it. She urged them to go to Page Park where the Crowd used to picnic in the old days.

With Carney, Bonnie, or Cab she often walked up

to the high school, closed now for the summer. She walked around it, looking dreamily up at the windows, the brick turret.

"No kids," she said to Carney, "ever had more fun going through high school than we did."

She went to the public library and called on the librarian. She went to the Opera House and gazed at the out-of-date posters on the billboards in front. She invited the girls to lunch at the Melborn Hotel.

"Isobel simply has to see the Melborn."

"I've seen the Waldorf Astoria, you know."

"It can't compare," Betsy said grandly.

She commanded white gloves, and the girls pushed through the swinging doors of the Melborn in supreme elegance, wearing their suits and their very best hats—wastebasket, peachbasket, dishpan hats. Loftily they inspected the red leather chairs in the lobby, climbed the broad, carpeted, grand staircase, past Winged Victory on the landing, and seated themselves in the dining room, two stories high, which overlooked the river.

"Oh," said Betsy, taking up the menu, "how I wish that Tacy and Tib were here!"

They talked old times furiously, until Isobel interrupted. "I'll never get over not having grown up in Deep Valley."

"You'd better come back often," Carney said. She

was surprised at her words for she didn't say things she didn't mean. She must really want Isobel to come again.

Betsy told them about Minneapolis. The Deep Valley girls went to the Twin Cities often, but they seldom ranged beyond the theatres and shops. Betsy described the chain of lakes which ran through the residential district, encircled by boulevards and joined by canals, so that you could paddle a canoe from one to another.

"It's like living in Venice," she declared.

That was just like Betsy, Carney thought. She made everything seem romantic. Her hazel eyes shone; she waved a white hand, bearing a jade and silver ring, to illustrate the canoe's venturesome course.

"Heavens!" cried Isobel. "I must stop and see this Minneapolis on my way back to New York."

"Come and visit us," said Betsy.

"That sounds like a Ray," said Bonnie, laughing. "How are your father and mother, Betsy?"

They were just the same, Betsy said. Her father still made sandwiches on Sunday night. Her mother still played her two tunes, a waltz and a two-step, when company wished to dance. Julia had gone back to Germany where she was studying singing. Margaret would soon be entering high school.

"Does she like Minneapolis?"

"Yes," Betsy said, doubtfully. "Of course, she's never gotten over losing Washington."

"Who was Washington?" Isobel wanted to know.

Betsy settled herself for a story. "Our cat. We Rays had a very distinguished cat and dog, Washington and Lincoln. They moved with the family to Minneapolis—in the baggage car, of course. Abie got along fine but Washington didn't like it, and shortly after we were settled in the new house he disappeared.

"We never found him, but what do you suppose? The people who bought our house here in Deep Valley say that he appeared one day, looking terribly forlorn. He took one last long look around and disappeared."

"How could they be sure it was Washington?" Carney asked skeptically.

"Washington," Betsy answered with conviction, "was unmistakable."

"He was just an ordinary gray and white cat."

"Ordinary!" said Betsy. "Ordinary! Don't you let Margaret hear you say that."

Bonnie told them about St. Paul, the capital, where her father had a pastorate.

"St. Paul and Minneapolis are supposed to hate each other but they have a bond now in Betsy and me."

They spoke about the Kellys. Bonnie and Betsy

were going to Katie's wedding in August. Tacy wasn't planning to be married until she finished her course in public school music.

"What about you and Joe?" asked Carney.

"It's an old story about Joe and me," answered Betsy. She looked mischievous. "What about you and Larry?"

Carney chuckled. She burst out suddenly, "We're having fun."

And that was exactly what they were doing together—having fun. At parties, she had noticed, people tried to leave them alone. They watched them surreptitiously with an interest they could not conceal, because Larry was supposed to have come back from California to propose. But he wasn't, as a matter of fact, anywhere near proposing. They weren't much better acquainted than they had been when he took both her hands out in front of the house the day of his arrival.

But Carney was floating on a cloud of content. He was here and she liked him. Her father and mother liked him. His good looks, modesty, and charm had captivated everyone.

Carney wished sometimes, with a touch of irritation, that Sam Hutchinson were more like Larry. Sam wasn't at his best these days. He not only went about unshaven and untidy, but he had lost his good nature.

His manner was often surly, almost rude.

"Something has come over him," Carney thought. "He acts jealous. Maybe he doesn't like our teasing Isobel about Howard Sedgwick."

Howard was certainly devotion itself. Isobel had a letter every day. She was reticent about him, of course. Isobel would always rather keep a secret than give one away. But she didn't seem to mind the teasing.

It cut through Carney's happiness, somehow, when she saw Sam scowling or glum. Sometimes she left Larry with Bonnie or Betsy and sought him out. But he was even ruder with her than he was with other people.

"What are you doing Sunday night?" she asked him, the evening after Betsy's luncheon. "Dad is making a rarebit for Bonnie, and Dad's rarebits are famous. He only makes them on special occasions and for very special people."

"Is church involved?" Sam asked.

"Why, we girls are going to Chapel with him first. You can come just for the rarebit, if you like. But church wouldn't hurt you," Carney added.

Sam was bitter. "I ought to shave! I ought to get a regular job! And now I ought to go to church!"

"I told you you could come just for the rarebit."

"Is it good?"

"Not always. But there's so much suspense about how it will turn out."

"Good Lord! I can't miss that." Sam began to grin. "The battle of the rarebit! The awful suspense of not knowing how it will turn out! Will it be grainy? Will it be rubbery? Hold my hand, girl! An ice bag, please!"

Carney laughed. "If you come, you have to shave."

"For the battle of the rarebit I'll even shave. But I won't," Sam added, "go to church."

Mr. Sibley's great interest, along with the bank and his family, was his church. He was an elder at the big Presbyterian Church on Broad Street. He taught a Sunday School class there, and for almost ten years he had been Sunday School superintendent at the little Mission Chapel which met every Sunday afternoon.

Many years ago his mother had given a lot for the building. The Mission services were being held then in the warehouse of an old knitting mill. Interested citizens had given materials. Will Sibley was only a boy but he had helped to rear the small frame structure. Now it had a membership of almost one hundred.

Bonnie was interested in the Chapel. She remembered it from the time of her father's pastorate in Deep Valley. She had suggested that the girls might like to go out for a meeting.

Mr. Sibley was delighted. "We'll all go to church and Sunday School and Chapel, and that night I'll make your rarebit," he said, ingenuously assuming that this stiff religious program would be a treat for them all.

But he was popular with the house party guests. They fell in with the plans.

Larry, although an Episcopalian, announced that he was coming to Chapel, too. So did Tom, and several of the other boys. To her surprise Carney was aware of a feeling of annoyance. Their decision to come put Sam in such a bad light. But when, after church and Sunday School and the usual Sunday dinner of chicken and ice cream, the Crowd piled into automobiles and started for North Deep Valley she could not help being gratified by the glow on her father's face.

The small Chapel was filled with children to whom the visit of the house party—already famous in Deep Valley—was a momentous event. The guests joined heartily in the congregational singing. They were devout when her father prayed, attentive when he spoke. He was so handsome, grave, sincere; Carney was proud of him.

Mr. Sibley asked Bonnie to make a speech and she did so happily, mentioning the new organ, promising to tell her father about the large attendance.

"Bonnie ought to marry a minister," Betsy whispered to Carney.

The boys attended Mr. Sibley's class for men, and the girls swelled the members of Grandmother Sibley's class for girls. Carney liked the golden text.

"What doth the Lord require of thee, but to do justly, and to love mercy, and to walk humbly with thy God?"

"I believe," she thought, "that's my favorite verse from the Bible. I can't get romantic about religion, like Betsy, going off to early church alone. It's nice to think that God will be satisfied with me if I just do the best I can."

When they started home, everyone was happy and hungry.

"Now for Bonnie's rarebit," Mr. Sibley said. "I certainly hope it turns out."

Carney repeated this remark to Sam when he arrived. But he only grimaced. He wasn't in a mood for foolishness today.

Mr. Sibley tied on a big white apron which aroused general laughter. But Sam didn't laugh. He looked cynical.

Mr. Sibley began to dice the cheese, saying he was glad it was creamy. You need a creamy cheese to make good rarebit, he explained. If the cheese was stringy it made the rarebit rubbery. Everyone listened respectfully except Sam who went to the parlor and played "Chopsticks" on the piano.

"Dad puts everyone to work," Carney said loud enough for Sam to hear. But he made no move. Larry offered to beat the eggs. Cab measured and mixed the mustard, salt, and pepper. Hunter scalded the milk. Sam suggested to Bobbie that they bring up Snow White's cage.

Mr. Sibley lighted the spirit lamp under the chafing dish. He mashed the cheese and stirred like mad while Larry, Cab, and Hunter poured in beaten eggs, the condiments, the milk. The house party watched admiringly; everyone was having fun. But Sam and Bobbie were busy with the mice. They had opened the cage and Snow White and her progeny were scampering about the parlors.

Mr. Sibley didn't notice the distraction but Mrs. Sibley frowned. Standing daintily erect, she called them to the table. Sam and Bobbie, however, had to catch the mice. At last Sam took the cage to the basement. Bobbie danced about, paying no attention to his mother's request that he sit down.

"Will," Mrs. Sibley appealed to her husband, "you tend to him."

Bobbie didn't like the sound of that.

"Well, I think I'll sit down now," he announced with elaborate carelessness, in a tone loud enough for his father to hear.

It was too bad, Carney thought desperately, that Sam couldn't be so easily handled. He sat down in silence. The rarebit was delicious but he didn't praise it. He was surly and withdrawn.

Larry, on the other hand, was at his most engaging. He claimed that the skill with which he had beaten the eggs was responsible for the rarebit's success. He praised Mr. Sibley by implication, and Mrs. Sibley said proudly, "You ought to taste the corn cake he bakes when we go on a picnic."

"It's swell!" shouted Jerry and Bobbie.

Larry inquired about the corn cake. He listened attentively while Mr. Sibley described the oven he used. It was a reflector oven.

"You let the fire die down and then you put the oven on the ground beside it. I bake the corn cake in an ordinary tin."

Bonnie beamed. "I remember your corn cake from when I was a little girl, Mr. Sibley."

"If it was as good as this rarebit . . ." Isobel said, and Betsy chimed in.

Sam drummed on the table, looking bored.

The telephone rang and Olga came to the dining room door.

"It's a long distance call," she announced.

"Betsy!" the girls cried teasingly, for Joe Willard telephoned from Minneapolis every Sunday night.

Betsy blushed and jumped up, but Olga cut in. "No. It's for Miss Porteous. It's a call from New York."

Silence struck the table, for the same thought came to everyone. A call from such a distance must mean illness or trouble. Isobel seemed less perturbed than the rest; yet she was unsmiling.

The telephone was in the hall adjoining the dining room. Everyone was quiet. But almost at once Isobel's tone made it clear that there was no need to worry.

"Howard!" she cried, pleasure ringing in her voice. "How very nice!" After a moment she said, "Oh, I adore it!" And then, at intervals, softly: "Yes. I do." "Of course I do." "Yes, I really do."

It sounded as though she were assuring Howard that she missed him . . . or loved him. . . .

Carney's glance fell on Hunter. He was looking at his plate and crumbling crackers.

She looked at Sam. He was playing absently with the rarebit on his fork.

Isobel shut down the receiver at last.

"It was nothing," she said, coming back to the table. "Just a friend who wanted to know how I liked the Middle West."

"The Middle West!" There was a chorus of jeers.

"You expect us to believe that?" asked Bonnie.

"A likely story!" said Betsy.

"Really," said Isobel, "I swear it. That's what he called for, to see how I liked the Middle West."

"Was it Howard?" asked Sam, although he must have known that it was Howard . . . if he had been listening.

"Yes," she answered. "It was Howard. And now, Mr. Sibley, could I have a little more of that divine rarebit?"

14
Roses for Carney

"WITHOUT DOUBT," said Betsy, inspecting the chart on which Carney listed their engagements, "we're the most popular young buds of the season."

"I never knew anything like it," said Bonnie. "I don't know how I'm going to settle down to ordinary living again."

"I don't believe," said Isobel, "that you Middle Westerners ever settle down. I think you live like this all the time." She, too, bent over the chart. "Two parties yesterday, and in between them Hunter took me for that wonderful drive."

Hunter had worn his best suit, Carney remembered, and his most becoming tie. The New York telephone call was forgotten, and his joy, when they started off, had made his face glow. But Carney had encountered little Ellen buying embroidery thread in the fancy-work shop down on Front Street. Ellen was so pale that her freckles stood out; she had been crying.

"And today," chimed in Bonnie, "we're going fishing."

"And tomorrow—" said Betsy, and paused. "By the way," she asked mysteriously, "what day *is* tomorrow?"

"It's Wednesday, isn't it?" Carney replied in pretended innocence. She knew that everyone knew it was her birthday. There was a something on embroidery hoops which Bonnie whisked out of sight whenever she entered the room. Isobel and Betsy had made an unexplained shopping trip. A few assorted relatives had been invited to dinner.

"Thursday we're going to visit your cousins in the country," continued Isobel. She had asked to see a typical Minnesota farm. "Friday is still free, but Saturday is the Hutchinson dance, and on Sunday we all leave."

"Boo hoo!" said Betsy.

"Boo hoo!" echoed Bonnie.

They fell on one another's shoulders in mock grief.

Carney jumped up and went out of the library. Sitting down at the piano, she began some agitated scales. The week was going by on wings! Larry would be leaving soon, and they didn't seem to be getting anywhere!

"I'm sure he likes me," she thought. Admiration was always plain in his eyes. "And I certainly like him. But I don't seem to know him very well."

It was queer. They talked easily—about Stanford and Vassar, about Larry's trip to Lake Tahoe and Carney's to New York. (To be sure, Carney thought, they didn't have much that was new to tell each other. They not only had written faithfully over the years but they had read and re-read one another's letters. She remembered all about Larry's camping on Lake Tahoe. Larry remembered all about her seeing the Wax Works down on Twenty-third Street in New York.)

They enjoyed doing things together, playing tennis or croquet. He joked and teased her in an affectionate way . . . like a brother, almost.

"But I don't feel close to him," she thought. She would, perhaps, if they were alone together more. But they were never alone. They never tried to be alone. They didn't even take advantage of the maneuvers by which their companions sometimes tried to manage it.

If only he were more aggressive! Some men . . . someone like Sam Hutchinson . . . would do something definite in a situation like this.

She pushed aside the disloyal thought. Larry was so attractive, so perfect! But if he was going to go away for another four years . . .

"Mail!" Betsy called. Betsy usually brought in the mail. She was always looking for letters from Joe. "Something for you, Carney."

Carney left the piano willingly.

"It's a letter from Vassar," she cried, examining it. "From the Secretary of the College. Do you have one, Isobel?"

"No," Isobel replied.

"I hope I'm not put out or anything."

Carney ripped open the envelope anxiously, but as she read a smile of real pleasure crossed her face. She was asked to serve on the Reception Committee for Freshmen. This group of upper classmen returned to school early. Wearing white dresses, rose and gray ribbons, and badges, they extended official welcomes and helped the freshmen register. It was an honor to serve on the committee.

Isobel echoed this thought.

"That's wonderful, Carney. Most of the committee are seniors. They only pick outstanding juniors."

"It's because of my work with the Christian Association, I suppose," said Carney.

"Oh," said Isobel, "you're in lots of activities. And you hold a class office. You're very outstanding."

Carney was surprised and pleased by this spontaneous tribute.

"Carney is a leader wherever she goes," Betsy remarked, and Carney felt some of her old assurance returning. Maybe she wouldn't have that feeling of inadequacy at college this year.

She was inordinately pleased by the letter. She told Sam about it that afternoon at the fishing. They had driven out to Pearl Lake laden with fish poles, straw hats, and a pail half filled with angle worms which Jerry and Bobbie had dug and sold for profit. Pearl was a small reedy lake lined raggedly with docks and faded summer cottages, but perch, sunfish, and crappies were abundant there, and boats could be rented. While Larry was concluding his bargain, Carney found herself seated in the boat with Sam. He had charged it, of course.

Her confiding in him seemed strange when she

thought about it afterwards. She had told Larry that she was asked to be on the committee. But she had told it as though it were nothing. To Sam, although he was unshaven and grumpy, she blurted out what was in her heart.

"I'm awfully pleased because . . . I never thought I was anyone at Vassar."

"Around here," he said, "Carney Sibley is pretty important."

"I know it. I think I was conceited when I went away. But Vassar took it out of me."

"Was the work hard?"

"Yes. I have a B average now, though. It wasn't the work . . . it was the people." She frowned at the cork bobber on her fishing line.

"Did you know anyone when you went there?" he asked.

"Not a soul. I just put on a hard shell and plunged. I got in with a group of dyed-in-the-wool Easterners who were very kind, but I was a sort of . . . curiosity . . . to them because I came from the Middle West."

"I suppose," he said thoughtfully, "the Middle West isn't very well represented at Vassar. But I don't think it took folks long to find out that you were quite a person."

Carney glanced at him gratefully.

His bobber dipped beneath the water and he pulled out his line. Finding only a bullhead on the hook he disengaged the ugly little creature and threw it back.

Carney spoke violently, "The East just . . . intimidates me. It has me buffaloed . . . or it did, until this letter came. This gives me back a little self-confidence."

"Then reach out and grab it," Sam said. "And don't ever let go of it again."

For a moment they were silent.

"I'm glad I'm doing well," Carney remarked presently. "It was good of Dad to send me."

"Do you know that you're awfully conscientious?"

"We were brought up that way. My family is different from yours. We were brought up to think we should have a serious purpose in life."

"Is the Presbyterian Church important to you?"

"I like to go to church. I like to organize my thoughts there every Sunday, see where I'm going wrong, plan things out. Of course, I don't believe what some Presbyterians do, that all those who haven't heard the word of God are damned . . . it wouldn't be fair."

"Of course not," said Sam.

"Lots of people don't think that any more. My father doesn't. I don't have deep thoughts," she added suddenly. "Not many of them." Then to her surprise she heard herself telling him the verse from Micah.

"What doth the Lord require of thee, but to do justly, and to love mercy, and to walk humbly with thy God?"

"That's darn good," said Sam. "It even lets me in."

"That's right," said Carney. "It does." She sounded surprised, which made him laugh; and she began to laugh, too.

"What are you two laughing about?" Isobel called from the next boat.

"The Bible," said Sam.

"The Bible?" Isobel sounded surprised. But Carney and Sam wouldn't tell her the joke.

Carney spent the rest of the day with Larry, and they told each other things they remembered already; they joked and fooled. Somehow it seemed a little colorless after the talk with Sam.

Larry was in her thoughts, however, when she woke the next morning. She wondered with pleasurable excitement what he would give her for her birthday. He would remember the day, she knew. He had never forgotten it in all the years he had been away. Of course, he had to give flowers, candy, or a book. That was all it was proper to give a girl until you were engaged. Her mother hadn't even liked his sending her that little abalone pendant. But his gift might tell her something.

He didn't come in during the morning. In the early afternoon a car stopped in front of the house, but it was Sam who bounded up the steps. The house party came running from all directions to meet him. He waved them off.

"Go back to your knitting, girls. I came to see Jerry. Brought him *Huck Finn*." Sam had taken to bringing books to Jerry from the big library in the house at Murmuring Lake. He turned to Carney. "Did he like *Tom Sawyer*?"

"Loved it. He read it out loud to Bobbie."

"Well, now that I'm here," said Sam, "how about a ride?"

The girls smiled at each other.

"We can't leave," Betsy explained in a stage whisper. "It's Carney's birthday."

"Is that the cake I smell?" Sam asked, sniffing. "Isn't there going to be a party?"

"Just a family party. Grandmothers, aunts, and such."

"Save me a piece of the birthday cake then," he said, departing.

Carney remembered that her mother had asked her to cut some flowers for the vases. Getting scissors and a basket from the kitchen, where Olga moved rapidly to conceal a cake fresh from the oven, she went out to the garden. By a happy chance she was still there, alone, when Larry came.

He strode toward her, removing his white straw hat, and extended a tissue-wrapped package.

"Something for you," he said, smiling.

Putting her basket full of cosmos and phlox on the ground, she untied the ribbons eagerly.

"It's a book," she thought to herself, and saw that it was a fine leather copy of the *Rubaiyat of Omar Khayyam,* illustrated with colored pictures.

"Oh, thank you!" she cried. "I'm glad to own this."

"Everyone at Stanford is reading it."

"Everyone at Vassar too. Thank you very much. Let's go in," she added nervously. "I've got enough flowers now."

He hesitated. "I can't stay. I was wondering whether we might get away for a picnic, just you and me? Would it be all right? Could you leave your house party?"

Carney swallowed hard. "They wouldn't mind."

"Is there a free day?"

"There's nothing planned yet for Friday."

"Let's go Friday then."

"I'll ask Dad for the car."

"No," said Larry. "I'll hire a livery team. Where shall we go?"

"To Orono?" asked Carney and then she felt confused, for she remembered what they had said—that they would save Orono for a very special occasion.

"Yes," said Larry with his charming crooked smile. "Let's go to Orono."

Carney went slowly into the house. She met her mother in the kitchen and showed her the *Rubaiyat*. Mrs. Sibley smiled approvingly. She had never read the Persian poet, but a book seemed a highly suitable gift. Besides, she had come to like Larry very much.

Carney wanted to talk to Bonnie. Fortunately Betsy and Isobel were deep in a game of Seven-and-a-half. Bonnie was sitting in the big chair, tatting, and it was not difficult to beckon her away.

"Let's go for a walk," Carney proposed, and when they were out in the street, she said, "Larry wants me to go on a picnic with him, Friday . . . all alone."

"Carney!" cried Bonnie. She looked at Carney solemnly. "This is it!" she said.

"It can't be."

"Don't you like him?"

"Yes. I like him awfully well. But . . . I haven't gotten to know him."

"You don't need to *get* to know him. You've known him all your life."

"But we're not close," Carney tried to explain. It couldn't be done, and she stopped.

"What will you say?" asked Bonnie excitedly.

"Let's wait to see what *he* says," Carney answered.

If it was going to be another four years before she saw him again, she'd better say "yes," she thought.

When they returned, her mother met them on the steps. She looked less serene.

"Carney," she said, "there's a box for you. A perfectly enormous box."

"Where is it?"

"On the back parlor floor."

Plainly, it was on the floor because there was no table long enough to hold it. It was a flower box, almost as long and as thick as a man.

Carney opened it with elated fingers. It held two dozen American Beauty roses, velvety and fragrant, unbelievably tall.

They could come from only one person. It wasn't necessary to search for the card. But when it was found it bore, as everyone knew it would, a scrawled, "Happy birthday—Sam."

"How ridiculous of him!" said Carney, but her cheeks were flushed with pleasure.

Mrs. Sibley looked critical. "I can't imagine what we'll put them in. The umbrella stand might do if it had a bottom."

Vases were borrowed from Grandmother Sibley and Grandmother Hunter. Jerry and Bobbie ran around the neighborhood excitedly borrowing vases. Soon the house was dizzily sweet.

It was turning very warm, and the heat seemed to make the fragrance all the sweeter. Cutting the cake, opening the modest packages from her family and the girls, Carney kept inhaling deep intoxicating breaths.

She remembered her thoughts the day she had first met the Hutchinsons. How different they were from the Sibleys in their extravagant lavishness! Purple and dove gray!

When Sam called the next day to drive the girls out to the country, she thanked him with the dimple shining.

"Did you like them?"

"I loved them."

"There's something I want to tell you." He encircled her shoulder with his big arm, which made Carney feel queer although he was only doing it, she knew, in order to whisper. He put his lips close to her ear.

"I paid cash for them."

"Did you really?"

"Yes, I did."

Larry came in presently, and like everyone else he immediately mentioned the forest of roses.

"Opening a florist shop?" he asked.

"Just birthday," answered Carney.

Bobbie piped up, "They're from Sam."

Sam turned to Jerry and Bobbie. "You boys coming along to the farm?"

"Nope," said Bobbie. "I'm playing *Huck Finn*."

"I'm reading it through again," said Jerry. "Gosh, Sam, it's good!"

That afternoon wasn't very successful, although the cousins were hospitable and their farm one of the finest in the county. The heat was growing more intense, and only Isobel seemed to have the energy to appreciate rural sights.

Of course, to the others, farms were homely and familiar. They well knew the pattern of small house, large red barn and outbuildings, windmill, windbreak of poplars and the rich flat land around. They were accustomed to handsome horses sweating in golden fields, to fat cows in verdant meadows, to grunting black and white pigs, bright hens, collie dogs and litters of kittens. They made the rounds apathetically and were glad to return to the shade of the door-yard elm, a plate of fresh-baked cookies and cold water from the well.

"It's almost too hot for sightseeing but there's one place we ought to take in before the girls go, and tomorrow's the last chance," Sam said.

"What is it?" asked the indefatigable Isobel.

"The dam at Orono."

Bonnie let out a startled gasp.

"Oh, we can't go there!" she cried, and stopped, looking distressed. Carney colored, and Larry began to dig in the ground with a stick he had picked up.

"Why can't we?" Betsy demanded. "It's a grand idea."

"I've heard so much about the dam," Isobel added.

Larry didn't speak.

Carney was exasperated. It wasn't like her to have concealed her plan for Friday, but she had dreaded telling Betsy and Isobel, and there hadn't really been a chance. The excitement of her birthday roses had almost blotted out the projected twosome picnic.

At least, she thought, she would be frank now. She spoke brusquely, interrupting Bonnie who was framing a suitable excuse.

"Larry and I are busy tomorrow."

There was a startled silence.

"Well," Sam said, "the rest of us could go."

"Oh!" exclaimed Bonnie. "But Orono is where they're going."

Still Larry didn't speak.

Carney sat rigidly upright. If she didn't say, "We'll all go," it showed how important their private picnic was. If she did say it, she destroyed the only chance she and Larry would have for a confidential talk.

She jumped up. "I'll get some more cookies," she said.

"I'll get some water," said Larry, jumping up, too, and seizing the pail.

But in spite of these fresh supplies the group didn't re-form.

Shortly Betsy found Carney.

"It's the most thrilling thing I ever heard of! I'm so thankful I was here when it happened."

"But nothing has happened."

"Oh, it will!"

Isobel seemed equally sure that the expedition was romantic.

"He's certainly a charmer," she said. "I'm awfully happy for you, Carney darling."

Even Sam sought her out.

"Did you know I was a good amateur carpenter?" he asked.

"No. Are you? Why?"

"I'm going to make you a shelf. You'll need one, I suppose, to climb up on after that trip tomorrow."

His eyes were crinkled into his bright smile. But there was something urgent and demanding in their gaze.

Carney opened her mouth to speak, but she shut it again. When she talked with Sam she always said too much.

On the return from the farm Isobel didn't get out of the Loco. The rest climbed out, but Sam said casually that he and Isobel were going for a ride. She wore her green and white tissue and a lingerie hat. In spite of the now torrid heat she looked enchanting.

For some reason Carney kept waiting for them to come home. The afternoon wore away. Kitchen sounds and odors indicated supper, but Isobel didn't return.

"Supper's ready," Mrs. Sibley called at last. "Shall we wait?"

"No," answered Carney. "Father hates to wait. And the Loco has probably broken down."

"Maybe," gurgled Bonnie, "she and Sam have eloped."

"What about Howard Sedgwick?" asked Carney.

"Well, he's in New York and Sam is here."

During supper the telephone rang, and Olga came into the dining room.

"It's Miss Porteous. She's been invited to stay for dinner with the Hutchinsons. She says she'll be home right after dinner. Is it all right, she wants to know?"

"Perfectly," said Mrs. Sibley, smiling.

A flutter ran around the table.

"What a romantic house party!" cried Betsy. "Larry and Carney going to Orono! Isobel eloping with Sam!"

"She *hasn't* eloped with Sam," Carney cut in almost sharply.

"Maybe she has! How do we know they're ever coming back?"

"What does 'elope' mean?" Bobbie inquired.

"To run away with someone."

"Huck Finn eloped. Gee, I should say he did!" said Bobbie, looking thoughtfully into his strawberry short-cake.

15

Orono

CARNEY COULDN'T SLEEP that night. It was too hot for anyone to sleep, she thought, even on a sleeping porch, without a top sheet. But Betsy and Bonnie were sleeping. Lifting herself on one elbow, she could see them plainly in the moonlight. Betsy's hair was done up in Magic Wavers, of course; Bonnie had pinned her yellow locks on top of her head for coolness.

Isobel was sleeping, too, although her loosened hair was scattered over the pillow. It made a wavy pattern. Heat caused Isobel's hair to curl even more endearingly than usual. Although it had been very hot when she and Sam returned last night, she had looked deliciously pretty. Her hair was twining into curls and curlicues about a flushed face. There had been a brightness lighting her from within. She had looked the way a girl ought to look when she got engaged.

"But I won't look like that if I get engaged to Larry tomorrow. I won't be that happy," Carney thought.

She wondered whether Isobel had become engaged to Sam. The idea seemed ridiculous because of Howard Sedgwick, but she couldn't be sure. Isobel was so mysterious. You couldn't figure out what she would or wouldn't do as you could with ordinary girls.

Carney felt a surge of resentment against her. She wished she hadn't invited her to come to Minnesota.

"But she's made a wonderful guest," she thought, trying to choke down this unworthy feeling. "Everyone likes her. I do myself."

She got up and went to the railing.

"I'm in a bad mood because of that picnic tomorrow. But I ought to be glad it's coming off. I usually hate things hanging fire."

The moon sailed in the sky above the hills in

golden indifference. It outlined the turret on the barn and threw large soft shadows of trees on the lawn. The shadows were motionless for there wasn't a breath stirring. It was stiflingly hot.

Carney longed for a cold bath but she was afraid the sound of running water would waken someone. Her parents and the boys had their bedroom doors open, seeking a nonexistent draft. She decided to get a drink instead, and tiptoeing down to the kitchen, she poured a glass of cold water from the earthen jug which Olga always kept in the icebox. The kitchen was stuffy.

"What weather for a picnic!" Carney groaned, wandering into the dark parlors. Even the ground floor windows were open but there wasn't a breeze. "I can't look pretty in weather like this. We can't make a fire. There has been plenty of nice cool weather. Why did he have to wait so long?"

And yet, she admitted, climbing the stairs again, there had been a reason for waiting.

"Even as it is, we don't really know each other. Of course he's only been here two weeks."

But she had known Sam only a week when they had had that talk about Matthew Lang.

Disgruntled, she returned to her bed. She was still disgruntled in the morning, and the girls annoyed her at breakfast.

"Do you know what we ought to read out loud to-day? *The Little Colonel's Hero*," Betsy said.

"What are you going to wear?" asked Isobel.

"I haven't any idea."

"I'm sorry it's such a hot day."

"Heavens!" cried Carney. "Don't act as though it were my wedding day."

Isobel and Betsy began to hum delightedly.

> *"Here comes the bride,*
> *Here comes the bride . . ."*

Carney gave them a crushing look.

She went out to the kitchen and made a jugful of lemonade which she put in the icebox to chill.

"Probably it will be as warm as soup by the time we drink it."

She got out a basket, slamming it down hard. She made deviled eggs and then decided she might as well make the sandwiches, too, while there was still a little morning coolness.

"It's going to be a scorcher," she thought.

Going to the garden for lettuce, she noticed Bobbie sitting underneath an old carpet which he had hung over the clothes reel to make a tent. Within this suffo-cating shelter he was wearing a leather jacket and knitted cap.

"Bobbie! Come out of there!" she cried. "Whatever are you doing?"

"I'm eloping," said Bobbie. "Huck Finn and I are eloping."

"Well, you don't need to elope in a leather jacket," said Carney, smiling in spite of her bad humor. She persuaded him to take off the jacket but looking out of the kitchen window later, she saw that he had it on again.

"That Sam!" she muttered. "Lending the boys books that give them crazy ideas!"

After dinner she took a cold bath and put on a clean middy blouse and her white duck skirt with a red tie and red ribbon as usual.

"You look very nice," said Bonnie.

"And so casual," added Isobel.

Betsy started to hum the wedding march again.

Carney snorted. "I hope you won't throw rice when we leave."

"Darling," Betsy answered mournfully, "we won't even be here. It's perfectly maddening. It would be invaluable to me, as a coming Mary J. Holmes, to watch you two start off, hand in hand down Honeymoon Trail. But Bonnie is dragging us over to your Grandmother's. In this heat! I'm sure we'll have sunstrokes."

"Bonnie," said Carney earnestly, "you are a jewel!"

Bonnie beamed.

Looking like a determined kitten, she did indeed shoo the reluctant house party out of the house at the proper time. Of course, Mrs. Sibley remained at home. She went about quietly as usual, a half smile on her face. Carney knew what she was thinking. She liked Larry. Her husband liked him, too. Neither of them would object if Larry and Carney reached some sort of understanding.

"Of course, you'll want to finish college," Carney could almost hear her saying.

Presently, with kindly tact, Mrs. Sibley went upstairs. Bobbie, still in his tent, was the only soul around when Larry came.

Larry called hello to Bobbie but he didn't cross the lawn to inquire about the tent. He wasn't as interested in the boys as Sam was, Carney thought. And Bobbie must have been deeply absorbed in his play, for he didn't rush out to inspect the rig Larry had hired, although it was magnificent.

It was the best Phillips' Livery Stable had to offer. The horses were groomed to a shine; the harness was polished; the nickel work gleamed. You could see your face in the surface of the buggy. A light-colored laprobe was folded over the seat, and there was a tasseled whip.

Larry looked as spruce as the livery rig. He was

even wearing a coat, but he asked permission to remove it, and rolled up the sleeves of his white shirt.

"Do you know the way to Orono?" Carney asked as they started up Broad Street.

"Out of West Deep Valley on the Indian Lake Road," Larry replied. "The Indian Lake Road! That certainly sounds like our childhood."

"Doesn't it?" Carney replied.

A wave of happy memories rolled out to meet them as they crossed the slough and started south through a high-walled valley.

"This hill on the right used to be the best place for flowers in the spring."

"May flowers, Dutchmen's breeches, dog-tooth violets . . ." Larry said.

"When we found an especially good patch we'd sit down to pick in order not to give away our prize."

Larry motioned with the whip. "There's some fine white sand a little farther on."

"We used to take it home. Bobbie still does sometimes."

But the glow induced by memory didn't last after they passed Indian Lake. They traveled now on the heights and now in the valley, following the distant Cutbank, and it was equally hot in both situations.

On the heights, where they rolled through level farmlands, the sun beat down on the buggy top. Dust was tossed by the horses' hoofs into their perspiring faces. In the valleys, the bluffs shut in the sweltering heat.

Talk languished, and Carney was glad when at last they reached the dam.

The sparkling blue water of the newly created lake made her feel better, and so did the crash of the waterfall. She wanted to sit in the shade of a willow and cool off, but Larry, who was studying to be an engineer, was interested in the dam. Hitching the horses, he walked about enthusiastically, inspecting it.

Carney tried to share his interest.

"There's been a mill here since pioneer days," she said. "First a flour mill and then a flaxseed mill which was the start of one of the biggest linseed mills in America, Dad says. Just two years ago the power company took it over."

"I want to find the guy in charge," said Larry.

He found him, and they were immediately boon companions. Larry bombarded him with questions. Did they use the reaction-type turbines? How much power did the plant generate? What was the hydraulic head?

Carney sat down beneath the willow tree alone.

On the west side of the bridge a small road descended to the gorge beneath the dam. On the other side rose a green hill where sheep were grazing. There was one dramatic promontory covered with pines and oaks and pale white birches with wild out-croppings of rock. It soared to a great height and commanded a view of the river valley. That would be a good place to picnic, Carney thought . . . if they were ever going to picnic!

"I like things *settled*," she said under her breath.

They were no farther along than they had been when they started. It grew hotter all the time, and now she was hungry, too.

Larry came back looking apologetic. "It was stupid of me to leave you so long in all this heat."

"Why, it's what people come to the dam for, to see the dam," said Carney. She tried to sound jocular instead of cross.

"It isn't what *we* came for," Larry said with laughing eyes. He took her arm. "Shall we picnic here?"

But Carney was sick of Orono.

"Let's drive on," she said.

They got back in the buggy and left the river behind.

"That place might be all right," said Larry, nodding toward a little hillside pasture. There was a small grove of scrub oaks. It looked cool.

"Fine," said Carney, and they tied the horses to a fence post.

"You'd better loosen the checkreins," she reminded,

and he did so. He lifted out the picnic basket, and they climbed through a barbed-wire fence.

The little oak grove was as hot as an oven. The grass was rough and hummocky, and the only birds were sleek unpleasant blackbirds with yellow eyes.

Carney unpacked her basket. The lemonade was still quite cold.

"I put a chunk of ice in it," she said.

"It tastes fine, and the sandwiches are swell. It's nice to get off by ourselves," Larry observed, slapping a mosquito.

Carney didn't answer. Was it?

For some reason she thought about Miss Salmon. She should, she realized suddenly, have thought about her long before. She should have analyzed her problem as Miss Salmon had taught her to do, as she had analyzed the problem of Isobel's coming, back on Sunset Hill.

Staring at a blackbird, she forced herself to think.

What was the matter with her? Was she afraid Larry wouldn't propose? No. She knew he was planning to do so. But it wasn't because he loved her. It was because he idealized their former relationship, just as she had always done.

Was she in doubt as to how she would answer him? She shouldn't be. She ought to say no. For it came to her now that she wasn't in love either. She simply wasn't in love.

❧214❧

As in Grandmother Hunter's kaleidoscope, she saw a medley of pictures: Hunter looking painfully downward when Isobel was talking to Howard in New York. Betsy running eagerly out for the mail. Betsy's face when Sam proposed inviting Joe down for the dance.

That was the way you felt when you were in love. She didn't feel that way about Larry. She used to, maybe. But she didn't now. And he didn't feel that way about her.

It had grown very dark in the little grove, although it was far from sundown. As a Minnesotan Carney knew the reason. A thunder storm was brewing. Larry would have to speak soon if he was going to speak at all.

He, too, had been thoughtfully silent, but now he cleared his throat.

"Carney," he said in his slow way, "it's been just grand seeing you again."

"Yes. We've had fun," Carney replied. He was going to propose, and she mustn't let him. It wouldn't be fair. She said impetuously, "But we're not in love any more. Do you realize that?"

Larry looked taken aback. "Aren't we?" he asked.

"No. I just like you, and you just like me."

"That's what I want to find out," he answered. "I'm not sure you're right. I like you a lot, Carney, better than any girl I know. You're so pretty and fresh and natural . . ." His voice trailed away.

"Yes," said Carney candidly. "But you're not in love. And neither am I." If she had been talking to Sam she might have been able to say more . . . that a magic which had lain over their relationship in the past had vanished, as when the lights of a Christmas tree are turned off leaving just an ordinary pine. Larry was the same, and she was the same, but the magic wasn't there any more.

"We're not in love," she said. "You can go back to California and fall in love with someone else."

"But I want to fall in love with you," he answered miserably.

Carney spoke firmly. "Falling in love is something you can't do anything about. You're in love or you're not, and that's all there is to it. We can be good friends, though. We can keep on writing to each other."

If they were just friends again, how much she would like him, she thought!

"Let's be friends all our lives," she said abruptly.

He still looked unhappy but her spirits now were as light as air. She felt as though she had been relieved of a great burden. She felt like flying or singing.

All of a sudden the rain started. There had been some forewarning—a flash of lightning, dull peals of thunder, birds scudding silently homeward. Larry and

Carney had been too much interested in their conversation to notice. But now a steady shower was rattling on the leaves.

Laughing, Carney jumped up and started to pile things into the basket. Larry ran to unfasten the horses. She looked upward.

Rain splashed on her face, but it was glorious. She was very, very happy. She wasn't going to marry Larry. He didn't love her, and she didn't love him.

"Hurry!" Larry called. "This is something terrific. The sky is black as ink."

"Coming!" she answered. She seized the basket and ran toward the barbed-wire fence.

16

Somebody Elopes

THIS WAS NO ORDINARY thunder storm, Carney realized when she reached the road. Even out in the open, the world was dark. Ominous black clouds were edged luridly with yellow. The rain seemed only a forewarning.

She was holding the reins while Larry buttoned on storm curtains, when the wind burst. It tore the curtains out of his hands.

"Never mind them!" Carney shouted, for the horses were rearing. It took all her strength to hold them. Larry grasped the reins just as a large branch snapped behind them. The horses plunged forward.

They ran as though the giant wind were blowing them, but Larry held the reins firmly. Branches were snapping off everywhere now. A big tree in a nearby pasture crashed.

Carney was frightened but she was exhilarated, too, and she knew that Larry was. The excitement was a relief from the strain of their afternoon. When the horses settled down, at last, into a fast trot, he turned and smiled at her.

"You all right?" he shouted.

"I'm fine."

They crossed the Orono bridge. The high land seemed mercilessly exposed to the wild glares of lightning, the deafening thunder. Cornfields were swept flat, as though a steam roller had passed over them. Down in the valleys the wind was like a broom sweeping the torrent of rain along the road.

They drove in silence because of the din of the storm, and reached the outskirts of Deep Valley at last.

Where the Indian Lake Road curved into Front Street they saw the owl-like glare of automobile lights. Larry slowed down and Carney cried, "Why, it's the Loco!" At the same instant the car's horn sounded, and Sam's voice swam through the rain.

"Carney! Larry! Is that you?"

Larry pulled the horses to a stop, and Sam jumped out.

"We're all right. It wasn't necessary for you to come to meet us," Larry said stiffly.

"Gosh! I wasn't worried about you two."

"What is it then?" Carney asked.

"Don't be scared, but Bobbie isn't around. He left a note saying he had eloped."

"Eloped!" Carney cried. She burst into laughter in spite of the fear which gripped her.

"That's what he said. 'Just like Huck Finn,' he said. He doesn't seem to have told his plans to anyone else in the family, and we wondered whether he had told them to you."

"No," Carney answered. "But he was playing Huck Finn all morning. I'll climb in with you, Sam. I'll get home quicker."

"I'll drive to your house," Larry said. "Maybe we'll need the horses."

She climbed out into the wind and the rain. Sam threw his coat around her. The collapsible top was raised and the storm curtains were on. Over the frantic drumming of the rain Sam told her what had happened.

"At supper time Bobbie didn't show up. No one thought much about it until the sky began to look so bad. Then your mother started telephoning around, but the other little boys were all safe at home, and Bobbie wasn't with any of them.

"I had stopped in to see Isobel, and I could see that your mother was getting nervous. For a joke I suggested that Bobbie might have left a note on her pillow. She went upstairs, and by golly there was a note!"

"What did it say?"

"'Have eloped like Huck Finn. Don't worry. Bobbie.' If it weren't for this storm it wouldn't be important. Every boy runs away once. But tonight it isn't so good."

"It certainly isn't." When the lightning flashed Carney saw telephone wires trailing on the ground.

The car drew up in front of the Sibley house where the Maxwell was already waiting. As Carney ran inside, a feeling of dread choked her. Her father, mother, brothers, and the girls were gathered in the front parlor. They looked up hopefully. Her father and Hunter were in raincoats.

"We were waiting for you," Mr. Sibley said. "We're hoping you can give us a clue."

"I can't," said Carney. "I wish I could." She glanced anxiously at her mother whose small face looked white and pinched. "Let me see the note," she added.

Mrs. Sibley gave it to her.

"Have eloped like Huck Finn. Don't worry. Bobbie." The large childish handwriting made the situation more poignant.

Sam was the first to speak. "Well," he said. "Let's see! He thinks he's Huck Finn."

Jerry broke in. "When Huck Finn ran away he went to the river."

"That's right!" Sam's face lighted up. "Bobbie is headed for water. There's no doubt about that."

Mr. Sibley, who had been pacing the floor, wheeled about. "He probably went to Page Park. That's the part of the river he knows best. Hunter and I will go there now."

"And I'll start up the Cutbank," said Sam, "unless . . ." He paused. "Bobbie knows Murmuring Lake, and he's been out in a boat at my place. I wonder . . ." He went to the telephone, but returned shaking his head. "The wires are down. I believe that's a good hunch, though. I'm going to drive home, and if I don't find him on the road I'll come right back here."

"I'll go with you, Sam," said Carney. "I can look for him while you drive."

"Take along some blankets in case you find him," her mother said.

"I have a hunch we're going to find him, Mrs.

Sibley," Sam replied. "But would you mind awfully if I didn't bring him back?"

"Why not? Why wouldn't you bring him back?"

"Because," said Sam, smiling at her, "he'd like it so much better if I didn't. We'd give him hot lemonade and a bath; all that stuff. But tomorrow he could play Huck Finn on our lake and get it out of his system."

"Why, of course!" Mrs. Sibley's smile trembled. "Wouldn't that be all right, Will?"

"A fine idea," Mr. Sibley answered. "You understand boys pretty well, Sam."

Carney knew that the warmth of her father's tone sprang partly from his gratitude at having Mrs. Sibley's thoughts diverted.

"He'd be there for the party tomorrow night," Sam added. The casual reference to the dance helped, too. It seemed to indicate that Bobbie was already as good as found.

While her mother was getting the blankets, Carney put on her raincoat and one of Hunter's caps. When she came downstairs Larry had arrived. It had been decided that he and Jerry were to go up the Cutbank. The automobiles were cranked, and the horses unhitched.

Sam and Carney started up Agency Hill. That was the greatest hazard of the trip. The wheels of the car could hardly engage the slippery mud. The wind came roaring down the steep incline, as though trying to push them back into the valley.

At the top they both shouted their relief. The road was flat now, all the way to Murmuring Lake.

They went slowly, Carney looking out closely on both sides. Sam's hands gripped the wheel, for driving was perilous. The road was littered with branches. Neither he nor Carney mentioned the possibility that they might encounter an obstacle big enough to stop the car. She was quite aware of that danger, though, and she knew that he was.

Carney concentrated on looking. Now and then lightning illuminated the landscape. She saw trees bending and swaying in the wind but no small boy eloping like Huck Finn.

They passed the Half-way House, and still no Bobbie.

"He could have fallen down. We could pass him without knowing it," she said.

"What would he fall down for?" Sam asked gruffly. "More likely he got a ride and is safe and sound at our house."

But he went more slowly than ever. The car barely crawled through the wind and slashing rain.

At last the lakeside trees came into view, tossing wildly. They reached the lake and saw that the water swept upward in sheets. Just inside the Hutchinson driveway a large tree had fallen across the road.

"It's too late to stop us now," shouted Sam.

They abandoned the car. He caught her hand, and they ran through the pelting rain, up the driveway to the lighted house. Sam opened the big front door.

"Now if he's here," he said in a low voice, "for Pete's sake, don't kiss him!"

"Why not?"

"You don't kiss Huck Finn."

Then he charged forward. "Is Bobbie here?"

"Yes," came a chorused answer from the library. Bobbie's voice rose above the rest in strident jubilation.

He sat in a big chair in front of a blazing fire, enthusiastically busy with a large well-filled tray. He was wearing a suit of Sam's pajamas, rolled up at ankle and wrist. His hair was wet, his cheeks were pink, and when he smiled up at them his big front teeth shone.

"Hello, Sis! What are you doing here?"

Carney went up to him but she remembered not to kiss him. She patted his head instead. "The next time you elope, tell us about it."

"Why," said Bobbie, sounding offended, "I told you about it tonight. Didn't Mom find my note?"

"Yes," said Sam quickly. "She found it. I told her you'd stay here and do some hoboing tomorrow."

"Fine," said Bobbie, returning to blueberry cobbler. "Gee," he added, "this grub is swell! Whipped cream and everything. You'd think it was a party."

"Fred found him down in the boathouse," said Mrs. Hutchinson, smiling out of the pillows on her chaise lounge.

"He picked up a ride," Mr. Hutchinson explained.

"Three rides," said Bobbie. "One of them had taken a pig to the butcher."

Sam's little sister Genevieve was there. She was gazing at Bobbie with an admiration of which he was not unaware. He licked whipped cream from his spoon with a grandly nonchalant gesture.

Carney said she would try to telephone her mother. It was no use, the Hutchinsons said, they had been trying without success.

"There's nothing for it but going back, and in a hurry, too," Sam said. "Rose is fixing some hot tea for you, Carney. You'd better go right to bed."

Carney snorted. "I certainly won't. I'm going back with you."

He looked annoyed. "Have a little sense. It's bad enough for a man out on those roads tonight. A tree might fall that I couldn't get over. I might have to hoof it."

"Well, I'm quite capable of hoofing it myself," Carney replied.

The Hutchinsons urged her hospitably to stay and Bobbie repeated that the grub was swell but Carney shook her head stubbornly.

"I'd like to tell Mother about Bobbie . . . and I've things to do at home. You'll be busy here tomorrow with the dance coming off at night."

"It's perfect idiocy," Sam answered angrily, "but I won't stand here arguing. I want to get back to your mother. Come if you want to."

He stalked out. Carney said hasty thanks and good-bys, patted Bobbie on the head again, and followed.

Mr. Hutchinson gave them a flashlight and Sam silently marked out her path as they descended. They climbed silently over the fallen tree. The car started without difficulty, and soon they were rolling along again through the howling wind and rain.

Carney hazarded one or two remarks but Sam didn't answer so she gave up. He was certainly mad, she thought. And he was certainly acting rude, but she couldn't really blame him. It had been insane for her to insist on coming back.

Riding along in the silence, with her anxiety relieved, her mind went back to the afternoon. In all the excitement about Bobbie, no one had remembered the importance of her picnic. No one, she was sure, had even thought to wonder about how it had come out.

She remembered the great decision with satisfaction.

"I'm happy," she remarked.

"Congratulations," Sam answered grimly. Now what did he mean by that? Was he congratulating her upon the engagement he thought had taken place? Or on Bobbie being found? Or on being happy in such inauspicious circumstances?

Before she could answer he swore under his breath. He swore violently . . . and didn't even apologize.

Carney was shocked. "What's the matter?"

"Don't you see? The lamps have gone out. I've run out of acetylene."

The car skidded in the soft mud as he stopped.

"What are you stopping for?"

"You don't expect me to drive on a night like this without lights, do you?"

"I suppose you can't. There's a very deep ditch."

"You're darn right there's a deep ditch!"

"Shall we walk?" she asked, although her heart sank a little. They weren't even half way home.

"Let me think," said Sam, in a furious voice. After a moment he went on more calmly. "I've got the flashlight. Maybe you could hold that so that I could see the ditch."

"I'll try."

She tried earnestly for a few minutes but it didn't

work. The feeble light didn't reach the roadside. After a narrow escape from the ditch, Sam halted the car again. He folded his arms on the wheel and sat thinking.

"If I got out on the running board I could do it," Carney said timidly.

"That's impossible, of course."

"I've got a raincoat on."

Sam didn't deign to reply.

"It would be easier than walking home," she urged.

"You're not walking home. I'll walk to a farm house and try to get acetylene."

"But there isn't a farm house anywhere near," said Carney. Her tone was almost a wail. "I don't want to be left alone, Sam. Please!"

He was silent.

"Please let me lie on the running board! Then I can keep the flashlight on the ditch and you can just crawl." As he didn't speak she pleaded, "Just as far as the next farm house!"

"All right," he agreed shortly. She scrambled out. Wrapping her raincoat around her tightly, she fitted her slim body onto the running board and aimed the flashlight downward.

Sam started the car. They progressed at a snail's pace. But they progressed. The flicker of a farm house light came into view.

"Sam!" cried Carney. Fearing that he hadn't seen it, she lifted herself up. "Look!" she cried joyfully. "The light . . ." and then she stopped, for she had rolled off into the road.

She wasn't hurt . . . the car was going so slowly. She struggled to her feet, wiping mud out of her face and ears. With a terrible leap of the heart she realized that the flashlight was no longer in her hand. She had lost it, and Sam would be madder than ever.

He had drawn the car to a sloughing, grinding halt. He was getting out. He was running toward her.

She realized suddenly that the rain had stopped. There was a delicious freshness in the air. And at that moment the heavy clouds overhead shifted. The moon came out, spreading the world with such light that it didn't really matter, after all, about the flashlight.

"Sam!" cried Carney. "I'm afraid I lost the flashlight, but . . ."

That was all she said for Sam took her in his arms. Holding her tightly he kissed her muddy face, not once but several times.

17

The Hutchinson Dance

"IT DOESN'T SEEM POSSIBLE that things were so awful last night," Bonnie said at breakfast.

The sun was shining over a world which seemed to have been washed in green. The air steamed with sweetness. Out on the side lawn Hunter and Jerry were piling broken branches and raking a litter of leaves.

"Last night is like a dream," said Betsy.

"It's like a nightmare," Isobel observed. "Isn't it, Mrs. Sibley?"

Mrs. Sibley nodded, twinkling-eyed.

Carney said nothing. She had said nothing to Sam after he kissed her. Her indignation was apparent in the force with which she tore herself away, in the stiffness with which she marched back and took her seat in the Loco.

Now it was Sam's turn to send remarks into the empty air. He had said that the moonlight was swell; that they would get home without any more trouble; that he hoped her mother hadn't been too worried. Carney didn't answer. He had said that if she didn't mind they'd put on a little speed. Carney hadn't said whether she minded or not.

None of her beaus had ever kissed her, and Sam wasn't even a beau. A man didn't kiss a girl of her sort unless he was serious. Far from being serious about her, Sam liked Isobel.

"I had stopped by to see Isobel . . ." he had said when he was telling her the news about Bobbie. He hadn't said he had come to see the house party, just Isobel.

And now he was kissing *her!*

Back at the house she had flown into the parlor to tell the good news. Sam had followed, smiling brightly. Speaking together in assumed accord, they had described the fire, the pajamas, the loaded tray of food. Mrs. Sibley had wept and tried to pretend that she was weeping from laughter.

Mr. Sibley and Hunter came in, and the story was told again. Larry and Jerry had returned from taking the horses, at long last, to the livery stable. They, too, were told the glad tidings. Mrs. Sibley and Bonnie had slipped out to the kitchen. There was hot cocoa presently. While they were drinking it Mr. Sibley asked Larry whether he and Carney had had much trouble getting back from Orono.

Carney saw Sam's head turn sharply. His glance slid down toward her left hand almost as though he expected to find a diamond there. A light had kindled, too, in the eyes of the girls.

Larry had told about losing the storm curtains.

"He handled the horses wonderfully," Carney put in. It was true, and besides it would serve as a needed rebuke to Sam.

Sam had stayed at the Sibleys all night, but he wasn't at the breakfast table. Mrs. Sibley explained now that he and Mr. Sibley and the boys had eaten early.

"Sam said he wanted to get out to Bobbie. And he insists on keeping Bobbie out there for the dance tonight. He took along his Sunday suit and a clean shirt. Wasn't that kind of him?" Mrs. Sibley asked, turning to her daughter.

"He's good with boys," Carney admitted grudgingly.

"He's very nice."

"Of course . . . ahem! He's not like Larry," Betsy put in mischievously.

"Ahem! Ahem!" added Isobel.

Bonnie beamed tenderly, and everyone looked expectant.

Carney chuckled. "All right. You might as well know. We came back mere friends."

"What?"

"Mere friends," she repeated, smiling at their blank astonishment.

"Did he? Did he . . .?" Betsy began, and stopped.

"It was mutual," said Carney. "We agreed perfectly. Neither of us is in love."

"Then you were very sensible to decide as you did," said Mrs. Sibley. She rose briskly and started to clear the table. But the girls rebounded more slowly.

"Oh, dear!" mourned Bonnie.

"He's awfully attractive," Isobel said regretfully.

Betsy frowned. "I like stories to have happy endings!" she declared.

"Well, this one has a very happy ending." Carney got up and stretched her arms. "I just love being a free woman."

She did feel thoroughly satisfied with the outcome of the trip to Orono.

"Betsy and Joe will have to provide the love interest tonight," she added.

"When does Joe get here?" Bonnie asked.

"On the two-five," said Betsy. "The beautiful two-five!"

"Let's all go to the train to meet him," Carney suggested. She was glad it was her turn to tease.

"Nothing could be more unnecessary," said Betsy. "I know the way to the depot."

"But don't you think it would be cordial . . . friendly-like . . . for all of us to go?"

"I think it would be cordial and friendly-like for all of you to stay home."

Bonnie sighed in mock dejection. "I wish there was a little romance in *my* life."

"Just wait till you get to the U."

"Your Minister is waiting somewhere!" The girls had told Bonnie, after the visit to the Chapel, that she was destined to marry a minister.

Bonnie's laughter bubbled.

They spent the morning packing, and Betsy cleaned her white shoes and bag. After dinner she dressed carefully in a lavender gingham with a wide flower-covered hat. When she came into the library, Carney sniffed loudly.

"Joe likes perfume," Betsy remarked, sauntering across the room in her best imitation of a show girl's alluring gait.

"Sure you don't want us to come along?"

"Positive."

"I suppose you'll hurry back home?"

"I suppose we won't," said Betsy.

"It's nice to see *some* love run smoothly," Isobel observed.

Carney laughed. "It didn't always run smoothly for Betsy and Joe."

"Well," said Betsy, "it's running smoothly now." She waved her hand, caught up the freshly cleaned white bag and ran out of the house.

It was four o'clock when they returned. They had gone to Heinz's, Betsy explained. Joe came in, walking with a swing as of old, to say hello before he left for the hotel. Carney greeted him with hearty liking.

He was blond with tufted golden brows above very live blue eyes, and a strong face full of humor and courage. He was a good one for Betsy, Carney thought.

"I suppose you hate me for snatching Betsy away from Minneapolis before she was hardly unpacked."

"I couldn't hate you, Carney," Joe replied. "But now she's going to come home and stay home."

"The voice of authority," said Betsy.

She was sparkling with happiness.

The house party had fun dressing for this last party. After an early supper they went upstairs to take turns bathing, to button one another's dresses, and make one another's puffs and psyche knots, and tie large graceful bows around one another's heads.

Annoyed as she was at Sam, Carney found herself wishing that she was wearing pink. But Isobel was wearing pink. Carney chose a white net with a hobble skirt which she hated. Miss Mix, the dressmaker, had persuaded her to have it because hobbles were the style.

Carney and Isobel wore the Liberty capes they wore to Chapel at Vassar. Carney's was red wool. She wrapped it about her haughtily as Sam came up to the porch where they were waiting. But after a genial hello he went straight to her mother. Carney heard him telling her about Bobbie. Fred had helped him rig up a boat on which Bobbie had played all day, pretending to be Huck Finn.

"I'll bring him home safe and sound tonight," Sam said.

Cars were arriving rapidly now. The Sibley home had been chosen as a point of departure for the Crowd. All the girls were in filmy dresses. It seemed as though bits of the sunset were drifting around the lawn. The boys were wearing blue coats and white trousers.

Everyone crowded around Joe Willard, especially members of the Class of 1910. The Crowd had not seen him since graduation night and it was a happy reunion.

So many boys had brought cars that some couples drove out alone. Sam and Isobel went alone.

The party left Deep Valley with the afterglow still in the sky, but by the time they arrived at Murmuring Lake the full moon was rising. The Hutchinson lawn was strung with Japanese lanterns, and the big house was blazing with lights.

Inside, the rooms were filled with great bowls of flowers: phlox, purple and white; dahlias, snow-on-the-mountain, cosmos and nasturtiums and daisies. An enormous cut-glass punch bowl was filled with fruit punch and surrounded by cut-glass cups.

The high dark-paneled dining room with its hand-painted ceiling and crystal chandelier had been cleared for dancing. The doors which led to the big screened porch were open. One could dance inside or out on the porch with a view of moonlit lake.

No piano-playing aunt furnished the music here. A three-piece orchestra—piano, violin and harp—was tuning up in the music room. Bobbie appeared in the Sunday knicker suit, very scrubbed and peachy. He and little Genevieve, whose hair was in glossy ringlets, passed out the programs.

These dainty cards had small pencils attached. Names were scribbled with jokes and compliments. Larry wrote his name five times on Carney's card.

"After all," he said, smiling, "I'm going home tomorrow. Nobody knows when I'll dance with you again."

Sam took just one waltz toward the end of the program.

Dancing began. The senior Hutchinsons looked on radiantly. Although Mrs. Hutchinson lay in her chaise lounge as usual, she was elegantly dressed with a corsage bouquet on her shoulder.

Bobbie and Genevieve devoted themselves to the punch. After watching her brother consume six glasses, Carney asked Cab to stop in the midst of a two-step.

"Bobbie! You've gone to dancing school. Why don't you ask Genevieve to dance?"

Bobbie put his arm stiffly around Genevieve's waist. They circled a few times, smiling broadly, bumping into everyone. But the punch bowl was more attractive. They soon returned to that. As soon as it was empty, it was replenished again.

The orchestra played all the most popular tunes— "Chinatown, My Chinatown" and "Come Josephine in My Flying Machine," "Alexander's Ragtime Band" and "Oh, You Beautiful Doll!" When they played "Down by the Old Mill Stream," everyone sang, of course, Dennie improvising a magnificent tenor.

The Crowd was happy, Carney thought, looking around. Winona and Dennie were clowning. Betsy and Joe were blissful, of course. Tom seemed to have forgotten Isobel and was giving Alice a rush.

Hunter looked wretched, and it appeared to Carney that he and Ellen had quarreled. They were never together, and Ellen—who could not dissemble—was dancing with stricken eyes.

Isobel and Sam were having fun. He liked to try out the new dances, and she knew them all. They danced a dexterous Turkey Trot which the Crowd stopped to watch and applaud. Isobel's hair came loose in curls around her laughing face.

Carney applauded with the rest, but she felt something hard inside her chest. She had never felt anything like it before. It was like an angry fist.

She was scornful of Isobel. "What about Howard?" she thought. "I wouldn't be that fickle!"

Another part of her nature spoke up in Isobel's defense. "She's never said she was serious about Howard. You're just mad because things didn't work out for you and Larry."

But she knew that wasn't true. The pleasantest feature of her evening was the fact that she and Larry were enjoying each other so much.

They hadn't got on as well as this since he came from California. He looked outstandingly tall and attractive in the blue coat and white trousers. They felt relaxed, at ease with one another. His eyes laughed down at her with genuine affection.

Bonnie pulled Carney aside. "Are you sure you were telling the truth about Orono? You and Larry seem devotion itself."

"It's platonic," answered Carney.

"Platonic friendships can be very dangerous."

"Not this one!"

Sam came up for his dance, his blue eyes squeezed tightly in his inflexible smile. The orchestra began a favorite song.

> "*Let me call you sweetheart,*
> *I'm in love with you . . .*"

The other dancers sang, but Sam and Carney didn't. Trying to erase their lingering embarrassment, she talked with unusual animation. Sam, at his most suave, kept talking, too.

"It's been a wonderful party, Sam."

"Well, we tried to think of everything," he answered. "Even a moon. Have you seen it?" And holding her elbow he drew her out to the porch, through the screen door, and down the steps.

The lawn smelled deliciously of white stock in the garden. As they strolled they fell into silence again. Passing beyond the lanterns, they reached an open knoll where there was a wide view of the lake.

The moon was high and majestic now. The golden path across the water seemed like a rug unrolled before a queen.

"Isn't that a nice show?" he asked. "I put it on just for you."

"Yes," Carney answered uneasily. "Larry and I admired it driving out."

He dropped her arm. "I suppose you're saying that on purpose."

"I don't know what you mean."

"Oh, of course not!" He sounded sarcastic. "Well, let's go in!" He hooked his arm into hers again, and turned her forcibly toward the house.

When they reached an elm tree so large and thickly leaved that its shadow defeated even Japanese lanterns, he stopped and kissed her.

Carney broke away from him. She was really angry now. It was possible to forgive what had happened the night before . . . they had both been wrought up. But this was different. It was inexcusable.

He still said nothing about . . . liking her or anything. He was stalking beside her toward the house.

Of course, maybe he thought that she was engaged to Larry? Well, he could ask!

At midnight the Hutchinsons served a supper which far outshone the usual Deep Valley ice cream and cake. Chicken salad, sandwiches cut in hearts and circles and half-moons, molded jellies, ices, and little frosted cakes.

Afterward there was one more dance. The orchestra (well fed and rested) played "Good Night, Ladies" and then switched to "Home Sweet Home."

Carney was dancing with Larry, and she smiled into his face as though she had been paid to smile and would be fined if she stopped. Larry held her closely and smiled in return. Across the dance floor Bonnie lifted warning eyebrows. They seemed to ask, "Are you sure?"

Genevieve was curled up on the library couch, winking in an effort to stay awake. Bobbie, on the floor beside her, was playing with a box of treasures which he had acquired during the day—important things like stones and shells and turtles.

The girls went upstairs for their wraps, and in the laughing hubbub of farewells Carney heard Sam say, "Come on, Bob! Got to get started! You and the turtles can have the back seat to yourselves."

Carney stepped forward grimly. "Bobbie will come with Larry and me," she said. "I wouldn't have him intruding on you and Isobel."

Sam stared at her. "What do you mean . . . intrude on me and Isobel?"

"Well," said Carney, feeling foolish, "it isn't very suitable for you two to have a little boy along."

"It's just as suitable for us as it is for you . . . more so, I would say. Bobbie certainly isn't going to intrude on you and Lochinvar."

"He's my brother and he'll come with me," said Carney. Her cheeks were as red as her cape.

"He's my guest and I shall take him home," said Sam.

They glared at each other until Carney burst into laughter. Sam didn't laugh. He looked at her wrathfully. He sought out Bobbie where he was playing with the turtles and swept him dramatically out to the Loco.

18
Betsy Gives Advice

It was the last night of The Little Colonel's House Party, and her guests were well aware of it. They could hardly fail to be, for Betsy Ray, who always took notice of "last times," had been saying for several days: "This is the last time we'll go down to Heinz's . . . This is the last time we'll take the Seven Mile Drive . . . This is the last game of Five

Hundred." And now: "This is the last night of the house party."

Moonlight favored the occasion. The sleeping porch was silvery bright. They could see plainly the outline of the hills, the little turret on the barn, the dooryard trees, which had grown so familiar over the summer.

Betsy and Bonnie went down to the kitchen to bring up a spread "for the last time." The four girls sat in their beds eating Nabiscos and cherries, corn bread and pickles and a nubbin of cold pork, discussing the house party with the greatest thoroughness.

They went in retrospect over the parties, drives, and picnics. They recalled the thrill of Larry's coming.

"All that excitement and then nothing happened!" Betsy groaned. "Nobody in the whole crowd eloped except Bobbie."

"But we thought Isobel had," said Bonnie, "the night she stayed to dinner with the Hutchinsons."

Isobel's laugh rippled. "There was nothing romantic about that."

"What do you mean? You didn't elope, but it was certainly romantic."

"Not a bit. I stayed in order to talk with Sam's father."

"His father!" everyone cried, and Carney felt that

hard fist churning in her chest again.

Betsy sat up straight in exasperation. "I knew that you and Sam were sweet about each other, but I didn't think it had gone *that* far."

Isobel swayed with mirth. "What do you mean?"

"Why, when you talk to the parents, things are getting serious."

"But Mr. Hutchinson and I were talking business," she replied.

Betsy and Bonnie pushed her over and crammed a pillow into her face. Carney looked on, smiling stiffly.

"I'll explain! I'll explain!" Isobel cried in muffled tones. She sat up, breathless. "I wanted to talk with Sam's father because I thought he might be able to help Howard."

"Howard!"

"Yes. Knowing someone like Mr. Hutchinson might mean a lot to a newcomer to the Middle West."

"Who's coming to the Middle West?"

"Howard. He has a job in Minneapolis, at one of the mills. It's a wonderful opening. And Mr. Hutchinson is going to pull a few wires to make it even better." She added softly, "I'm very glad. It's so important to me."

"Why?"

"That's what I want to tell you. The last night of

the house party seems a suitable time." She threw back her curls and smiled. "I'm engaged to Howard Sedgwick."

"You're engaged!" There was a triple shriek.

"Yes. We were engaged before he came to see me at Vassar. That's why Mrs. K let him stay to dinner, because he was my fiancé."

Bonnie and Betsy threw their arms around her rapturously. They hugged and kissed her and pelted her with questions. Carney couldn't seem to join in. She sat stiffly, thinking.

It all fitted in—or almost all. Isobel had wangled the invitation to the Sibleys because she wanted to see Minnesota. She wanted to know whether she could bear to come and live among the Indians. Carney remembered the ring of truth in her voice when she came back from the phone and said that Howard wanted to know how she liked the Middle West. And she had wanted to meet the influential Hutchinsons so that she could forward her fiancé's interests. Yes, it all fitted in.

"But, Isobel!" Bonnie was saying. "How you've been acting all summer!"

"What do you mean?"

"Why . . . flirting with everyone!"

"Pooh!" said Isobel. "It doesn't hurt a little boy like Hunter to like an older girl. Tom and I were just having fun, and as for Sam . . . I don't say I'd have forgotten Howard if I could have hooked Sam, but I'd have been tempted. He's so attractive, don't you think so, Carney?" Her tone was meaningful.

"Moderately," said Carney.

"You admit now, don't you, that he's not a baby hippo?"

"He's lost weight," said Carney furiously, "worrying over you."

"That's nonsense," answered Isobel. "He's known about Howard for days."

And that, too, fitted in. Carney remembered his almost bored inquiry after the New York 'phone call, "Was that Howard?"

What didn't fit in was Isobel telling all this with such frankness. It wasn't a bit like her.

She was looking at Carney searchingly now. "Maybe it's you he's worried about."

"Fiddlesticks!" said Carney.

"Sam and I talked about you when we were driving in last night."

"Did you? What did you say?"

But Isobel slipped down in the bed and stretched luxuriously. "Don't ask me any more questions. I'm tired, and I want to go to sleep."

"Isobel Porteous!" cried Carney. "If I ever knew anyone who liked to make a mystery of things, it's you!"

Isobel yawned and stretched in the moonlight.

"*Bon nuit,*" she murmured. "Tomorrow night and the next night on a sleeper!"

"I'll be back in St. Paul," said Bonnie.

"And Joe and I will be back in Minneapolis. He's coming to Sunday night lunch. Isobel, your news is wonderful! It puts just the finishing touch to the house party. Don't you think so, Carney?"

"Yes," answered Carney. She was too mixed up to say more.

Once again she lay awake, faced by a problem. She had done that more this summer than ever before in her life. She was still offended at Sam, but her heart was singing because of what Isobel had said. Isobel seemed to think he was crazy about her, Carney.

Carney couldn't help admitting that she liked him. "Or I might, if he didn't go around kissing everyone!"

But how was she to let him know she liked him . . . and still save her pride? She didn't want him thinking she was used to being kissed by every Tom, Dick, and Harry.

Bonnie, the usually perfect confidante, could be of no help. She had had no experience. She had hardly seen a boy from the time she left Deep Valley until she returned to it.

Isobel had had experience, but Carney wouldn't

ask her for the world. She liked her again, she discovered. All her affection had come pouring back in the strangest, most mystifying way. But she couldn't ask advice from her. Isobel wasn't . . . kind enough.

That left Betsy. And Betsy wasn't ideal. She was too romantic—she dramatized everything—while Carney was matter-of-fact. But she was sympathetic and kind; and she understood boys.

Carney resolved to talk with Betsy. And in keeping with her habit of leaving nothing unsettled longer than necessary, she crept to the adjoining bed.

"Betsy! Wake up!"

"What?"

"Wake up! Come on in my room. I want to talk with you."

In her bedroom Carney lit the gas. Betsy came in, rubbing her eyes. She had put her arms through the sleeves of her silk kimono, bright red with large green dragons on it. She curled up on the high-backed bed while Carney shut the door and sat down in the bird's-eye maple rocker.

"What's the matter?" Betsy asked drowsily.

Carney said without preface, "Sam Hutchinson kissed me."

"He did?" Betsy was wide awake in an instant. "How did he happen to do that?"

"He just did. Coming home from Murmuring Lake

the night of the storm, and again last night on the lawn."

"He *does* like you!" Betsy cried. "Isobel was right. Carney, do you like him?"

"I'm terribly offended at him."

"Why?"

"It isn't right to just kiss me like that. I'm not a spooner."

"Of course not." Betsy went off into hushed laughter. "Excuse me, Carney. I'm not laughing at you but at something I happened to remember. I'll tell you about it. Maybe it will help you.

"You know, I'm not a spooner, either, but a boy in California kissed me."

"Was it Herbert?"

"No. A friend of Herbert's. He didn't know about Joe. He kissed me, and yet he didn't say a word about being serious, or getting engaged, or anything. I was offended just as you are."

"What did you do?"

"I'll tell you, and you can do the same thing. It worked like a charm." Betsy's face shone beneath the crown of Magic Wavers. "I saw him the next night, and broke our engagement."

"Your engagement! But you hadn't gotten engaged."

"Of course not," said Betsy blithely. "But I pretended

we had. I said: 'I laid awake all night thinking about our engagement, and I decided that it was a mistake. I can't marry you after all because I don't love you. Good-by, forever!'" She declaimed the last two words in a tragic voice.

"What did he do?" asked Carney, choking with laughter.

"He was furious. He was a little bewildered, too, but mostly he was furious. He started right in giving me all the reasons why we ought to get engaged. But I turned him down flat. I think I taught him a lesson . . . not to go around kissing girls. Now you must do the same thing."

"I couldn't," said Carney gloomily. "I'm not made that way."

"I'd write out what to say and you could memorize it."

Carney shook her head. "It's no use; I'm so darn truthful."

"Well, I'll tell you what!" cried Betsy. "Listen! Here's something you can do, something awfully subtle. Tell him that he *should* have asked you to marry him and that if he had you would have turned him down. Then he'll propose and you *can* turn him down."

Carney looked grim. "I will," she said. "I'll do it tomorrow after you all go."

Betsy jumped up in such elation that even the drag-ons on her robe seemed to be smiling. She ran to Carney and hugged her. "Will you write and tell me exactly what happens?"

"Exactly," said Carney. "Thanks for the idea, Betsy. Come on, let's go back to bed. I think I can sleep now."

The next morning was cool, with a heavy dew. It suggested fall, although it was barely August. And the talk was all of school, of things that would happen in September.

"It's the house party ending, not summer," Carney reminded herself. But she couldn't shake off that au-tumnal feeling.

All the travelers were leaving together. They were taking the four forty-five for Minneapolis. In the morning they went to church. Betsy went to her own Episcopal Church with Larry, Tom, and Joe. Isobel went with Bonnie and the Sibleys.

"Do you know," she said to Carney, "I rather like this family church-going. In my family we don't go to church much, and when we do we don't go together. The way you and the boys start off with your father and mother, all of you so neat and shining . . . I think it's nice. When I have a family I'd like to do the same."

Carney remembered her qualms about Isobel and

the Sibley Sunday morning. How unnecessary most of her qualms had been!

After church Isobel left Carney and Bonnie. She was going to walk home with Hunter, she said. He was waiting a little way off and Carney saw Isobel slip her hand into his arm, smiling sweetly upward.

They took a long way home. They must, Bonnie remarked, have gone by way of Page Park or even Orono.

"She's telling him about her engagement," Carney said soberly. "I hope she makes him feel all right."

They appeared just as dinner was being put on the table. Hunter looked pale but he had an exalted, not unhappy look. He went to the telephone and when he returned Carney heard him say to Isobel, "I called her. It's all right."

So! She had sent him back to little Ellen. Isobel was wonderful, Carney thought, shaking her head.

Shortly after dinner Larry appeared. He, too, suggested a walk. He and Carney left Broad Street at the Episcopal Church and took the road up Cemetery Hill. They passed the watering trough, and the little candy store, and the road began to climb. It was the hill down which they had coasted as children.

"You could certainly steer," Carney said. "I always wondered how you missed the watering trough."

They sat down beside the road. The ditches were

full of August's rich tangle of flowers. The trees had August's lush deep green. The day had turned warm and sunshiny.

"I hope you'll keep on writing to me," Larry said. "I wouldn't feel right without your letters. It would be like the week losing Thursday, almost."

"I'll write you. I'd miss your letters, too," Carney replied. "Maybe," she added, "we'll always write each other even when we're married to other people."

Larry took off his straw hat and stared at it.

"Carney," he said, "are you sure we haven't made a mistake?"

"Positive," she replied. He looked up, and she looked at him with frank friendly eyes. Then she smiled and jumped to her feet. "I'll race you back to the watering trough."

They didn't race, but they joined hands and ran to the very foot of the hill.

Sam was sitting on the porch with the Crowd when they returned. He was shaved and looked trim in a navy blue suit. He had brought boxes of candy—gigantic, of course—for the girls. Winona and Alice had brought fudge and divinity.

"We're not going to starve on the four forty-five," Joe remarked.

It was time to say good-by, and Bonnie kissed Mr. and Mrs. Sibley with almost a daughter's affection.

She kissed Jerry and Bobbie, who grinned sheepishly. Hunter was coming to the train with the Crowd—and Ellen.

"We've had the most scrumptious time," said Betsy.

"You were so good to have us!" Isobel's tone was like honey. "I hope we haven't exhausted you?"

"Not a bit," said Mr. Sibley. "We'll miss all the phoning, and the giggling on the porch at night."

"We won't be making so many doughnuts," joked Olga, flushed with the praise the girls had heaped upon her.

They piled into the usual three cars; Carney and Larry went with Ellen and Hunter. They drove down Broad Street, and across to Front, and down Front to the station.

Isobel, Bonnie, and Betsy were wearing their suits with fluffy jabots, basket-shaped hats, and gloves. Carney was hatless and gloveless, wearing her pink linen. Sam looked at her more than once.

"It's just because he likes pink," she told herself. "Still, I think he's going to get quite a surprise when I tell him I won't marry him."

The boldness of her plan brought on premonitory chills.

They waited on the platform, laughing and joking. Isobel was talking to Tom now. She was making him promise that he would come to Vassar to a dance. She paid no attention to Hunter who walked up and down with Ellen.

Larry stayed close to Carney. They looked at each other with warm liking.

"There's lots to be said for friendship," Carney thought.

The train whistled, distantly. It whistled close at hand. It rushed into the station with the bell swinging and clanging. The house party fell upon Carney with kisses.

"Thank you for asking us! . . . Thank you! . . . It's been simply glorious!"

Larry shook hands, holding her hand tightly.

The engine was noisily getting up steam, the whistle sounded again. The conductor called "All aboard!" and the three girls, Larry, and Joe hurried into the parlor car. They came out on the observation platform. Larry and Joe took their stand behind the house party which stood together, arms entwined.

Bonnie was beaming. She looked cute and cozy in spite of the mature dark red suit.

Betsy was smiling, showing her parted teeth.

Isobel was smiling, too, but sadly. Her dark blue eyes were fixed on Hunter. He stood rigidly, holding Ellen's arm, as the train began to move.

When Carney turned around, she found Sam beside her.

"It *was* a wonderful house party!" she said, still breathless.

"It certainly was," he agreed. He took her arm possessively and the other boys, who might have joined her, turned away to the other girls. Carney climbed into the Loco.

"Shall we drop off at Heinz's for a sundae?" he asked.

"I don't mind," she answered. She braced herself with small shivers of fear for what she planned to say.

19
And Carney Follows It

THERE WAS NO CHANCE to bring up the subject at Heinz's. Over their sundaes, which Sam told the waiter genially to "put on the book," they talked about college. The house party had left a vacuum, but it began to fill up as Carney told Sam about her plans for getting ready for college. Miss Mix was coming to sew; she and her mother would be shopping . . .

"Do you ever wish you were going back to college?" she inquired.

"Sometimes. There was one prof I liked a lot, and I enjoyed the Orchestra in Minneapolis. But I like working around the mill, and Dad wants me to learn the business." He added with unaffected casualness, "Isobel seems to think this Sedgwick guy is going to make a miller."

Carney tried to sound natural. "What do you think of her plans?"

"Swell. It will be fun to have her around. She's such a good scout."

A good scout! Carney was astonished. It was the last term she would have thought of applying to Isobel.

The conversation wasn't one into which you could throw remarks about engagements. She would have to wait until they got home, Carney thought. But she was resolved to have her say, although it was late when they returned. Slanting sunlight glimmered over the lawn, over the zinnias and marigolds and dahlias which stood up straight in their beds. Jerry and Bobbie were playing with the sprinkler.

Sam swung up the steps behind her, and they sat down on the porch, in a faded, rain-beaten settee behind the curtain of vines.

"Now is the time," Carney thought, "to make that speech if I'm ever going to make it." She turned to him desperately. He was telling her how much he would like to take her up to Minneapolis in the Loco to hear a symphony concert before she went back.

"But I'm afraid the season won't have started," he was saying when Carney cut in.

"Sam!"

"Yes?" he answered, startled.

"You know how you kissed me at your party and the night before?"

"I remember something about it," he answered. He reached out and took her hand. "Did you think it was a good idea?"

Carney took her hand away.

"No," she said, "I didn't. I don't believe in people kissing unless they're serious about one another. You didn't ask me to marry you, and I just wanted to say . . ." she stopped and swallowed for it sounded ridiculous. It had sounded all right when Betsy had said it in her persuasive voice. But it didn't now.

"What do you want to say?" Sam asked.

"I want to say, that if you *had* asked me to marry you, I'd have said no," Carney replied.

For a moment Sam sat in stunned silence and Carney's heart misgave her. First, she was afraid that she had hurt his feelings. Then she was even more afraid that she had told a lie. Looking at him as he sat there in the golden light which filtered through the vines, so warm, so protectively big, with that dimple in his chin—she wasn't at all sure that she would have said no.

She felt almost weepy and was quite unprepared for what Sam did. He laughed. He laughed uproariously, and it was obviously a spontaneous reaction. He laughed as she had never heard him laugh before. She sat in a hurt, embarrassed silence.

Then he turned and took her in his arms and kissed her. He kept on kissing her so that she couldn't say a word. And when he stopped and she had a chance to speak, she could think of nothing to say.

It was Sam who spoke. "You'd say no, would you?" he asked. "Are you sure of that? Will you put it in writing so that I won't get roped in if I ask you? But I'm not going to ask you. I'm going to tell you. If you're not marrying Lochinvar, you're going to marry me."

Carney said what she had said to the girls. "Larry and I are mere friends."

"That's what Isobel told me, after the dance. I guess she could see I was jealous," Sam added. "Why couldn't *you* have told me?"

"Why couldn't you have asked me?"

"Oh, well! I'll forgive you!" He smiled expansively and drew her back in the settee. "Then we're engaged," he said.

"Oh, no!" said Carney. "Not until we ask Dad and Mother. And I think we'd better ask them now because . . ."

The boys had come nearer. They were glancing curiously in. Carney didn't want them to see their sister being kissed by a young man to whom she wasn't engaged.

"Do you mean right now?" Sam asked.

"Right now." She was delighted because he seemed confused.

"I don't believe your father likes me too well."

"You should have made more fuss about his rarebit."

"I don't believe your mother likes me either."

But Carney couldn't bear to tease him. "As a matter of fact," she said, "you won their hearts the other night when you were so good to Bobbie."

"You think they'll think it's all right, then?"

"They may not want a real engagement," Carney answered, "until I'm through college."

"What's the difference between an engagement and an understanding that you're going to have an engagement?" grumbled Sam, but he got up and started inside. Carney followed.

In the library the gas had been lighted, and her father and mother were reading.

"You two looking for some supper?" Mrs. Sibley

asked. "I was just going out to see what I could find."

Olga always had Sunday evening off.

"I don't want supper," Sam answered. "I want Carney."

He took hold of her hand, partly as though he were seeking courage and partly as though he wanted to show her parents that they might as well agree. He smiled his engaging smile.

Mrs. Sibley's lashes fluttered and she didn't say a word. Mr. Sibley asked him to sit down. He told Mrs. Sibley and Carney that they had better go out and rustle up that supper. Sam was obliged to let go of Carney's hand, but he yielded it reluctantly.

Out in the kitchen Mrs. Sibley and Carney felt awkward with each other.

"When did this happen?" Mrs. Sibley asked sternly. "I never heard of such a thing."

But Carney knew that she wasn't angry, she was just embarrassed. Carney walked across the room and looked out into the sunset.

"I'm in love with him," she said.

There was a long pause, such a long pause that Carney turned around at last. She saw that her mother's eyes were wet. Mrs. Sibley stooped to a drawer and got out an apron, crackly with starch.

"Then," she said, "I can't think of any reason in

the world why you shouldn't marry him. I hope your father won't think of any."

She began to make white sauce for the creamed potatoes. Carney got out the cold tongue and started slicing. She peeled and quartered tomatoes from the garden. They talked about the house party, but their ears were pricked toward the sound of conversation continuing steadily in the library.

When the creamed potatoes were finished, Mrs. Sibley made tea. Carney filled glass dishes with sliced peaches and arranged cookies on a plate.

"I wish they'd hurry up," she said. "The boys will be coming in."

"That's just what I was thinking," her mother said.

They went to the dining room door, and Mrs. Sibley coughed gently. Mr. Sibley called, "That supper almost ready?"

"It's all ready," Mrs. Sibley said.

"Will you two come in here then?"

They went, and Carney could see at once that everything was going to be all right. Her father was standing, and he looked grave, as he did when he presided at the Chapel Sunday School, but he looked good-humored, too.

Sam reached out for her hand. He squeezed it as though to say, "It's all right. Don't be afraid."

Mr. Sibley said almost what Mrs. Sibley had said.

"I don't see any reason why you two shouldn't become engaged if you want to. Of course, Sam understands that you would want to finish college."

"Oh, of course!" Carney cried.

Sam squeezed her hand again. He didn't let go of it even when her father said, "Well, let's go in and get some supper."

After that, August slipped by on wings. The August lilies came and went. In the vacant lots Queen Anne's lace grew birds-nesty, but goldenrod was burnished yellow, and purple asters bright as paint.

Jerry and Bobbie had forgotten baseball; they played with a football salvaged from the garage. Hunter and Ellen told Carney happily that they planned to "go together" in their senior year. Miss Mix came to sew, and Carney was busy with a hundred errands—shopping, going to the dentist, paying farewell calls. But she went in the big Loco, or else it was parked in front of the Sibley house. To Bobbie's satisfaction Sam practically lived there.

Every few days Sam drove Carney out to Murmuring Lake. Mr. and Mrs. Hutchinson were delighted with the engagement. They deluged Carney with affection.

"What ails that boy of mine that he hasn't bought you a ring yet?" Mr. Hutchinson wanted to know.

Carney was happier than she had ever been in her

life, and yet she didn't mind going back to Vassar. That was because Sam was willing for her to go. He would be proud, he said, to have her graduate. And he wanted her to get more lessons from Miss Chittenden.

"When you play for me after we're married, I want you to be good!"

He didn't even mind that she had to go back early. He thought it was splendid that she was to be one of those outstanding juniors in white dresses, with rose and gray ribbons and badges, who would be welcoming the freshmen.

On Labor Day Mr. Sibley proposed that they take Sam on a picnic. The Sibleys had many family picnics. It was time Sam was initiated, Mr. Sibley said. The boys whooped with joy, and Mrs. Sibley and Carney packed a lunch. Mr. Sibley carefully got out his reflector oven.

They went to Two Falls Park. As they walked toward the bridge, memories of the earlier picnic there caused Carney's dimple to flicker. Sam whispered to her, "Don't you wish I were a baseball star?"

The day was as warm as summer, but the waterfall was now only a spun-silver thread. There were touches of yellow in the trees lining the canyon. There were red vines garlanding some of the trees. The wild grapes would be ripe, Mr. Sibley said.

As they unpacked the basket, a flock of yellow-headed blackbirds crossed the horizon, headed south.

"How about some hunting this fall?" Sam asked Jerry and Bobbie. "There'll be lots of ducks on Murmuring Lake. And I've got a couple of extra guns."

Sam made the fire. He was good with his hands. It burned up brightly, but according to Mr. Sibley's exact instructions he let it die down. Mr. Sibley mixed the corn cake, equal parts of yellow corn meal and flour, and egg and milk. He put the tin in the reflector oven and while it was baking he fried bacon and eggs, and Sam made coffee.

Carney laid out plates and cups, knives and forks and spoons, on a blue cloth. She poured glasses of milk and heaped platters with doughnuts, peaches, plums. She smiled all the time.

After eating they talked about nature. They always did, Carney told Sam; her father knew a lot about it. They watched a squirrel storing nuts and Mr. Sibley told them about the habits of squirrels. Mr. Sibley explained how the ironwood tree got its name—because it was so hard. He showed them how tough the ironwood sapling was. Jerry tried to break one, but he couldn't. Bobbie begged his father to make him a willow whistle. Whistles, Mr. Sibley explained wisely, belonged to the spring when the willow bark slipped off easily.

Later they all played "duck on a rock"; even Mrs. Sibley played. Sam ran so fast when Mrs. Sibley knocked his duck off, that she said she thought he could beat Dan Patch.

After "duck on a rock" Bobbie brought out the football, and he and Sam kicked it around.

"Bobbie thinks he owns Sam!" Carney said to her mother with irritation.

But presently Sam remarked to Bobbie that there were lots of chokecherries on the trees up on the hill. He offered him a nickel for a capful. Bobbie ran off, and Sam and Carney did just what Winona and Dennie had done. They went down below the falls and threw sticks and watched them sail away; they threw more and followed them.

They were talking about a trip they were going to make to Minneapolis. He had offered to drive her and her mother up for shopping. He wanted Carney to meet that favorite prof. He wanted to take her to a concert, too, if the Orchestra was playing, and explain the instruments.

"And I want to take you to a bootmaker."

"For heaven's sake, why?"

"I'm going to have him make you some hiking boots. Girls never get the right kind. This fellow will make them to my order, and I can get exactly what I want."

"But what do I want hiking boots for?" Carney asked.

"For our honeymoon. That is, if you'd like to go to the north woods."

"And camp? Oh, Sam! I'd love it!"

"I'll do the cooking."

"But I like to cook. I'm a good cook."

"If we get to fighting about it, we'll let our Indian do it."

"Are we going to have an Indian?" Carney asked excitedly.

"You bet. Indian guides are fine on honeymoons. They don't pay a bit of attention to you."

Carney's dimple twinkled again. "You've been on so many honeymoons!"

"Well, I'm going on one two years from next June."

"Unless there's a war or something," she joked. She knew, as everyone did, that there was never going to be another war. Wars belonged only to history classes.

"There's something I want to get for you besides boots," said Sam. He spoke haltingly. "It's a ring. I have one all picked out, a whopper."

"Sam!"

"But I'm not going to . . . that is . . . I'm waiting to dig up some money. I'm getting to be a regular miser, saving to buy that ring. I won't charge it, but it's hard for me, Carney, to let you go East without it. All the guys you'll be meeting at dances, and your left hand perfectly empty . . ." He stopped.

"You don't need to worry," Carney said. She felt like crying. There was something else she wanted to say, but it was always hard for Carney to be romantic. She swallowed hard and made herself say it.

"You don't need to worry. When I love someone, *I love someone,*" she said.

20

Sunset Hill Again

THE CAMPUS SEEMED STRANGE without Isobel, Win,
Sue, and Peg. Only Winkie of the Tower crowd had
been called back to serve on the Reception Committee. And it seemed strange not to be living in Main any
more—but juniors never lived in Main. On the day
of room-drawing last spring, Carney and Isobel had
been given two rooms and a sitting room in Lathrop.

They would be together again, at least.

The rooms smelled of varnish and looked unnaturally neat, as dormitory rooms always did at the beginning of the year. They wouldn't look right until she and Isobel got out their banners and pictures, their pillows and books, the tea set with the spirit lamp. And Carney didn't want to do any of that until Isobel arrived because settling was such fun. Besides, her trunk had not come. She had only the suitcase which she had carried herself from the Poughkeepsie station to the trolley.

The little bobtailed trolley had been filled with girls she knew. None of them belonged to her gang, but they were Vassar girls and so they seemed like friends. They had climbed off at the Old Lodge Gate, and Carney had carried her suitcase beneath the clock on to the campus.

The tall Norway spruces stood like majestic ladies. The maples were turning their coppery gold, and scarlet vines covered some of the buildings. The campus had looked even more beautiful than she remembered it.

She had changed into a middie blouse and skirt, and was unpacking when Winkie came in.

"Hi there! Carney!" she cried.

She looked just the same; so small that she was almost topheavy under her big blond braids. Her face was one jubilant smile. Carney was very glad to see her. They went outside and sat down on the steps.

The air was full of the scent of evergreens.

"It smells like college," Carney remarked, sniffing. "Do you know, this place grows on you."

"You really glad to be back?"

"I really am. But we had a wonderful summer. I guess you know all about it from our letters."

Winkie said she did, and Carney was relieved. The summer had moved so far away; it didn't seem to be the thing to talk about, sitting on the steps of Lathrop. And she didn't want to tell the news of Isobel's engagement. Isobel would want that pleasure herself.

Carney had a plan. She thought they would give a spread, the night the gang got back, to announce both their engagements. She would tell Isobel about her own first, of course. Isobel would have her diamond, and Carney wouldn't, but she didn't care. She loved not having her diamond.

"You've been down to the Circle, I suppose?" she asked. The Athletic Circle, where they played tennis and basketball, was the center of college for Winkie.

"Not yet. I've been trailing my trunk."

"I'm anxious to get back to the music building," Carney said. "To my horse stall!" She chuckled. "It will seem good to be starting piano again."

"I want to lay in some Whitman's Instantaneous Cocoa."

"And I have to collect Suzanne from Professor Bracq."

"Did you bring back the dress suit?"

"You bet I did. What would you all do for masculine company if I didn't have my dress suit?" Winkie grinned. "When do we start looking after freshmen?" Carney asked.

"We get our instructions tomorrow," said Winkie. "Then we pin on those badges and start shoving the children around—to the Lady Principal's office, and the Secretary's office, and the Treasurer's office."

"There's nothing so deaf as an adder," Carney put in. It was a joke the old treasurer always made when they tried to talk while paying their bills. "I suppose the freshmen will be feeling awfully strange, just as we did."

"Remember how we all hit it off the first night at supper?"

"I should say I do! It's too bad the whole gang couldn't get into Lathrop this year, but we'll stick together."

"No doubt of that," Winkie said. She stood up. "Well, I guess I'll run down to the Circle, see what sort of shape the courts are in. Want to come along?"

"I have to unpack," Carney replied. "I'll meet you

at the Class Tree in an hour."

When Winkie was gone she tossed a coin to see who would get which bedroom. They were both small, exactly alike. Then she unpacked and settled in her usual orderly fashion. She had learned in previous years to put a roll of shelf paper and scissors in her suitcase. She lined all the bureau drawers, Isobel's as well as her own.

She put away her toilet articles and hung her night gown and kimono in the closet. There was left *Bleak House* which she had been reading on the train, her Bible, and her photographs.

Larry's photograph had stood on her desk for two years. And she hated the way some girls gave the place of honor to a different picture every year.

"I'm going to put Larry right back where he always was," she said aloud, and placed him on her desk.

She picked up Sam's picture and held it in her hands a moment. Looking at his smiling eyes, his firm mouth, and the dimple in his chin, she knew that he would be the one to whom she would say good night and good morning. She realized that wherever Sam's picture stood would be the place of honor. It made her think of that Frenchman who had said that wherever he sat was the head of the table.

She put Sam's picture on the bureau, and went out into the crisp bright air.

It was wonderful to have this free day before her duties with the freshmen began. She was so busy during the school year that she never saw enough of the campus and the adjoining woodlands. She wanted to stroll around the Pine Walk, and go down to the brook, and up Sunset Hill.

"I believe I'll go up Sunset Hill right now. There's time before I meet Winkie," she thought.

On the lower slopes the grasses were full of goldenrod and asters, thistles and Joe Pye weed. A few dried yellow leaves were drifting down from Matthew Vassar's ancient apple trees. The apples were ripe, but they were very small.

She came to a bench with a view of the brook, the roofs of the college, and the flag on Main, but she kept on climbing. She went through a thicket of tall dark pines, past the outdoor theatre, along a path bordered by wine-red sumac, to the summit and the bench she loved.

Carney sat down and looked off at the rolling blue hills. This was the bench to which she always brought her problems. She didn't have a problem at the moment, but it was nice to be here anyway.

The last time she had come she had been trying to decide whether to invite Isobel to Minnesota. She was glad she had invited her. She hadn't grown to love her as she loved Bonnie and Betsy. A girl just didn't love

Isobel that way. She was too much like that smiling and inscrutable Mona Lisa who had been stolen last month from the Louvre Museum in Paris. Carney liked her, though; she had enjoyed her. And it had been darn nice of Isobel to tell Sam that Carney had turned down Larry. But would she have done it if it hadn't been for Howard Sedgwick? Carney would never know.

"I'll never understand her," she thought.

It didn't matter, because Sam had preferred her to Isobel. Sam's choosing her had built up her self-confidence more than any one thing had ever done. Larry had liked her. He would have proposed if she had let him. Perhaps she could even have made him fall in love if she had tried. But Sam had picked her out all by himself.

Her junior year was starting, and everyone said it was the nicest year of all. It was starting wonderfully, for tomorrow she would be standing on the steps of Main in a white dress with rose and gray ribbons and a badge, a member of the distinguished Reception Committee. Juniors looked after freshmen all through the year because they were sister classes. The junior party for freshmen would be coming along soon. And the juniors and the freshmen would be singing together every night before Chapel on the steps of Strong. Last year, as sophomores, her class had sung with the seniors at Rockefeller.

Change! Change! Life was full of change, but the gang would stick together and classes would go on.

It would be good to see Miss Salmon. How surprised she would be if she could know how much she had influenced Carney's life! Miss Chittenden might take her to play for Matthew Lang again, and he could say all he liked against her playing, but she would remember what Sam had said:

"Probably your husband will hound you to play for him every night after supper. Of course, as the kids grow older, you'll play less and less. But you won't feel bad about that for one of the kids will be musical, maybe . . ."

And he would look like Sam!

Carney jumped up. She wanted to run down to her room and write to Sam before she met Winkie. It was amazing! She used to write to Larry on a certain day every week, and it never occurred to her to write at any other time. But she was always wanting to write to Sam.

He wasn't good about writing letters, he had warned her. She had cautioned herself not to expect too many. But since he was Sam she knew he would telegraph and even telephone at unexpected times. It wouldn't surprise her, she thought, to get back to her room and find it filled with roses.

It would be full of Sam anyway. Vassar would be full of him. Sam at Vassar! And all the chaperones in the world couldn't keep him out.

Carney began to laugh, and laughing she ran down the hill, through the spicy pine grove, through Matthew Vassar's orchard, and over the brook to meet her junior year.

Winona's Pony Cart

For
STEPHEN *and* CATHY BOND,
BONNIE CROWE,
and
LEA *and* ANN AVERY

Contents

1

Winona and Toodles

WINONA ROOT and her pug dog Toodles were sitting on the wall which hemmed in one side of the large Root lawn. Winona was cross.

"*Dignified! Dignified!*" she was saying crossly. She kicked her heels against the white stones of the wall. It hurt, but she didn't care.

She was saying "dignified" because her mother had told her that she ought to be more so.

Her mother had come out of doors a little while before to call Winona in, and had found her sitting on top of the bird bath. This marble bowl stood on a tall pedestal out on the front lawn. Winona had been calling, "Giddap! Giddap!" and bouncing up and down and slapping imaginary reins. She was pretending, of course, to be riding a pony.

Naturally, she had gotten wet—her dress, her two petticoats, even her panties. There was water in a bird bath; wasn't there? Was *that* her fault? If she had a pony she wouldn't have to go riding on so many other things.

But her mother hadn't waited to hear these explanations. She had been much annoyed, perhaps because she was entertaining the Ladies' Foreign Missionary Society, and Winona was wearing her very best dress. She had been supposed to pass the candy around.

"Well," her mother had said slowly, "you can't pass candy now."

"But I *want* to pass it!" Winona had wailed.

"And you can't have any refreshments."

"But I *want* some refreshments!" Winona had scrambled down from the bird bath, dripping and crying.

Her mother had paid no attention. She spoke gently, as she always did, but her voice was as firm as a rock. "Go in the back door and up the back stairs. Change your clothes, and then take Toodles and sit out on the wall until my guests go home."

She picked up the skirt of her gray silk dress and started to go away. But she stopped and gave Winona a look. It was a sort of sad, discouraged look as though she was thinking, what on earth am I going to do with this child!

"Winona," she said, "you're almost eight years old. You ought to be more dignified."

"*Dignified!*" Winona said now, as she sat on the wall with Toodles.

Toodles was asleep. Winona knew he was asleep because his tail was uncurled. When Toodles was awake his tail curled up as tight as a doughnut on his smooth yellow hip. But when he was asleep it hung as straight as a sausage.

Winona kept on kicking the wall. "This house is too dignified whatsoever," she said.

The house stood on a corner, catercorner to the school house. It was dignified, all right. It was a large brick house, painted white, with dark green shutters and porches on every side. The lawn was full of trees: tall oaks and elms and maples. The leaves were turning red and yellow and orange and brown and pink.

"Getting ready for your birthday," her father had told her at dinner. The trees were always brightly colored for Winona's birthday because it came in October.

On the side nearest the school, the lawn followed Pleasant Street down a steep hill. It was hemmed in by that wall on which Winona was sitting. On the other side it ran flat along School Street and ended in a hedge. The bird bath stood here with flower beds on either side.

From this upper lawn a terrace rolled down to the lower lawn, which Winona especially liked. There was a swing down there, and room for the croquet set. Best of all, there was lots and lots of grassy space to play in. On the alley was the small corral where Ole, the hired man, exercised her father's bangtailed riding horse, Bob, and her mother's carriage horse, Florence. The carriage house stood near, and the barn where Bob and Florence lived.

There was an empty stall in the barn, just the right size for that pony Winona wished she had. And Ole had plenty of time to take care of a pony.

"He wouldn't mind at all," Winona thought. Old Ole liked horses better than people. He told her so often, especially when he found her climbing on Bob or Florence, or playing with the harness in his tidy harness closet, or pretending to ride in her mother's carriage—an elegant surrey with a brown fringed top.

All of a sudden Winona had a wonderful idea.

"I might," she thought, "ask for a pony for my birthday."

Of course, she had already asked for a little printing press, and her father had said he couldn't afford it. And she had asked for a doll as big as a baby, jointed, with yellow hair and eyes that opened and shut, and he had said he couldn't afford that. But he always said he couldn't afford the things she asked for. He would say he didn't have any money, and then he would laugh and jingle some in his pocket. And, oftener than not, she got what she wanted.

"He spoils me. Everyone says so," Winona thought hopefully.

Maybe she'd ask him tonight! Or maybe she shouldn't, because it would remind her mother of how she had gone riding on the bird bath? Her mother hadn't liked that a bit.

"My mother is too *dignified*," Winona thought, kicking the wall hard with her black high-buttoned shoes.

Her mother was very dignified. She was president

of the Ladies' Foreign Missionary Society. She was slender and frail and always beautifully dressed, with never a hair out of place.

Winona's sisters were dignified, too. Of course, they were young ladies. Bessie was fifteen and Myra was thirteen; they wore shirt waists and skirts and pompadours. They liked to study and to do embroidery, and Bessie painted place cards and fans and copied Gibson Girl heads. Myra was planning to marry a minister. Not any special minister; she just liked ministers.

Winona wasn't a bit like either of them.

Winona had black eyes that snapped and flashed with mischief. Her face was tanned, and a mane of black hair was always flying out behind her. She liked to be outdoors, to play wild games, and run, and climb trees.

"This is my *western* daughter," Winona's mother always said when introducing Winona. She would explain with a loving smile that the two older girls had been born back in New York state while Winona had been born here in Deep Valley, Minnesota.

"She means I'm a tomboy," Winona thought bitterly and kicked the wall so hard that she yelled, "Ouch!" and Toodles woke up.

He looked at her with his bulging dark eyes.

He had a comical little black face full of worried-looking wrinkles.

"Prob'ly he worries about me," Winona thought. "Toodles," she said, putting her face down on his soft yellow back, "I'm the only one in this whole family that isn't dignified. Even Father is, a little."

Her father was a tall, important-looking man. Across his starched white vest he wore a heavy gold watch chain with a Knights of Pythias fob. He had black hair and eyes like Winona's, and white teeth like hers, and perhaps when he was a little boy he hadn't been dignified either. Certainly he always understood what made her do the things she did. He always helped her out when she got into fixes.

"He isn't *very* dignified," Winona said. "Not any more than he has to be, when he's editor of the paper."

He was publisher and editor of the *Deep Valley Sun*. Winona liked to go down to his office and watch the busy presses. Not long ago he had bought a self-setting type machine. A linotype machine, it was called. He said it was a wonderful new invention. He had shown it to her and explained it to her just as though she were grown up. He had let her sit on the operator's lap and push the keys and spell out her name in type.

It was on account of this that Winona had asked

for that printing press for her birthday.

In September, when school began, he let her walk around the printing shop and pick out whatever she wanted—ink and pencil tablets, and clean note pads, and a full new box of pencils sharpened to fine points. He had her name printed on her note-books. Betsy Ray, a girl in Winona's class at school, always envied her that.

"I'd like *my* name printed on a notebook. I'd write a book in it," she said.

Winona's father was having the invitations to her birthday party printed at the paper. He was going to bring them home tonight.

Winona remembered how nice her father was.

"Yes, I *will* ask for a pony," she decided. "But perhaps I'd better go in and practice my music lesson."

Her father often asked her at supper whether she had practiced. He was anxious for her to learn to play the piano. She was supposed to practice half an hour twice a day. But she didn't always do it. There was too much to do out of doors.

"But, Winona, you like music, just as I do. You'd be good at it," he would say. "After you learn to play, you can play for me in the evening."

"Yes, I'd better go in and practice," Winona thought, jumping up. But then she remembered the

Ladies' Foreign Missionary Society, and she sat down again.

"I can't practice," she thought with satisfaction. "And it isn't my fault. Prob'ly they'll stay so late I can't practice at all. Too bad! I might get so I could play beautiful pieces for Father. I might get to be a famous piano player, if it wasn't for that old Foreign Missionary Society . . . in there eating up the refreshments."

Toodles growled sympathetically, but after a minute he fell asleep again. And Winona grew crosser and crosser. It was lonesome, sitting on the wall.

2

Winona and Her Friends

SOME SYRIAN children came toiling up the hill. They were coming from the Catholic school on the north end of town and going to their homes on the south end of town in a valley called Little Syria.

Winona liked the Syrians. They were dark and foreign-looking and talked in an exciting way, waving their hands. They loved bright colors, and she did, too. Her father had asked her mother please to let Winona wear bright colors because she loved them so. Her mother favored dark blue sailor suits, with white dresses for Sunday.

The Syrian girls wore gay-colored head scarfs, and red ribbons woven into their braids. They wore earrings and glass bracelets, and the boys put feathers in their caps and flowers in their buttonholes.

They had come to know Winona, passing her house so much. Sometimes they stopped and turned her jump rope. Sometimes they joined her in hop scotch on the walk. A boy named Scundar often threw her a ball as he passed, and Winona would throw it back to him, and he would throw it back to her. A little girl named Marium often stopped to pet Toodles.

She stopped to pet Toodles now, and Scundar asked, "Would you like to toss the ball?"

But Winona had to shake her head.

The Syrian children went on.

Winona looked dismally across at the school house, a red brick building trimmed with yellow stone. There was a flight of steep stone steps leading to the big front door. Whenever it was time for school to begin, a boy stood on those steps and rang a bell. Winona lived so near that she didn't

need to start to school until she heard that bell—unless she wanted to. Sometimes she ran over early for the fun of playing in the girls' yard.

School was over now. The girls' yard and the boys' yard were empty. But after a while Winona saw a boy named Dennie come running down the school house steps.

He had been kept late because he had brought a garter snake to school and put it in a box of erasers. Miss Canning, the teacher, hadn't liked it.

"What did she do to you?" Winona called as he came near.

"Aw, she just scolded me!" Dennie tossed his curly head. He stopped beside the wall. Dennie liked Winona. He had once left a stick of gum on her desk.

"I'll race you down the hill," he said.

Winona wished she could do it, but she had to say no. She had to sit on the wall.

Lottie and Lettie Pepper came up the hill next, pulling an empty cart. They had come to fetch the laundry. Their mother did the washing for the Roots. Lottie and Lettie were twins and looked just alike, thin and wiry, with bright blue, interested eyes.

"Want to do tricks?" they asked.

They often stayed to do tricks when they came to

get the laundry or to bring it back. They could stand on each other's shoulders, and were teaching Winona to do it.

"Yes, I *want* to, but that doesn't mean I can," Winona answered.

Lottie and Lettie took their cart around to the back door and received a brimming laundry basket from Selma, the Roots' hired girl. They pulled the cart back down the hill and disappeared.

For a while there were only horses going up and down the hill, pulling surreys and buggies and delivery wagons. A load of hay went past, and Winona wished on it; she wished for a pony.

The street-sprinkling cart went past. That was fun, as a rule. It sprinkled water as it moved along the street, and you could run out and play in it and get wet. She couldn't today.

The rag man went past in his mysterious wagon. He was calling, "Rags! Rags! Any rags today?" If she hadn't had to sit on the wall, Winona could have followed him down the street. She might have seen him weigh somebody's bundle of old clothes and give them a shiny pan or muffin tin in return.

"Double darn!" Winona said, although she knew it was practically swearing.

Three little girls came out of Mrs. Chubbock's candy store, next door to the school house. They were in Miss Canning's room too. Their names were Betsy, Tacy, and Tib.

Betsy Ray, the one who liked Winona's notebooks, had a round face with short braids sticking out behind. Her front teeth were parted in the middle. Tacy Kelly had long red ringlets and Tib Muller was little and cute with yellow curls.

"Want to play?" they called now, running across the street.

This was too much, Winona thought! Everyone could play except her! The Syrian children, and Dennie, and Lottie and Lettie.

"If I did, I'd have plenty of people to play with," she answered, scowling.

That made them mad.

"You think you're pretty important," said Betsy, "just because your father runs the newspaper. Well, my father is so handsome that people stop him on the street to tell him how handsome he is! Just last night old Mrs. Murphy stopped him right in front of his shoe store. She said he got handsomer every day."

"He gives her shoes for nothing," Tib explained. Winona saw Betsy and Tacy poke her to keep still.

"My father can play the violin," said Tacy quickly. "He's as good as Ole Bull, just about."

Tib thought only a moment. "My father can eat

spoiled catsup," she said. "He did it once and it didn't make him sick."

The three of them looked at Winona defiantly.

"Who's talking about fathers?" asked Winona. "I'll bet you can't guess who kissed me once?"

Betsy, Tacy, and Tib burst into scornful laughter.

"We don't like kissing talk!"

"We hate it!"

"We don't like boys!"

"Joke on you!" said Winona. "It wasn't any old boy. I'll tell you who it was because you never could guess. It was Buffalo Bill!"

"Buffalo Bill!" They were astounded.

Winona nodded importantly. "Yup!" she said. "Buffalo Bill kissed me."

He had, too.

It was over a year ago when she was only six. He had been in town with his Wild West Show, and after the parade down Main Street, he had brought his band to serenade the office of the *Deep Valley Sun*. Winona had been hoisted up into the glittery wagon. Buffalo Bill, with his broad-brimmed black hat, his piercing eyes, his mustaches and spike of beard, had held her by the hand.

The band had played, and the music had sounded frighteningly loud, and the bandmen in their gaudy uniforms had looked frighteningly strange. Buffalo

Bill had stood straight as an Indian holding Winona's hand, and at the end he had picked her up and kissed her.

Winona had been terribly afraid. She knew better than to cry with her father and a whole crowd of people looking on. She hadn't liked it, though.

"I didn't like it," she said now to Betsy, Tacy, and Tib. "His mustaches tickled."

That made them laugh.

"Want a jelly bean?" asked Betsy, holding out the bag.

"Yup!" Winona answered, and Betsy, Tacy, and Tib hopped up on the wall beside her.

It was nice sitting there in the late afternoon sunshine. Red and yellow leaves drifted down upon their heads.

"You have a lot of leaves on this big lawn," said Betsy. "Do you ever play in them?"

"I should say I do," Winona answered. She munched a jelly bean and gave one to Toodles. He wasn't supposed to have them, but she didn't care today. "My father doesn't burn up the leaves until after my birthday," she said. "He leaves them just on purpose so I can play in them."

"What do you play?" Tacy asked.

"I rake them into a house. You know—parlor and dining room and kitchen and bedrooms with piles of leaves for walls."

"I'd be good at that," said Tib, "because my father is an architect. I could tell you where to put in closets and halls and things."

"Betsy could make up a story about us all living in that leaf house," said Tacy.

"Could you?" asked Winona.

"Of course," said Betsy. "We could have a big fight with the people next door."

"A terrible fight! We'd get so mad we'd all throw leaves," said Tacy, and her eyes began to sparkle.

"We'd throw so many leaves it would be the end of the house!"

"Why don't we do it now?" asked Tib. "We can stay a little while."

Winona wriggled uncomfortably. "Maybe your mothers wouldn't want you to stay," she suggested.

"Oh, they wouldn't mind!" Betsy replied.

"Betsy and I were playing over at Tib's house," Tacy explained. "We found a nickel down a crack in the sidewalk, and Tib's mother let us come and buy candy."

"She wouldn't worry if we were a little slow coming back," added Tib. "Where do you keep your rake?"

But Winona had to shake her head.

"Toodles and I have to sit here on this wall," she

said hastily. "We're . . . we're waiting for something. I can't tell you what it is, but it's something awfully dignified!"

"What does 'dignified' mean?" asked Tib.

"Important," said Betsy. "Oh, well! We'll come and make the leaf house some other day."

"When is your birthday?" asked Tib. "Are you having a party?"

"A week from today. Of course, I'm having a party."

"Ice cream?" asked Betsy.

"Of course."

"Birthday cake?" asked Tacy.

"*Of course!*"

Everyone looked interested.

"What do you want for your birthday?" Tib inquired.

"A pony!" said Winona. It was wonderful to say it. Saying it right out loud like that sort of made up for having to sit on the wall.

"A pony!" cried Tib. "Why, I don't know anyone that's got a pony!" Betsy and Tacy nudged her to keep still.

"Oh, a pony isn't so much!" said Betsy. "Maybe *you'll* get one for *your* birthday, Tib. I'll bet you will. Don't you bet so, Tacy?"

"I'm practically sure of it," said Tacy.

"Oh, my papa couldn't afford one!" answered Tib. Betsy and Tacy nudged her again.

"Maybe Tacy will get one," said Betsy. "Her father has a horse, and so has mine."

"Would you like a pony, Betsy?" Tacy asked in a careless voice.

"Well, sort of! I wouldn't mind!"

"I'll bet you wouldn't mind!" Winona jeered.

The front door of her house opened and the ladies of the Foreign Missionary Society began to come out. They were wearing hats and jackets, or short capes, and they caught up their sweeping skirts in their hands as they started down the porch steps. They were telling Winona's mother that it had been a splendid meeting and the refreshments were delicious.

Several of them got into a surrey that had driven up in front. And others got into a phaeton that Ole brought around from the driveway. The rest started off down the walk, still holding their skirts daintily off the ground.

When everyone was out of sight, Mrs. Root came to the door.

"Winona!" she called. "You may come in now and practice your music lesson."

Betsy, Tacy, and Tib whirled upon Winona.

"Winona Root!" cried Betsy. "You were just sitting here because you had to!"

"You were being punished!" cried Tacy.

"But you said it was something dignified!" cried Tib, bewildered.

"Yes," said Betsy crushingly. "She said she was going to get a pony, too."

"Winona!" called Mrs. Root again. "You *must* come in and practice. It's almost time for supper."

Toodles heard the word "supper" and struggled to his feet. Toodles loved to eat. That was why he was so fat. He curled his tail and started up the walk, but he stopped and waited for Winona.

Winona was dancing a jig on the wall. This was to show that she didn't care because they had found her out.

Betsy, Tacy, and Tib started to go home.

"Can we come over and rake?" asked Tib.

"Sure," said Winona teasingly. "But come before my birthday. After that, I'll be busy with my pony."

"Pony!" cried Betsy in exasperation.

"Pony! Pony!" cried Tacy and Tib.

"Pony!" they all cried together.

"P-O-N-" began Winona but she stopped. She wasn't sure whether she should say "Y" or "I-E." Winona wasn't very good at spelling.

"Winona!" called her mother sternly and started down the steps.

"I'm coming," shouted Winona. "Ta ta," she said over her shoulder to Betsy, Tacy, and Tib.

"Ta ta," they answered, waving.

Winona was laughing but inside she felt determined.

"I have to, I just have to get a pony for my birthday," she thought as she hurried up the walk.

3
Party Invitations

THAT EVENING Winona's mother addressed the party invitations. Mr. Root had brought them home at supper time, elegantly printed on gold-edged pink cards. There were fifteen of them.

"For fifteen children! And Winona makes sixteen. Two children at the party for every year of her life," Mrs. Root said, smiling. She was happy about the invitations. She hadn't even mentioned Winona going riding on the bird bath. Maybe she had forgotten about it, Winona thought. She hoped so, on account of the pony.

Mrs. Root looked nice in her gray silk dress. The yoke and high boned collar were of gray lace over pink. Some of the pinkness seemed to have crept up into her soft pale cheeks. The skirt swirled out around her slender figure as she sat writing at the library desk.

This was really Mr. Root's desk, and the library was really his room, but the family liked it. They often sat here in the evening.

There was a fire in the fireplace tonight. Toodles was stretched out in front of the dancing flames. Toodles loved the fire. You couldn't persuade him to go for a walk after a fire had been lighted. He would cough or wheeze and pretend that he had a cold. Now he was sleeping, with his tongue hanging out—his tail uncurled, of course.

The library had tall shelves full of books. There was a red plush lounge with a bolster, and above it hung a gold-framed oil painting that Winona particularly liked. An artist had painted it down at her father's office. It showed a table and upon it were a copy of the *Deep Valley Sun*, a half-smoked cigar, a violin and a mouse.

What, Winona always wondered, was a mouse doing there? And the violin was almost as mysterious. Her father couldn't even play the violin. But the newspaper looked as though he had just put it down, and she could fairly smell that cigar.

He was smoking one now as he sat reading in his big leather chair.

Bessie and Myra were doing their homework beside the center table which had a gas lamp with a green glass shade. It was good to study by. There was a basket chair where Mrs. Root liked to sit and crochet, but tonight she was sitting in front of the desk.

She sat very straight, as she always did. Mrs. Root was sick a good deal, but she never acted sick. She never complained and always tried to do whatever she was supposed to.

"Win," Winona's father had said to her one day, "I know your mother expects you children to be perfect. And it's hard on you sometimes. But don't forget, Win, that first of all she tries to be perfect herself."

Winona leaned on her mother's chair and watched her address the party invitations.

One went to a little girl named Joyce. She and Winona had started to be friends because she came from a town named Winona, and Winona's name was Winona, and they thought that was a joke. She was a fat, jolly girl with a fat braid of butter-colored hair.

Another invitation went to a boy named Percy. Mrs. Root liked him better than Winona did. Winona thought he was a sissy because he wore ruffled blouses. And he had curls—not merry, tousled curls like Dennie's but neat, blond curls that used to be long. His father had insisted on cutting them, Mrs. Root had remarked one night at supper.

"Hooray for him!" Mr. Root had answered. Mr. Root liked Percy's father. They went riding together.

"Do we have to have Percy?" Winona asked as her mother addressed his invitation in her graceful, precise handwriting.

"Certainly," her mother replied. "He's one of your best friends."

Invitations went to every child in Winona's Sunday School class, and the rest went mostly to children whose mothers were friends of Winona's mother. Just as Mrs. Root finished the last invitation it dawned on Winona that there were lots more children she'd like to have invited.

"Mother," she said, "I'd like to ask Dennie."

"Dennie?" said her mother. "I don't believe I know him."

"He stopped to talk to me just this afternoon when I was sitting on the wall," Winona said. "He had been kept after school."

"Why?" asked her mother. "What for?"

"Oh . . . nothing much!" Winona was sorry she had mentioned it. "He just put something into a basket of erasers."

"What was it?" her mother persisted.

"Oh . . . just a garter snake."

"A garter snake!" Her mother jumped as though one had run up her silken skirt. Bessie and Myra squealed delightedly, and Mr. Root laughed out loud.

"It was a very little one," Winona cried. "And garter snakes can't hurt you. You know that; don't you, Mother?"

"Never mind!" said her mother. "All our invitations are used up. See? Father had fifteen printed and we've addressed them all, so we couldn't possibly invite anyone else."

"Oh, dear!" Winona cried, for the more she thought about her party, the more she thought of people she would like to invite—the Syrian children, and Lottie and Lettie, and Betsy, Tacy, and Tib.

"Couldn't Father . . ." she began, but her mother stood up. She shook the invitations into a neat pack between her slender fingers.

"Just fifteen," she said firmly, smiling. "And every one is written. It's bedtime, Winona."

"Oh, dear!" Winona said again.

She kissed her mother, and she kissed Bessie and Myra. When she reached her father, she climbed into his lap. She put her black head on his shoulder, and he gave her a hug. It seemed like a good time to ask for a pony.

"Father," she said, "I practiced my music lesson after school today."

"Did you, Win?" he asked. He often called her Win because it was a boy's name and he said she was the only boy he had.

"I practiced awfully good," Winona said. "I think I can play pieces pretty soon. I'll play them for you in the evening."

"That will be nice," he answered.

Winona snuggled down cozily. "Father, do you know what I want for my birthday?"

"Of course. You told me."

"What?"

"A printing press, and a doll as big as a baby."

"And a pony," said Winona dreamily.

"A pony!" He spoke loudly in surprise. Mrs. Root, who had gone to her basket chair and picked up her crocheting, looked up quickly. Winona thought perhaps she had better tell her father what had happened that afternoon.

"I really need a pony," she said, speaking fast. "I have to go pony-riding on the bird bath, and I get all wet, and it's a wonder I don't break it."

"It certainly is," he cut in.

"But that's the only pony I've got," said Winona. "The only pony whatsoever."

Mrs. Root put down her crocheting. She looked at her husband earnestly.

"Horace," she said. "About that bird bath incident! It made me see more clearly than ever that Winona must be trained to be more ladylike."

"See here!" said Mr. Root, and he patted Winona's hair. "Win is the only boy I've got."

"But she isn't a boy. She's a girl and will soon be a young lady. And I want her to be quiet and gentle and modest like her sisters . . ."

Bessie and Myra looked up at Winona and smiled. Myra almost winked, but of course she didn't. She was going to marry a minister.

Her sisters liked Winona just as she was. She was so much younger that they made a pet of her. Bessie had made her a set of hand-painted paper dolls. And Myra curled Winona's hair for Sundays and parties; she put it up on rags.

They were smiling at her fondly, but Mrs. Root wasn't smiling.

"A pony," she said, "would only encourage Winona in her tomboy ways."

"Hear that, Win?" her father asked, and Winona knew what he meant. About some things he always minded Mother. He said Mother knew more than he did about raising girls.

Winona slipped off his lap and looked up at that picture she liked. She looked hard at the mouse. What *was* it doing there? She was trying not to cry.

"I'm afraid you'll have to be satisfied with Toodles," her father said. He sounded sorry.

Toodles heard his name and got to his feet, stretching and curling his tail. He always went to bed with Winona. He was supposed to sleep in his basket, in a corner of the library. It was a comfortable boat-shaped basket with a red and brown blanket inside. But he went upstairs when Winona did and curled up on the foot of her bed.

When Mr. and Mrs. Root went to bed they called him down and put him in his basket. It didn't do any good. As soon as the door of their room was closed, he sneaked back to Winona.

He ran upstairs ahead of her now, as fast as his short legs would take him. At the top he paused and

barked for her to hurry. Winona followed glumly.

She liked her room. It had fluffy yellow curtains, and the yellowish-brown matting on the floor smelled pleasant, like hay. All her toys and books were here. Her doll house stood in a corner.

Selma had lighted the gas jet and turned it down low.

Winona went to the east window. There were two windows in her room. One looked north down Pleasant Street Hill. The east one looked over the roof of the back porch to the barn where Bob and Florence were sleeping. She wondered whether they were standing up or lying down. Horses could sleep standing up; Ole had told her so.

"It can't be very comfortable," Winona thought. "If I had a pony, I'd teach him to sleep lying down. I'd want my pony very well took care of." She winked back tears.

Toodles, who had jumped up on her bed, began to whine, and Winona went over to him. He fell upon her, bouncing and sniffing and licking her hands and face. Winona pushed him off and he bounced back again. He barked and she laughed. It was fun.

"Yup!" said Winona, breathless from laughing. "Yup! Yup! I love you, Toodles. But I wish I had a pony. And I wish there were more than fifteen party invitations."

4

A Different Kind of
Party Invitation

AT SCHOOL the next afternoon Winona
heard about a different kind of party
invitation.

Miss Canning's room was the Third Grade. It
was on the ground floor, and through the tall windows you could see the girls' yard, a sandy play-
ground with two maple trees, good for playing

Prisoners Base. Their leaves were colored yellow now.

Dennie sat across the aisle from Winona, and that afternoon he gave her another stick of gum.

Winona was always glad to get gum; she wasn't allowed to chew it at home. Of course, she couldn't chew it in school either, but she could chew it at recess. She chewed this gum all through recess until the girls' line and the boys' line formed to march back into the school house. Then she stuck it on her signet ring. She squeezed it into a very tight ball and she thought it looked like a ruby.

But Miss Canning saw it and recognized it for gum. She took it away.

Dennie and Winona walked across the street to Winona's house together.

"That was good gum," Winona said. "I'd invite you to my birthday party, Dennie, only I haven't got any more invitations."

"Can't you just write some more?" he asked, sounding surprised.

"No. You see, my father had them printed down at the paper, and there were just fifteen, and my mother has sent them out to fifteen people. She's terribly sorry but there aren't any more."

"Heck!" said Dennie. "I don't need a printed invitation. You can just invite me, and I'll come."

"Will you?"

"Of course. When I have a birthday party, I don't print invitations or write invitations or stuff like that. My mother just tells me I can invite some kids and I invite them."

Winona gazed at him, her black eyes growing bigger and brighter.

"That's all there is to it," Dennie said. "I'd have asked you to some of my parties, Winona, but I've always had just boys. Maybe this year I'll have girls, too. I'll say to you, 'Say, can you come to a birthday party at my house tomorrow?' and you'll say sure, you can come."

They had reached her wall. Toodles was waiting for her, as he always did, wagging his tail and wriggling all over with pleasure.

"Toodles always seems to be waiting for you here," Dennie remarked.

"Yes," answered Winona. "He is. Toodles knows just as well as anybody does when school is over. Toodles is smart."

But she wasn't thinking about Toodles.

"Say, Dennie," she said carelessly, "can you come to my birthday party?"

"When's it going to be?"

"Next Thursday afternoon at half-past three."

"Sure, I'll come," he answered. "I'll bring a present, too."

After Dennie ran off down the hill, Winona stood smiling broadly. This was glorious! Dennie's way of inviting people to parties settled all her problems.

When Scundar and Marium came toiling up the hill, Winona called out to them.

"I'm giving a birthday party. Next Thursday afternoon at half-past three. Can you come?"

They were surprised but very, very pleased.

"We would be honored," said Scundar, taking off his hat.

"We are full of thanks to you," Marium exclaimed. Her small face was as bright as the scarf tied over her head. But after a moment it dimmed.

"I *think* I can come," she said. "But in the afternoon my mother goes out selling the embroideries. My Aunt Almaze takes care of my little brother Faddoul until I get home from school, but then *I* take care of him." She looked worried.

"Why, bring him to the party!" cried Winona hospitably.

Marium breathed deeply. "Would that be all right?"

"Of course! Bring him! Bring him!" Winona urged.

When Lottie and Lettie brought the laundry back, Winona invited them.

"I'm giving a birthday party. Can you come?"

The twins looked at each other and smiled. Their smiles would have been exactly alike except that Lottie had just lost two front teeth, and Lettie's matching ones were only loose. She wiggled them all the time so they would hurry and come out like Lottie's. But she stopped wiggling them now.

"Oh! Oh! We'd love to!" she cried.

"When's it going to be?" asked Lottie.

"Next Thursday afternoon at half-past three."

Winona invited people and invited people. She invited Betsy, Tacy, and Tib when they came to make the leaf house. They accepted promptly, but Betsy looked a little puzzled.

"Don't you send out invitations to your birthday parties?" she asked.

"Oh! Sometimes I do," said Winona airily. "And sometimes I don't. It's an awful bother. If you send out invitations, somebody has to print them, and somebody has to address them, and you have to decide how many kids you're going to have. Just asking people is lots easier."

They all agreed.

"Well, I'm practically sure we can come," said Betsy. "When is it?"

"Next Thursday afternoon at half-past three."

They ran down the terrace and scuffled through the leaves that covered the lower lawn. Toodles ran

after them, yelping joyfully. Fat squirrels with plumy tails dodged each other on the branches, and blue jays were flashing about.

The girls ran out to the barn and Ole gave them rakes. Ole took care of the lawn in summer and the fires in winter and the horses all the year round.

Winona and Betsy, Tacy, and Tib began to rake.

They had a wonderful time making the leaf house. There were leaves of every kind and color. Oak leaves and maple leaves and elm tree leaves. Orange-brown and red-brown and pink and pure gold and red and yellow and green.

Winona and Betsy, Tacy, and Tib raked them into walls. They made a parlor and a back parlor and a dining room and a kitchen and bedrooms.

Tib put lots of closets in the bedrooms.

"People never have enough closets. That's what my father says," she declared.

They made a porch. And Winona ran up to the side porch of her house and picked a piece of bright red vine to drape around the leaf house porch.

That gave Betsy an idea. She picked some of Mrs. Root's frostbitten zinnias. (Winona said she might.) She and Tacy stuck them in a row along the front of the leaf house.

"I want a barn!" Winona cried. So they raked some more leaves and made a barn. As soon as it was finished they sat down in the middle of it and started to talk about Winona's pony.

They all believed in the pony now. Or if they didn't, they pretended they did, which made it just as nice.

"Let's play a game of Naming the Pony," said Betsy. So they began.

Winona suggested Dolly because she liked that name. But Tib didn't want it, because she had an aunt named Dolly.

"It wouldn't be respectful to name your pony Dolly," she objected.

Betsy suggested Dixie and Tacy suggested Trixie. Tib suggested Buster, because of Buster Brown.

Winona suggested Sparkle; she had heard of a pony named Sparkle.

"Once," said Betsy, "I heard of a pony named Question because he had a question mark on his face."

"But maybe my pony won't have a question mark!" Winona protested.

Tacy suggested Dumpling. "That would be very good if he's fat," she pointed out.

Tib suggested Sugar because she knew ponies like sugar.

"They like carrots, too. But Carrots would be a funny name."

"Hay would be a funny name."

"Oats would be a very funny name!" Tacy shouted.

They were all laughing now. Tacy's face was red from laughter, and her blue eyes were streaming.

"You could name him Buffalo Bill," shrieked Tib, "because he kissed you one time!"

Winona pushed her into the leaves. Betsy and Tacy pounced upon Winona, and they all rolled over and over, screaming. Toodles barked and raced about.

It was a very humorous game.

When Mrs. Root called Winona in to practice her music lesson, Winona's face was shining with delight. It was dirty, though, and her mother sent her to wash it.

While she was washing, Winona thought and thought about how she could get a pony.

She went into her mother's bedroom, across the hall from the library. This was a beautiful room, with a canopy bed. The bed was white iron with a gleaming brass rail and pale green decorations, and the canopy stretched above like an awning. It had ruffles of white silk and pale green chiffon. The dressing table and bureau were white; so were the chairs; and all of them were decorated in pale green. At the foot of the bed was a large white bearskin rug.

Mrs. Root sat by a window, mending.

"Mother," said Winona, holding out her hands so her mother could see how clean they were, "if I got a pony I wouldn't ride him bareback. I'd hitch him up to a little cart. I could act very dignified in a little pony cart."

Her mother finished sewing on a button. She snapped off some thread.

"Now be sure to practice half an hour," she said.

Winona went into the parlor because that was where the piano stood. The parlor wasn't so cozy as the library. Everything here was upholstered in rose pink. It had to be kept clean.

The upright piano had a rose pink scarf across the top. It had a stool to sit on. Winona had to whirl the stool to make it the proper height. Sometimes she whirled it and whirled it just to use up time when she was supposed to be practicing.

Today she didn't whirl a minute longer than she had to. As soon as the stool was high enough, she sat down and began to practice.

There was a clock beside the piano and Winona was supposed to practice half an hour. Sometimes if she got very tired or was very anxious to get outdoors and play, Winona would push the minute hand just a little bit ahead. After a little while, she would push it again.

"This clock is always gaining time," Winona often heard her mother say. Mr. Root took it to the jewelry store one time. He told the jeweler that he wanted it fixed, but the jeweler couldn't find anything wrong.

Today Winona didn't push the clock ahead. She practiced and practiced.

"Did you hear me playing those scales?" she asked, when she got back to her mother's bedroom after she had finished. "Didn't they sound exciting? If Father knew how good I played, maybe he'd get me a pony."

Mrs. Root was mending a ripped seam. She said they were going to have peach cobbler for supper.

Winona stood swinging back and forth on the tips of her toes.

"I can peel potatoes," she remarked. "I peeled one one time. Would Selma like to have me help her peel potatoes, do you s'pose?"

She knew it wasn't likely. Selma knew how to peel potatoes and peel them fast. She didn't need any help from little girls.

Mrs. Root looked at Winona gravely. "Why do you want to help Selma?" she asked.

Winona glanced away, embarrassed. "Oh, I just thought . . . Father likes me to learn . . ."

Mrs. Root laid down her mending. She put her arm around Winona.

"Winona," she said, "I don't want you to keep asking your father for a pony. I don't want you to have a pony. I don't think it's best for you."

Winona pulled away. She put her fists in her eyes.

Her mother got up and walked across the room. She felt bad, too.

"Winona," she said. "You've outgrown your party dress. Miss Flanders is making you a new one. I was planning to surprise you, but I'm going to tell you *now*. It's red."

"Red!" Winona leaped to her mother's arms.

"Bright red," Mrs. Root said. "And it has a red sash, and you'll wear a red hair ribbon to match."

"Oh, goody, goody!" Winona cried. "Is it done yet? Can I see it?"

She danced around the beautiful white and green room.

"It won't be finished until the day before the party. But you can see it. You can go and try it on," Mrs. Root said.

She was smiling tremulously. It made her glad to see Winona happy.

Winona was very happy about having a red

dress. She talked about it all through supper. She didn't mention her pony and she tried not to think about him. That was hard, though.

In spite of herself Winona kept wondering whether to name him Dumpling, or Sparkle, or Buster, or Buffalo Bill.

5

Getting Ready for the Party

INONA SAW her new red party dress
the next day. She went with her mother
to try it on at Miss Flanders' house.
Miss Flanders' house was little, but on the outside
it looked as dignified as though it were big. It had
a tower on top, and curliques up in the gable, and

blood-red glass framing the front door.

Inside, it didn't look dignified at all. The sewing machine was open. Chairs were heaped with half-made dresses. And the floor was strewn with pins and buttons and hooks and eyes and snips and scraps of cloth.

Miss Flanders didn't look dignified either.

"Sewing is such messy work," she always apologized as you came in. Wisps of grayish-brown hair fell down from her pompadour, and her shirt waists were continually pulling out of her skirts.

She was a good dressmaker, though.

Winona's dress was even more beautiful than she had imagined it would be. It had short, puffed sleeves, and the skirt was accordion-pleated below a wide sash. It was a lovely vivid red.

"Oh, Mother!" Winona exclaimed, parading up and down in front of Miss Flanders' mirror, which swung in a frame and was long enough so you could see yourself from top to toe. "Oh, Mother! It's lovely! I look just like a gypsy!"

Mrs. Root looked at Miss Flanders and sighed. "Well, if you and your father are happy, I am!" she said.

"I'm sure," Miss Flanders put in brightly, "it's going to be a wonderful party!"

"Oh, it is! It is!" Winona whirled. The accordion-pleated skirt swelled out like a balloon. "Joyce can come," she added.

Joyce lived a long way away on the other side of town. She went to a different school, and Winona didn't see her very often.

Joyce had telephoned to say that she could come. It had made Winona feel very important to get a telephone call. Not many people in Deep Valley had telephones in their homes; these inventions were too new. But Mr. Root had one at home, as well as in his office, because he was editor of the *Deep Valley Sun*. And Joyce's father had one in his store. So Joyce had gone to his store to telephone Winona.

The other fourteen children who had received the printed cards wrote notes to Winona, or their mothers did. Everyone was pleased to accept her kind invitation.

Betsy, Tacy, and Tib could come. They had told Winona so at school. Their mothers had been a little surprised, Betsy said, that they hadn't received regular invitations.

"What did you tell them?" Winona asked.

"Oh," answered Betsy, "we explained that you were just asking people. I told my mother that Tacy and Tib were invited and *they* didn't have any invitations."

"And I told *my* mother that Betsy and Tib were invited and *they* didn't have any invitations," Tacy said.

"And I told *my* mother that Betsy and Tacy were invited and *they* didn't have any invitations," said Tib.

"That made everything perfectly all right, Winona," Tacy assured her kindly.

Dennie wanted to know what games they were going to play. He wanted to know whether they were going to have prizes. Winona asked her mother, and she said that they were.

Every day after school when the Syrian children came toiling up the hill, they stopped to talk about the party. They didn't go to many American parties.

"My little brother Faddoul says 'party, party, party' all day long," Marium chattered. She pronounced it 'par-r-rty,' for the Syrians always rolled their *r*'s. It made the word sound very exciting.

"See you Thursday if we live," Marium and Scundar called gaily as they departed. They didn't expect to die; that was just a Syrian saying.

Lottie and Lettie came up to Winona's house although they didn't have a basket to deliver or one to collect. They didn't even do tricks. They just sat on the lawn and talked about the party.

"Mamma is washing and ironing our party dresses and putting on new ribbons," Lottie sang.

"Hers are pink and mine are blue," sang Lettie.

"And we're going to wear white shoes. Mamma bought us some!"

Everyone was in a joyful dither.

The party came nearer and nearer all the time. And the trees grew more golden, and the vines grew redder.

"All getting ready for Winona's birthday!" her father kept on saying.

"And my dress will fit right in!" Winona cried. She was thrilled about the new red dress. She had told everyone at school about it. How red it was! How it flew out when she whirled!

But she still talked about the pony.

She didn't mention him to her father any more. And, of course, she didn't mention him to her mother. She didn't even mention him to Bessie and Myra. But to everybody else she did.

She and Betsy and Tacy and Tib tried to decide whether Winona should ride astride or sidesaddle, or whether she should have a pony cart.

"With a pony cart you could take more people riding," Betsy pointed out.

Dennie said jubilantly that with her pony and

Toodles she could give a dog and pony show, like Gentry's Dog and Pony Show that came to Deep Valley every summer.

"That's right!" Winona cried. "Of course we could! Lottie and Lettie could do tricks."

She told the postman that she was going to get a pony. She told the milkman and the baker's boy. It seemed as though, if she told enough people, she would make it come true.

She told the lamplighter who was a special friend of hers. Every night he came up the hill with his ladder. He set it against the lamp post on the corner and climbed up to light the lamp. His name was Mr. Dollar.

"Mr. Dollar," Winona said, "I'm going to get a pony."

"Is that a fact?" he asked.

"Yup!" She crossed her fingers behind her back, because, of course, it wasn't a fact, exactly.

And yet that pony got realer all the time.

Every spare minute Winona went down to the barn. She had always loved the barn, with its smell of hay and leather and the sounds Bob and Florence made, chewing and stamping in their stalls.

Winona went to the empty stall where her pony would live. It would need some nice clean straw on the floor, she decided.

"What's all this talk about a pony?" Ole asked. He was a bald, thin little man with blue eyes as faded as his overalls. "You're not going to get a pony. If you were, I'd be the first to hear of it."

"If I got one," Winona said, "he wouldn't be any work for you, Ole. I'd brush him and curry him and exercise him and bring him nice cold water."

"Ponies can't have cold water," Ole interrupted sourly.

Winona asked why not. And she asked how much hay a pony ought to get, and how much oats.

"Not many oats," Ole replied. "It makes them too frisky."

"But I *want* my pony frisky!" Winona insisted.

By and by Ole grew interested in the pony. He started telling Winona stories about ponies he had known.

Once a pony he was taking care of got into a field of buckwheat. He ate so much buckwheat that it made him blow up. Ole was able to save him from an early grave.

Another pony, named Traveler, knew how to get out of his pasture.

Traveler liked to go to the house next door because the lady there always gave him sugar. He would get out of his pasture, although the gate was closed, and go over and paw on her door. And when he had eaten his sugar he would go back to the pasture. He would get back in the same way he had gotten out.

"But how had he gotten out?" Winona demanded.

Ole put on his you'll-never-believe-this voice. "He'd crawl under the fence like a dog," he declared.

That same pony had a kitten for a friend. She would rather sleep in the barn with Traveler than in the house, Ole said. She slept in the straw in a corner of his stall. She liked to eat and drink with him and she never left his pasture in summer.

"Ya," said Ole, "she used to sit on a fence post with her four little paws as close together as though they were tied. Traveler would lean against the post, and they'd stay like that for half an hour. You'd swear they were talking."

Winona, who had climbed to the edge of the manger, bounced up and down.

"Oh, maybe my pony and Toodles will be friends like that!" she cried.

But then Ole told her again that she wasn't going to get a pony, and Winona walked slowly back into the house.

She found Bessie painting place cards for the party.

"Sixteen of them!" she said, laying the last one

aside to dry. They were pretty cards with pictures of birthday cakes on them.

But just sixteen! Winona looked at them uneasily.

"Maybe you ought to make a few extra, Bessie," she suggested. "There might be a few extra children."

"Why, no!" Bessie answered. "There can't be. There are only fifteen invited."

Myra showed her the favors. Sixteen paper hats and sixteen little tin horns.

"Do you have any extra ones?" Winona asked.

"Of course not! Why should we have extra ones?" Myra replied.

Winona was a little worried. Maybe she ought to tell someone about those children she'd invited? Or maybe it would be better not to.

Maybe it would just be borrowing trouble, she thought. She had heard her father say that.

And just then her mother asked her whether she would like to see the prizes.

She was allowed to see them because she couldn't possibly win one. She was the hostess. And even if she pinned the tail on the donkey on the exact spot where it was supposed to go, she couldn't win a prize. She'd have to give it to the child who had come next closest. Her mother had explained this to her.

There was a little iron cookstove for the girl's

prize—a real one; you could cook on it. The boy's prize was a bat and ball. Dennie would like a bat and ball, Winona thought with satisfaction.

"Oh, I can hardly wait for my birthday!" she cried, and her mother and Bessie and Myra smiled at each other.

"Fortunately," her mother said, "it's just day after tomorrow."

The next day, after school, Bessie and Myra gave Toodles a bath. Winona helped, of course. They didn't bathe him often; they didn't need to.

"Pug dogs are just naturally clean," Mrs. Root often said.

They bathed him in the kitchen, in his own round tub. Toodles didn't like to be bathed. He whined and snorted and tried to get out. Bessie held him while Myra scrubbed and Winona screamed and pranced.

First they put him into suds, and then they rinsed him, and then they dried him. It was easy to dry Toodles; his coat was so short.

After he was dry, they brushed him, and he acted pleased and strolled around with his tail curled tight as though he knew how nice he looked. His coat was like yellow satin; his ears were like black velvet.

"Oh, Toodles, you are beautiful!" Winona

exclaimed, and Myra and Bessie tied ribbons in his collar in honor of the party.

"Look at Toodles, Father!" Winona cried at supper.

Toodles ate beside her chair, from a low brown bowl. Mr. Root served him after he had served the family but before he served himself. Toodles got everything the family did, although Mrs. Root always protested. She thought he was too fat.

"But he does love to eat!" Bessie and Myra and Winona would plead. And Mr. Root kept on giving him tidbits.

Mr. Root regarded him admiringly now.

"Do you remember, Agatha," he asked his wife, "the night I brought Toodles home? I had asked Dr. Dodds to look up a pedigreed pug; you didn't know a thing about it. I brought him home in a baby's shoe box. He was just three weeks old."

Mother began to smile. "He was so dear!" she said. "He was the tiniest, softest, yellowest, loose-skinned, black-faced, pug-nosed little creature! Tiny as he was, he had those wrinkles. I didn't want you to have a puppy, Winona. I thought you were too young to take care of one properly. But when I saw him, I gave in."

"It was a good thing I surprised you," Mr. Root chuckled. He looked around the table. "Well, tomorrow I have a surprise for Winona!"

Winona put down her spoon in the midst of floating island. "A surprise? For me?"

"Who else is having a birthday?" her father teased. He was a tease like she was.

Winona thought fast. He had just been saying that Toodles was a surprise. Would this surprise be a pony?

She flashed a look toward her mother for if it was, her mother wouldn't like it. But Mrs. Root was smiling.

"Yes," she said. "Your father has a very nice idea."

This was discouraging. But the more Winona thought it over, the more it seemed to her that she must be getting a pony. A printing press wouldn't be a surprise. A big doll wouldn't be a surprise. A red silk dress wouldn't be a surprise. It must be a pony!

She tried to hide her joyful excitement. A surprise ought to be a surprise! She said, "Excuse me?" and burst out of the dining room and played with Toodles, singing loudly, "Won't you come home, Bill Bailey?" until her mother asked her please to stop singing that vulgar song.

Winona and Toodles went up to bed; and Myra came, too, and put Winona's hair up on rags for the party. She parted and combed the long, black locks and wet them and twisted them and wound them around the rags. Then she rolled the rags up tight and tied them in knots.

Winona looked in the mirror and howled with glee.

"You'll look pretty tomorrow," Myra said. "Prayers, now." And when prayers were over and Winona had hopped into bed, with Toodles settled at her feet, Myra kissed her goodnight. "Father's surprise . . . it's the cutest idea! I don't know how he ever thought of it," she said.

"*I* know how he thought of it," Winona said to herself. "He thought of it because I *asked* him for a pony, the night Mother addressed the party invitations."

She didn't say a word out loud, though, and Myra turned out the gas and went away.

Winona couldn't get to sleep. She was almost sure the surprise would be a pony. And yet . . . she couldn't be entirely sure.

She felt as though she were going up and down on a see-saw.

6

A Surprise for Mrs. Root

INONA WORE her hair in curls to school next day. And the Third Grade knew that her birthday had come at last. Miss Canning said, "Happy Birthday, Winona!" And all the children shouted, "Happy Birthday!"

Whenever a girl came to school looking particularly fancy, everyone knew that something was up.

Either she was giving a party or she was going to one. And in Winona's case there was no doubt about which it was. She had talked for days about her birthday.

Everyone knew that Betsy Ray must be going to the party, for her hair was not in its usual braids. It was curled to a friz.

"My sister Julia put it up on rags last night," Betsy told Winona at recess.

"My sister Myra put mine up on rags, too," Winona answered.

Winona and Betsy thought it was interesting that they each had two sisters and no brothers. They talked about it often.

Tacy's hair looked just as usual, and so did Tib's, for they had curls all the time. But they looked partyish, just the same; they looked so excited.

Dennie looked excited, too. After recess he leaned out to whisper to Winona.

"I hope there's plenty of birthday cake."

Winona nodded with gusto. Selma made wonderful birthday cakes, and Mrs. Root frosted them herself, putting on little birds and bouquets of flowers, and printing "Happy Birthday" in red candies.

It was hard that morning for Winona to keep her mind on arithmetic or geography or spelling. Her spelling was even worse than usual. Miss Canning, smiling, asked her to spell 'birthday' and Winona put in a *u* instead of an *i*.

In the afternoon she couldn't keep her eyes off the big clock on the wall. She wished she could fly up and push *that* minute hand ahead.

But at last, it pointed to three.

The Third Grade children went into the cloakroom for their jackets and caps, and then they formed lines. Someone played a march, as usual. The music always set Winona's feet to dancing, but today she positively jigged.

Birthday cake! Red silk dress! That surprise! *Could* it be a pony?

The marching lines went out the front door and down the steep steps into a crisp bright day.

"Ta ta! See you at my party!" Winona called to Betsy, Tacy, Tib, and Dennie, as she rushed across the school yard. They were rushing homeward, too. They had to change into their party clothes.

Toodles, waiting on the wall, was wearing his ribbons already. His tail seemed to be curled tighter than usual in honor of her birthday.

Inside the house there was a smell of freshly baked cake. And the dining room, when Winona peeked in, was a scene of gracious beauty. The long table was set with lace, candles, and flowers. There was a paper hat and a little tin horn at every place.

Of course—there were only sixteen places! Winona felt that pang of worry again.

"But it doesn't matter," she assured herself. "I can hold Joyce on my lap. And Lottie would just as soon as not hold Lettie. And Scundar and Marium could sort of squeeze in Marium's little brother."

She rushed upstairs.

"Be sure to wash," her mother called. "Myra," she added, "you'd better go and help her."

Bessie and Myra had hurried home from school in order to assist with the party.

Myra helped Winona wash her face and neck and ears. She helped her put on the new dress. It was like a dress out of a dream with its short puffed sleeves, and the wide sash, and the accordion-pleated skirt— all gloriously red.

Myra combed Winona's curls afresh and tied a red bow on the top of her head.

Winona rushed back downstairs and into her mother's bedroom. That was where her presents were always waiting, under the pale green canopy of Mother's bed. Her father was there. He had told her at breakfast that he would come home early.

"I'll be on hand," he had said. "I have to be . . . for that surprise."

He and her mother and sisters watched eagerly as Winona dashed for her presents.

There was the doll as big as a baby, jointed, with yellow hair and eyes that opened and shut. It was the doll she had asked for, the one her father had said he couldn't afford.

"Is this the surprise?" Winona asked.

Her father said no.

Beside the doll was a wardrobe full of doll clothes from her mother.

"Some of them are your own baby clothes," Mrs. Root said tenderly. "This doll is almost as big as you were when you were born, Winona."

Winona riffled through the doll clothes. "Are they the surprise?" she asked.

Her mother said no.

On the table beside the bed was a little printing press. It was just what Winona had wanted.

"Is this the surprise?" she asked.

"No, not that," her father answered. "The surprise is coming later, Win. It isn't a present, exactly."

Then it wasn't the hand-painted ribbon box from Bessie or the copy of *Black Beauty* from Myra. Winona hugged and kissed her sisters and her mother and father.

The doorbell rang.

"Why, it isn't half-past three yet," Mr. Root chuckled.

"Oh, they always come early," Mrs. Root laughed.

Winona flew to open the door. "It's Dennie!" she shouted.

Dennie looked very spruce in his blue Sunday suit with long, ribbed stockings and polished shoes. He wore a sateen blouse, striped blue and red, and a neat blue tie. His curly hair was brushed to a peak above a rosy face.

"Happy birthday! Here's my present," he said, extending a package.

It was a Noah's Ark.

"Watch me whirl!" cried Winona, and whirled to show him how her skirt flew out.

"Gee!" said Dennie. "You can wear that for the circus."

Winona's mother looked surprised to see Dennie. She looked very surprised. She didn't say anything, though.

In just a minute the doorbell rang again. This time it was Joyce, fat and jolly, her thick braid swinging. She said, "Happy Birthday!" and gave Winona a cup and saucer. Winona whirled for her, and they jumped about for joy.

A girl from Winona's Sunday School class came next, bringing a game of Authors. A carriage stopped outside and Percy came in.

His blond curls were neat as usual, and he wore a velvet suit and a waist with a ruffled collar and ruffles down the front.

"Who's that sissy?" Dennie whispered to Winona.

"My mother knows his mother," Winona whispered back.

Percy brought a bouquet of flowers in a holder.

"My mother bought it," he said crossly, thrusting it at Winona. He walked to the window and looked out, acting haughty. Nobody followed him.

After that, children came in a steady stream. Each one said, "Happy Birthday!" and gave Winona a present. The presents were unwrapped and put on that table in her mother's room where the printing press was. Soon the beautiful white and green room was a sea of tissue paper, and the table was crowded with cups and saucers, silk embroidered handkerchiefs, games and books, a tea set, and a ring with three pearls and twelve rubies in it.

Lottie and Lettie brought a pair of mittens. They were red and green, with tassels.

"Mamma knitted them herself," Lottie said to Mrs. Root who was admiring them with a strange look on her face.

Lottie and Lettie looked nice in their starched white dresses. They looked a little summery, but the pink and blue ribbons streamed from rosettes on their shoulders. And they wore their new white shoes.

Winona saw her mother go out to the dining room. She picked up all the place cards and came back.

Betsy, Tacy, and Tib arrived together, each one with a present. Tacy stayed close to Betsy at first; she was bashful at parties. And none of them had been inside Winona's house before.

Betsy's party dress was brown, piped in pink. She, too, had an accordion-pleated skirt. Tacy's dress was dark blue silk with a tucked yoke of lighter blue. Tacy usually wore blue because she had red hair. Tib's pink wool dress was belted low; that was the newest style.

"My Aunt Dolly sent it to me from Milwaukee," she said, pirouetting.

That reminded Winona to whirl, so she whirled, and Betsy whirled, too. They whirled and whirled to see whose skirt would spread out the widest.

Winona's mother was looking absolutely mystified.

"Winona," she said, "won't you introduce me to your friends?" When she heard their names, she said faintly, "Oh, yes! I think I know your mothers."

Children came and came and came.

There was one little boy, five years old, who lived down the block; Winona took care of him sometimes. He was wearing a clean sailor suit.

Two other little boys, about his age, were wearing Indian suits. They thought it was a Halloween party!

Winona's father had disappeared. Her mother and sisters were whispering in a corner. Shortly her mother beckoned Winona to join them.

"Winona," she said, speaking gently, but with something urgent in her voice, "just how many children have you invited, dear? They're very welcome but I have to know how many there will be, on account of the refreshments."

"Won't there be enough ice cream . . . on my *birthday*?" Winona asked indignantly.

"We don't need to worry about the ice cream," her mother answered. "Myra will run down to the drug store and buy more. But it's hard to stretch a birthday cake."

"But Dennie especially asked about the cake! I told him we had plenty!" This was terrible.

Before Mrs. Root had a chance to answer, the doorbell rang a last time, and in came Scundar and Marium and Faddoul. Scundar looked very handsome. He was wearing a red tie, and his black hair was plastered down with oil.

Marium looked like a picture out of *The Arabian Nights*, in a purple dress, very long and full. She was wearing purple ribbons on her long, black braids, and earrings, and even more bracelets than usual. Her eyes were rimmed with something black which was very becoming.

"Happy Birthday," she said like everyone else. She was holding her little brother tightly by the hand.

Faddoul was very chubby with fat red cheeks. His eyes were like ripe olives as he stared around the house. Marium nudged him, and he murmured something and gave Winona a box of candied fruit.

Marium's package held a handmade lace doily. It was exquisite, Bessie said.

Scundar balanced his gift carefully on outstretched hands. He carried it over to Mrs. Root who was looking more and more amazed all the time. In fact, she was looking pale.

"My mother hopes you will like this poor baklawa cake," Scundar said, and bowed.

"Cake!" cried Mrs. Root in a tone of thankfulness.

"Cake!" cried Winona and hurried over to look. It was an odd but delicious-looking cake, crisscrossed like a checkerboard and oozing honey.

"Oh, Mother!" cried Winona. "Now there'll be plenty of cake!"

"Yes," said Mrs. Root, "thanks to this Syrian mother!"

"Oh, the Syrians are lovely people!" cried Winona, dancing about.

The children were all looking at her presents. Betsy was charmed by the printing press.

"I'm going to get out a newspaper for children," Winona said importantly.

"Can I write stories for it?" Betsy asked.

"I could make you a funny paper," offered Tib. "I can draw Buster Brown and Happy Hooligan and the Katzenjammer Kids."

"I could peddle the papers," chimed in Tacy. She wasn't feeling bashful any more.

Lottie and Lettie liked the big doll. Winona told them they could undress it and put on different clothes. So they did, while Marium watched admiringly.

The boys were asking when the games would begin.

Nobody asked about the pony. Perhaps, Winona thought, they had forgotten about him in the excitement of the party. Perhaps they were being polite, or perhaps they had thought all along that the pony was just a sort of game.

But Winona didn't forget him. She couldn't help expecting him. After all, she hadn't had the surprise!

They went into the library, and she pointed out

that picture she liked. It was the one an artist had painted down at her father's office, showing a copy of the *Deep Valley Sun*, and a cigar, and a violin, and a mouse.

"What do you s'pose that mouse is doing there?" Winona asked the company.

"I could make up a story about it," Betsy volunteered. "You could print it on your printing press."

"Do it now!" Winona commanded. But there wasn't time. Her mother had started blindfolding children for Pin the Tail on the Donkey. Lottie won the cookstove, and Dennie won the bat and ball. Winona was glad about that.

Afterward, they ran out to the lower lawn for London Bridge. After that they played Go In and Out the Window. And then Lottie and Lettie did some of their tricks. Lettie stood on Lottie's shoulders. They were acrobats, practically.

Little Faddoul had a good time rolling down the terrace.

He would lie down with his arms at his sides, making a fat little bundle. And he would roll over and over, down the steep slope to the bottom, where he ended in a nest of colored leaves. Then he would get up solemnly and climb to the top of the terrace and roll down again. Toodles followed him, barking, because he liked that game.

The little boy in the sailor suit was busy counting leaves. He could only count to ten. When he reached ten he would start all over again.

The two little boys dressed like Indians were playing by themselves, giving war whoops and waving sticks that they pretended were tomahawks.

Winona kept looking around for her father. Where was he? And what was the surprise?

Her mother and Bessie and Myra seemed to be looking for him, too . . . or for something. They kept rushing out to the barn. Even Ole acted queer.

He had marked out a white circle on the lower lawn with ground lime. It was big, something like a race track.

"What game is this for, Ole?" Winona asked. But he wouldn't answer.

Instead, he yelled to the children to stand back.

"Back! Back! Behind that circle," he yelled.

"Stand back, children!" Winona's mother echoed, lifting her long skirts and running to and fro.

When everyone had crowded back, Ole turned toward the barn. He opened the gate that led to the corral where he exercised Florence and Bob. He opened it wide, and Winona's father came out, smiling.

"Winona!" he called. "Here is your surprise!"

7
A Surprise for Winona

WINONA STOOD staring at the gate of the corral. Something funny was happening inside of her. Something had swelled up and was pushing into her throat. She wanted to cry, but she wouldn't, of course. Not any more than she had when Buffalo Bill kissed her.

She knew that a pony would come through the gate, and he did.

First she heard a jingling of little bells, then the beat of tiny hoofs. Then the pony trotted out, hitched to a pony cart. It was a small wicker cart with red wheels and two seats, set back to back.

The man who held the reins wasn't sitting in the cart. He was running along beside the pony, laughing.

"Giddap, Jingle! Giddap, Jingle!" he was calling in a laughing voice. He was a thin young man with reddish hair, and he was wearing a green velvet jacket.

Winona looked at him and at the cart because she could hardly bear to look at the pony. It made her too glad.

At last, she stole a fearful glance.

He was a stocky shaggy little pony. He was black, but his bushy forelock, mane, and tail were white. Later Winona was to discover that he had a little chocolate on one ear and a little vanilla on the other; that was a joke she made up.

Now she noticed chiefly that his ears stood up jauntily and his eyes were large and bright. His tail was lifted gaily as though he enjoyed coming to a party.

"Giddap, Jingle!" the young man kept crying.

Jingle! Winona looked toward Betsy, Tacy, and Tib. They needn't have bothered trying so hard to think of a name for her pony. He had brought his own name—Jingle, like his little jingling bells.

Jingle came straight to Winona and stopped. The young man smiled and put the reins into her hands.

"Jingle, at your service, miss!" he said, touching his cap.

Winona couldn't speak.

Her father came up. He looked pleased with himself.

"Wasn't this a nice surprise?" he asked. "I thought you might like to have a pony come to your party and give the children rides."

"Father!" cried Winona. She dashed into his arms and rubbed her eyes on the sleeve of his coat so that no one would see they were wet.

"Who will you choose to take for the first ride?" her mother asked. She was smiling, too. Her mother didn't mind after all, Winona thought, because her father had given her a pony!

There was no doubt about whom she would choose.

"Joyce!" she called, and Joyce ran over, her butter-colored braid swinging proudly.

"There's room for two more," the young man said.

"Anybody!" Winona yelled. There was a wild rush, but Tib and Dennie reached the pony cart first. They clambered up into the back seat.

The young man took the reins again, and Winona and Joyce climbed into the front seat. The cushions were black, tufted with red. The whip was red.

"That whip is just for decoration, miss," the young man warned with a wink of his blue eye. "Jingle doesn't like the whip."

"He doesn't like the whip whatsoever!" Winona shouted to her interested guests.

She didn't feel at all like crying any more. She took the reins back and sat up straight and looked around radiantly at the crowding, clamoring children.

"Just touch him with the reins when you want him to start," the young man said.

"Drive him around that track," her father directed, pointing to the circle Ole had marked out. He was as excited as Winona was, almost.

"Ya, but I'll lead him the first time," Ole cut in. He was excited, too.

Toodles was most excited of all. He had come rushing down from the terrace to see what was going on, but when he found Winona sitting in the pony cart looking such a picture of bliss, he didn't seem to like it. He began to bark furiously. He ran around the pony, barking.

"Better put Toodles in the house," Mr. Root said.

"He might make the pony nervous."

So Myra picked him up and carried him in. She told him severely that he must be good.

"Toodles will get to like Jingle soon," Winona thought. "He'll like him as well as that kitten Ole told me about liked the pony named Traveler."

"All set?" her father asked.

Winona nodded, her eyes like black stars. She slapped the reins gently on Jingle's back.

"Giddap, Jingle!" she said.

Jingle started to walk around the circle. The bells on his harness jingled merrily. After the first round, Ole let go of the bridle, and Jingle broke into a merry little trot. When he had gone around three times, he stopped.

"Me, next! No, me! Me! Me!" the children clamored, swarming around the pony cart.

"Remember me, Winona!"

"I'm your friend, Winona!"

Mrs. Root was afraid that someone would get hurt. But no one did. And everyone got a ride . . . except Faddoul, who didn't want one. He was having too much fun rolling down the terrace.

Scundar and Marium got a ride, and the little boy in the sailor suit, and all the girls from Winona's Sunday School class. The little boys dressed as Indians stopped being Indians long enough for a ride.

Lottie and Lettie waved to the crowd. Betsy and Tacy sat close together, holding hands. Percy had been acting stand-offish all afternoon but he cheered up after Jingle came. He smiled as Winona drove him briskly around the circle.

Winona didn't always drive. She didn't even always ride. There were too many children screaming and waving and jumping for their turn. And she was hostess, her mother reminded her gently. Winona didn't mind.

"I can drive him tomorrow," she thought, climbing out. "And the day after that."

She liked to watch the shaggy little pony pulling the cart around and around under the bright trees.

Jingle didn't seem to mind how many times he went around. He seemed to be used to giving children rides.

"He likes children," Winona thought. And so did the young man in the green velvet coat. She wondered whether he used to own Jingle. He understood him pretty well.

"Would you like to have me unhitch the pony?" the young man asked Mr. Root. "Let the youngsters ride?"

"A fine idea!" Mr. Root replied. "I'll give them some lessons." Winona's father knew how to ride very well.

The young man unhitched Jingle and put a blanket on his back, and then a saddle. But when Mr. Root came up, Jingle turned around and looked at him. He put his ears back. He acted cross.

"Jingle won't let a man ride him," the young man said. "He doesn't like men, except me."

"He doesn't like men!" Winona shouted to the crowd. "He doesn't like men whatsoever!"

"He's always all right with children, though," the young man added.

"We'll let Winona try it then," her father said, and Winona skipped joyfully over to Jingle. She climbed into the saddle and put her feet in the stirrups.

Jingle walked around the circle, cheerful once more.

Tib rode next, as triumphantly as Winona. Tacy acted a little timid; she rode round the circle, though.

When Betsy's turn came, she said, "Thank you very much. Just a *little* ride, please."

She was slow getting on. And once on Jingle's back, she refused the bridle.

"I'll just ride this way," she said, putting her arms tightly around the pony's neck. Jingle didn't seem to mind, but after a few steps he paused.

Betsy scrambled off.

"You didn't get all your ride!" Winona protested. "Get back on!" she added generously. "You can go around three times."

But Betsy backed hurriedly away. "Oh, I got plenty. Thank you. It was lovely," she said.

Most of the children seemed a little in awe of Jingle. And no one knew exactly how to ride. Mr. Root shouted directions from the sidelines, but he only confused them.

Nothing confused Jingle. He trotted around and around in his usual business-like way . . . until Percy's turn came.

Percy climbed on, and he seemed to know exactly what to do. He lifted the reins commandingly and pushed his knees into the pony's sides. Perhaps he rode like a man.

At any rate, Jingle turned around and looked at Percy. He looked at him just as he had looked at Mr. Root. He put his ears back. He acted cross. And then like lightning he bolted the track Ole had marked out on the lawn and headed for the alley.

There was an uproar.

"Wow! Look at that!"

"Help! Help!"

"God save!" cried Scundar and Marium.

Bessie and Myra ran to their mother. Mr. Root and the red-haired young man raced in pursuit of the pony.

Winona jumped up and down in a panic. She didn't mind having Jingle run away. It was thrilling to have a wild pony. But that Percy, of all people, should be on his back in this moment of danger! Percy, with his curls and velvet suit and ruffled blouse!

"Percy will faint dead away!" Dennie said.

But Percy didn't.

As Jingle galloped down the alley, Percy kept his seat. He wasn't, Winona saw with amazement, even tugging on the reins. Jingle galloped and galloped, his white tail flying, but Percy held him firmly and at last even succeeded in turning him around.

Mr. Root and the red-haired young man had almost reached them, but Jingle veered away into somebody's back lawn. Still Percy kept his seat and held the reins.

Jingle kept galloping, but at least he was galloping in the right direction now. He galloped from lawn to lawn, stepping into flower beds now and then, dodging a big bonfire in which a neighbor of the Roots was burning leaves!

At last he reached the lawn of the house next door.

There was a low hedge between that lawn and the lower lawn of the Root house. Jingle jumped. He went up and over in a stunning leap, and Percy didn't fall off. He bent low like a cowboy. His yellow curls were blowing. He was smiling.

Once across the hedge on the Root lawn, Jingle stopped. He stood still and put his head down, acting ashamed. Percy jumped off and patted him, and Jingle nuzzled Percy's arm.

Everyone crowded around, shouting and exclaiming.

"Percy!" cried Winona. "You were perfectly wonderful!"

"Maybe you'll ride in a circus we're going to have!" Dennie urged.

"You certainly know how to ride," said the young man in the green velvet coat, running up out of breath.

Mr. Root clapped Percy on the back. "Your father would have been proud of you, son," he said.

Winona looked at Percy, thinking hard.

"Maybe," she thought, "if I were a boy, Mother would make *me* wear a ruffled blouse."

No one else rode Jingle after that. Instead they fed him sugar and carrots. Selma brought out an apple, and he ate that. They picked some clover, and he ate that.

"He'll eat anything," the young man laughed. "He even eats ice cream."

"He shall have some then," Mrs. Root said kindly.

"Children!" she called. "It's time for refreshments!"

Bessie had started playing the piano, and Myra formed the party into a line. They marched around the house and into the front door. They must be going to the dining room, Winona thought, and she could not help feeling a little anxious.

They could hold each other on their laps, of course. And her mother had taken off the place cards. But there were only sixteen caps and sixteen tin horns!

To her great relief they didn't go into the dining room after all.

They went into the library, where sheets had been spread on the carpet. They sat down in a circle, and Bessie and Myra passed dishes of ice cream. There was plenty of ice cream because Myra had gone down to the drug store and bought more.

Winona's mother came in carrying the birthday cake. It was a beautiful cake with little birds and bouquets of flowers in the frosting. Everyone sang "Happy Birthday" and Winona blew the candles out. But she didn't know what to wish for because now she had a pony.

The cake wasn't enormously big for so very many children but it didn't matter. Right behind Mrs. Root came Bessie with the cake Scundar had brought.

"There's going to be lots of cake," Mrs. Root said, "because Scundar brought Winona this beautiful present."

The baklawa cake was rich and sweet, covered with honey. It was delicious.

Everything turned out all right.

It was even all right about the favors. There were just sixteen caps and sixteen tin horns but instead of giving each one a cap and a horn, Mrs. Root gave each one a cap *or* a horn. Everyone got something, and they had fun exchanging.

Toodles came out from under the lounge. The children played with him and gave him bites. They talked about the pony.

Joyce said she would rather have the big, jointed doll.

"And I'd rather have the printing press," said Betsy, looking thoughtfully at that picture with the mouse.

Scundar looked up at the sparkling chandelier hanging from the ceiling.

"How do you light it?" he wanted to know.

Winona showed him the lighter, a long-handled stick with a taper in the end. You lighted the taper, then turned on the gas with the stick and lighted the gas with the taper.

Lottie and Lettie went out in the hall to look at

the telephone. The long, dark box was attached to the wall, with a bell on one side that you cranked to get Central.

"If Mamma had a telephone we'd telephone her," Lettie cried.

At last the doorbell began ringing. Parents were coming to take their children home. Children who lived near enough to go home alone ran into the bedroom for their jackets. They all told Mrs. Root they had had a nice time.

"We are full of thanks to you," Scundar said, bowing, and Marium added demurely, "You are welcome at our home at any time."

Winona's mother looked at them with a wondering smile.

"Pro'bly," Winona thought, "she didn't know Syrians were so nice."

Mrs. Root thanked them again for the cake. She thanked Lottie and Lettie again for the mittens.

Betsy, Tacy, and Tib left together, hand in hand.

Usually Winona hated to have a party end, but she was glad tonight when the last child was gone. Now she could take some ice cream out to Jingle. She could hardly wait to see him again.

Her mother sat down on the lounge. "Winona dear," she began. "Come here! I want to talk to you."

But Winona ran toward the kitchen pretending that she hadn't heard. She did so want to see Jingle! And the talk would only be about those children she had invited to the party.

"Winona!" Mrs. Root repeated, and then Winona came back and sat down. She had to, when her mother used that tone. She kept thinking about Jingle, though.

Her mother took hold of Winona's hand and looked at her for a long time without saying a word.

"I'm not going to punish you," she said at last, "because it's your birthday, but I want to be sure you understand what a foolish, thoughtless thing you did. Why, we might not have had enough ice cream! We might not have had enough cake! Even as it was, you caused great inconvenience. All those beautiful place cards Bessie made were wasted! And she had worked on them so hard!"

Winona hadn't thought of that. She was sorry.

"I hope," Mrs. Root said gravely, "you will be more thoughtful, Winona, now that you are eight."

Winona bounded upright.

"That's right," she thought to herself, "I *am* eight. Eight years old!" She'd been too busy with the party and the pony to think about it before.

"Oh, Mother!" she cried. "I'm sure I will! I'll be

more thoughtful . . . and more ladylike . . . and more . . . more . . . dignified. I did such foolish things when I was only seven, Mother. It's different now that I'm eight."

Her mother said she hoped so.

"Now may I go?" Winona asked, swinging on her toes.

"Where do you want to go?"

"Why, to take . . ." But suddenly Winona decided not to stop to get ice cream. Her mother might think it was too late to go outdoors, or that she ought to put on a jacket or something. Her mother wouldn't understand—nobody could—how much she wanted to see Jingle in his own little stall.

"I'll be back in a sec," Winona cried.

She ran through the kitchen and out into the twilight.

8

Winona and Jingle

IT WAS growing dark outside. Mr. Dollar had lighted the street lamp. A wind had come up and was bringing down the leaves. They had almost covered the track Ole had laid out that afternoon.

Winona hurried into the barn. She was cold in her party dress. And Jingle, she thought, had better have a blanket. She wanted to get to him quickly, to pet him. He was such a little pony! He might feel lonesome the first night in his new home.

She passed Bob and Florence in their stalls. They stopped eating their oats and turned their heads to look at her. But the empty stall which she had planned would be Jingle's was empty still. Ole hadn't even put fresh straw on the floor.

And where was Ole? He wasn't in the barn. He wasn't in the corral. Winona ran out into the alley. And there she saw the young man in the green velvet coat leading Jingle down toward Pleasant Street.

"Wait! Wait!" Winona ran after him as fast as her legs would carry her. The wind whipped the skirts of her accordion-pleated dress.

"What's the matter, little girl?" the young man asked.

She looked at him with imploring black eyes and caught Jingle's bridle.

"Why . . . what's up?" He was trying to joke.

"Where are you going with my pony?" Winona demanded.

The young man passed his hands over his red hair. With his smile gone, he looked tired and his expression was anxious.

"You don't understand," he said. "Your father hired me to bring Jingle this afternoon to entertain the children. Jingle is my pony."

"No! No!" Winona cried.

"I take him around from town to town so children can ride him. That's my business. When I reached Deep Valley yesterday I went to the *Sun* to put an ad in your father's paper . . ."

"No!" Winona stopped him. She began to cry wildly. "Father! Mother! Ole!"

Ole came running out of the kitchen, where he had been eating his supper. Selma ran out after him, her apron flying. Mr. and Mrs. Root, Bessie, and Myra came from the dining room through the back porch.

Winona flung herself into her father's arms, crying and sobbing.

She heard the young man say, "The little girl seemed to think the pony was hers. She didn't understand."

Her father hugged her and murmured comforting words. Winona heard him speak to the young man.

"Let the pony stay here tonight," he said in a low voice. "Ole can put him up in the barn. There's an empty stall."

An empty stall! Jingle wasn't supposed to sleep in it just one night. That was supposed to be his home, forever.

With her father and mother on either side and

her sisters behind, Winona went sobbing back into the house. In the library, she pulled away and threw herself down on the rug in front of the fire.

Toodles whined and licked her ear. He found her cheek and licked that. Winona put her arm around him, but she kept on crying.

Sometimes when Winona wanted something she cried in order to get it. She knew that wasn't a good thing to do. She felt ashamed after she did it. But that wasn't the way she was crying tonight. She was crying because she couldn't help it.

Her father and mother and Bessie and Myra tried to make her stop, but she couldn't.

"We'd better just leave her alone a few minutes," her father said.

"She's tired out from the party . . . all that excitement," said her mother.

"No," answered her father. "It's more than that."

They went to the end of the room and talked softly.

Winona's sobs grew quieter at last; she could hear what they were saying. It didn't seem important at first. It was like what you hear when you're half asleep and people are talking in another room. But it began to make sense.

"You know, Agatha," her father said, "a Shetland hasn't any vicious traits. He loves children and enters into their play just like another child."

"Winona has Toodles and two sisters to play with," Mrs. Root replied.

"A pony keeps a boy or girl out in the sunshine and fresh air," her father said. "It's a wonderful source of health."

"Winona is perfectly healthy," her mother answered. "And she's out of doors more than I want her to be."

"Owning a pony develops a sense of responsibility," her father said. "The child should take care of him, of course. Winona should be taught to feed and water him and to give him exercise. It would be good for her."

"Oh, Horace!" Mrs. Root cried despairingly. "You don't know the trouble I have making Winona ladylike. She isn't like the other girls. She's more like you."

"I had a pony," Mr. Root said. "I didn't grow up until I had a pony."

"But you were a boy! And a Westerner, too!"

Winona heard her father give a little laugh. She was listening hard now. She knew very well what was being decided. Maybe, she thought, she ought to pray. But she couldn't stop listening.

"Agatha darling," Mr. Root said, "you've never gotten over the feeling that when you came to

Minnesota, you came to the Wild West. But more ladies ride back East than they do here. You've seen them yourself in Central Park. Mrs. Vanderbilt, Mrs. Astor, Lillian Russell . . ."

Father's voice was teasing now; it seemed a little risky.

"Why, Queen Victoria rides!" he said. "Or she did when she was young."

"Mother," said Bessie, and Winona could tell from the sound of her voice that she was crying, "Winona could wear divided skirts."

"She could ride sidesaddle," pleaded Myra between sniffs. "Our minister would think it was all right. I'm sure he would."

"All I want," said Mrs. Root, "is what is best for Winona."

Her voice was trembling and Mr. Root answered gently, "Of course, dear! We all understand that. Well, you know more than I do about raising girls!"

There was silence.

It was decided, Winona realized feeling empty inside. She couldn't have a pony.

She didn't want to cry any more. She had cried all the tears she had. She had lost Jingle; that was all there was to it. But she would never forget him.

"I'll love him as long as I live," she thought. "I'll love him whether he's mine or not."

She remembered him trotting around and around under the red and yellow trees.

It had been a wonderful party, she thought, almost smiling. And after all she had her big doll. And the little printing press. They weren't as nice as Jingle but they were very nice. How Betsy Ray had liked that printing press!

Winona remembered the newspaper they were going to have. Betsy was going to write stories for it, and Tib was going to draw pictures, and Tacy was going to peddle the papers. She herself would be editor like her father.

"Maybe we'll make money enough to buy Jingle!" she thought, and jumped up, and dried her wet cheeks with her hands, and shook out the crumpled red dress.

She didn't really believe they would, but it was fun to pretend.

Her father and mother and Bessie and Myra were looking at her anxiously.

"Father," said Winona. "I'm going to get my printing press. Will you show me how it works?"

A smile broke over his face. "You bet I will, Win," he answered.

"What a little brick!" she heard him say as she went out. That made Winona feel proud.

She got the printing press from the bedroom

where her presents were arranged, and when she crossed the hall again she saw through the open library door that her father was walking up and down with his hands behind his back. He wasn't smiling any more.

"It was all my stupid fault!" he burst out unexpectedly, to Winona's surprise. "I should have told her the pony was just rented for the afternoon! I should have known what she'd think . . . after she'd asked me for a pony."

"So should I," said Mrs. Root. "She asked me, too. It was my fault, too."

Suddenly her voice took on a different tone. She sounded happy and excited.

"Horace!" she said. "Horace! Let her have the pony!"

Winona stood perfectly still. She had to. Her feet seemed to be rooted to the carpet. And something rushed over her; it was like a wind full of joy and love and gratefulness. She was grateful for everything—not just the pony. For the party, and her presents, and her father and mother and sisters.

"Winona!" her mother called.

"Come a-running, Win!" her father shouted.

Winona's feet came loose. She went a-running.

"Winona," her mother began, "we've decided. . . ."

But Winona interrupted. "Oh, Mother!" she cried.

"You don't need to tell me. I heard."

She threw her arms around her mother's neck and hugged her. She hugged with such violence, and her mother was so frail, that Winona almost knocked her over. But Mrs. Root seemed to like it. She hugged back.

"I'll ride sidesaddle, Mother," Winona cried. "I'll wear divided skirts. And I'll drive out in the little cart just like you and Bessie and Myra drive with Florence."

Her mother started to cry.

Winona flew to her father. She hugged him and kissed him and hugged him.

"Father," she said, "I'll learn to play the piano good. I'll never whirl the stool when I ought to be practicing, and I'll never, never push the clock ahead."

"Why, you little monkey!" said her father. "Is *that* what was the matter with that clock?"

Winona got up and danced around the room. She kissed Bessie. She kissed Myra. They looked funny with their faces streaked with tears when they were still wearing their party dresses. The library still looked like the party. The white sheet, full of crumbs, was still on the floor.

Selma came to the door. She had been crying, too.

"Selma," Winona cried, running to hug her, "I

can keep Jingle! Jingle is my pony!"

Ole came running in, blowing his nose on a bright red handkerchief.

"Ole!" Winona cried. "I can keep Jingle. And he won't be a bit of trouble to you, Ole. I'll feed him and water him and curry him and clean out his stall. He'll give me a great sense of re-re-responsibility, Ole."

"Ya, ya!" Ole said.

"See here!" said her father. "You're going to have a pony. But maybe you don't want Jingle . . . he's had a hard life. He's gone around with that young man for years entertaining children."

Winona gazed at her father with black reproachful eyes. "Why, *of course* I want Jingle! He's my pony!" she said.

"Oh, all right, all right!" her father replied.

In the morning when the young man returned, Mr. Root bought Jingle and his harness and the pony cart. He wrote the young man a check.

"Glad to get it!" the young man said, looking at it with a pleased expression before he folded it up and put it in his pocket. "I've been wanting to get out of this business. I think I'll find a merry-go-round."

"I'll take good care of Jingle," Winona said.

And she did.

Ole insisted upon cleaning his stall. He thought Winona was pretty little to clean stalls. Besides, her mother didn't want her to do it. But Winona learned how to feed Jingle; she learned how to give him his oats and hay . . . and a little bran mash now and then.

She learned that his drinking water should be fresh but never cold and that she shouldn't feed or water him while he was hot. If he was warm when she brought him home, she unharnessed him and threw a blanket over him.

She learned how to brush him and curry him.

This wasn't easy in the winter. Then Jingle had a very heavy coat. It was almost waterproof. In the spring his shaggy coat hung in untidy rags and tatters. He would rub himself on the ground to try to get rid of part of it. Ole clipped him then, while Winona watched. He trimmed Jingle's white mane and tail.

In the summer Jingle's coat was shiny and handsome.

Winona learned how to harness him to the little cart. She learned how to saddle him. Jingle didn't like to be saddled.

"He doesn't like to be saddled whatsoever!" Winona would shout. For whenever she started to put on the saddle he would blow out like a balloon.

Later, of course, the girth wouldn't be tight enough.

Ole suggested giving him an apple when she came out to saddle him.

Jingle loved apples. In fact, as his late owner had said, he loved to eat. He would nose into people's pockets for sugar. He crunched on carrots with delight.

He loved freshly cut grass. He loved clover. He liked to graze on the lower lawn and nibble. But once he ate some little evergreens Mr. Root had bought to plant along the alley. Once he ate some flowers from Mrs. Root's garden. Once the baker's boy left four loaves of bread on the back porch, and Jingle chewed into them all.

He would go up to Selma's kitchen door and whinny, and Selma would say, "You're as bad as Toodles!" but she always found something for him to eat.

Jingle liked to come into the house. If he found a door open he would walk right in and down the front hall. Winona's mother didn't like that. Winona had to train him not to do it.

Toodles didn't like it either.

Toodles loved the pony cart, though. He was so fat that Winona had to lift him in and out, but he would ride contentedly for hours. He would sit beside her looking around at the streets, with his tail curled as tight as a doughnut.

He never came to love Jingle as much as that kitten loved the pony named Traveler. Toodles wouldn't have liked sleeping in the barn. He liked to sleep with Winona. And when winter came he liked to lie by the fire. But he did love riding in the pony cart.

Sometimes Winona used to drive up to the high school to call for Bessie and Myra. She would wait for them out in front, sitting up straight, holding the whip in her hand. Of course, she never used it.

Mrs. Root used to smile with pleasure when Jingle came trotting up the street with Winona driving her sisters home from school.

Winona used to hitch up Jingle and drive downtown to see Joyce. It didn't matter now that Joyce lived far away. Winona could go to see her just as well as not and take her riding in the pony cart.

Winona took Lottie and Lettie riding. They went out to Page Park for a picnic.

She took Scundar and Marium riding, and little Faddoul. Her mother never forgot how much they had helped her by bringing a cake to Winona's birthday party.

She took Dennie riding. She and Dennie would plan about her Dog and Pony Show. They would teach Toodles to do tricks, Dennie said.

"And maybe Percy would ride standing up on Jingle's back," said Winona.

"I'll bet he could!" Dennie replied.

Sometimes Percy and his father and Winona and her father went riding together. They liked to go early on a summer morning before it got hot.

Betsy, Tacy, and Tib went riding in the pony cart, of course. But only once or twice. They got busy giving a show, or playing store, or having a club, or something. And of course they lived several blocks away. And Winona made friends with lots of other children, near at hand on School Street.

For a long time Winona and Betsy and Tacy and Tib didn't see each other except in school. Later on, though, they had lots of fun together.

Maud Hart Lovelace and Her World

Maud Hart Lovelace in her 1910 high school graduation photo

MAUD HART LOVELACE was born in 1892 in Mankato, Minnesota. She always believed she was born to be a writer. From the time she could hold a pencil, she was writing diaries, poems, plays, and stories. When Maud was ten, her father had a booklet of her poetry printed, and by age eighteen, she had sold her first short story, for $10, to the *Los Angeles Times*.

The Hart family left Mankato shortly after Maud's high school graduation in 1910. They settled in Minneapolis, where Maud attended the University of Minnesota. In 1914 she sailed for Europe and spent the months leading up to the outbreak of World War I in England. In 1917 she married Delos W. Lovelace, a newspaper reporter and popular writer of short stories. They had one daughter, Merian.

In 1926 her first novel, *The Black Angels*, was published. Five more historical novels followed. Maud wrote two of them, *One Stayed at Welcome* and *Gentlemen from England*, in collaboration with her husband.

With the publication of *Betsy-Tacy* in 1940, she

began the successful series known as the Betsy-Tacy books, which were based on the lives of Maud (Betsy) and her best friend, Bick (Tacy). The stories of her childhood in Mankato (the fictionalized Deep Valley), small-town life, family traditions, and enduring friendships continue to capture the hearts of her fans.

Maud died on March 11, 1980, in Claremont, California, and as she requested, she was returned to her beloved Mankato and is buried in Glenwood Cemetery. Her legacy lives on in the books she created and in her legion of fans, many of whom are members of the Betsy-Tacy Society, a national organization based in Mankato, Minnesota.

—Based on *Maud Hart Lovelace's Deep Valley* by Julie A. Schrader. Copyright © 2002 by Julie A. Schrader. Published by Minnesota Heritage Publishing.

The Betsy-Tacy Society
P.O. Box 94
Mankato, MN 56002–0094
www.betsy-tacysociety.org

The Maud Hart Lovelace Society
277 Hamline Avenue South
St. Paul, MN 55105
www.maudhartlovelacesociety.com

About
Carney's House Party

Marion Willard at Carleton College in 1910

"I WOKE UP the other morning with an idea for a Deep Valley story which I thought I'd like to do, but before beginning it I want to consult you, for it's a book about Carney."

Such is how Maud Hart Lovelace described her idea for a book about Carney Sibley to the real-life Carney, Marion Willard Everett. It was Carney's popularity with readers that inspired Lovelace to expand her story after completing *Betsy and Joe*. As with the other Betsy-Tacy books, the fictional story is based on actual people, places, and events.

"I want to ask your permission to write such a story because of course Carney is really you," Lovelace wrote in that 1948 letter. "And although I will embroider the tale and put in all sorts of fictional incidents, the outline of the plot will be true to your story, as I know it. From reading the Betsy-Tacy books, you know pretty well how I work. I use the actual facts just as a spring board. Nevertheless Carney will be recognizably you, and I wouldn't write the book unless you were willing."

Marion Willard's house, with the sleeping porch on the back, in 2009

Marion Everett was happy to oblige and shared detailed memories and information about her years at Vassar, her husband's family, their courtship, and countless other details that make *Carney's House Party* come to life.

After graduating from Mankato High School in 1909, Marion "Marnie" Willard went to Carleton College in Minnesota for a year. She was unhappy there and transferred to Vassar in the fall of 1910. Vassar placed Marion in the freshman class, dubious perhaps about the educational standards at her small Midwestern college.

Vassar College was less than fifty years old when Marion moved into her room in Old Main's North

The Daisy Chain at Vassar in 1912, the semester before the House Party takes place

Dorothy Brinsmade, "Isobel," in her Class Day dress, 1914

Tower. The idea of higher education for women was still relatively new, and the stringent guidelines for students' behavior were designed to keep students focused solely on their studies. The strict rules described in *Carney's House Party* were indeed enforced, but Marion and her friends still managed to have lots of fun without male companionship. Sports, plays, step-singing, and evening "bats" filled their free time.

In *Carney's House Party*, Carney's roommate, Isobel Porteous, is a glamorous, slightly devious beauty from the East who wangles an invitation to Deep Valley. Marion's roommate, Dorothy Brinsmade, was very beautiful and popular, but she lacked the guile of her fictional counterpart. "Dot" was a star tennis player and all-around athlete. Whereas Isobel is engaged to Howard Sedgwick, a Harvard man with a future in the Minnesota milling industry, Dot's husband was a Princeton-educated doctor. Dot met Arthur Jackson at their Connecticut tennis club, the Washington Club, where both were frequent champions. In 1914—the year Dot graduated from Vassar—they were the mixed-doubles champions, thereby sealing their fate.

Marion had a talent for making and keeping friends. Her children recall her saying that one of the reasons for her popularity at Vassar was that she never tried to steal anybody's beau. Some of Marion's closest friends—Adeline deSale, Annie Green, and Margue-

Marion rowing in 1914, the year of her graduation from Vassar

Marion in her Class Day photo carrying the roses that Tom Fox sent to her

Rupe Andews (Larry Humphreys) in his high school track team photo

rite Butler—appear as Win, Winkie, and Peg. They remained close friends throughout adulthood, writing, visiting, and even vacationing together.

Other Vassar characters are also based on Marion's time there. Her favorite teachers became Carney's favorite teachers: Miss Chittenden for piano and Miss Salmon for history. Marion even kept her doll, Suzanne, at French Professor Bracq's house in the summers. Mrs. Bracq was a hometown friend of her mother's, and the Bracqs' daughter, Florence, was a friend and classmate.

Throughout her college years, Marion corresponded weekly with Rupe Andrews (Larry Humphreys) at Stanford, just as Carney does. And, like Carney, Marion was piqued by a letter Maud Hart sent from California, where she was visiting. Marion wrote her mother:

> *Mamma I don't know what to think, but Maude [sic] seems to think from the way people in San Diego talk that it's all fixed between Rupe and me. Now that's the first I knew about it and I'm mad. Do they expect to carry me off like a cave-dweller or have you performed one of those proxy-affairs in my infancy. I'm as peeved as I can be and it's a good thing I don't hold it up against poor Rupe or he'd get biffed in the eye by the next mail.*

Bill Everett (Sam Hutchinson) in 1916, the year he and Marion were engaged

Marion camping on her honeymoon, 1919

Marion with her children, Ted, Willy, and Louise

In the summer of 1912, Rupe Andrews came back to Mankato for a visit, just as Larry does in the book. Like Larry and Carney, the young couple agreed they weren't in love and Rupe returned to California. However, there was no "Sam Hutchinson" waiting in the wings—Marion didn't meet her future husband until 1915, when she was a schoolteacher in Waseca, Minnesota.

Sam Hutchinson is based on William "Bill" Everett, the only son of the richest man in Waseca. Bill was an easygoing, fun-loving man who played the saxophone, enjoyed practical jokes, and didn't worry about money. Like Sam, he rarely carried cash, and like Carney, Marion was horrified.

Shortly after they became engaged in 1916, Bill joined the Army Signal Corps Reserve. When the U.S. entered the war in April 1917, Bill was mobilized and didn't return from France until 1919. One month after his return, he and Marion were married. True to form, he had forgotten to order flowers for her, so bought a lavish, last-minute cascade of two dozen cabbage roses that nearly hid the bride from view.

Not wanting to work for his overbearing father, Bill struck out on his own. He and Marion settled in Minneapolis, where they had three children. As Sam prophesies in the book, their eldest child was a boy, Ted, who was markedly gifted in music. All of the children took music lessons—daughter Louise even took voice lessons from Kathleen Hart, the model for Julia Ray. Marion continued to play the piano, sometimes accompanying Bill on his sax.

The years of World War II were hard for Marion. Louise went to Vassar, fifty years after her mother did; sons Ted and Willy joined the Armed Forces. In 1943 Bill died at age fifty-two of an aortic aneurysm. Less than a year later, Ted was killed in combat in France.

The Old Crowd—a reunion in California with old friends in the mid-1960s. From left to right: Bick Kenney Kirch (Tacy), Marion, Narcissa Fox, Maud Hart Lovelace, Tom Fox (Tom Slade)

Marion faced her losses stoically, as she (and Carney) had been brought up to do. She found comfort in Willy's safe return from war and Louise's happy marriage and children.

When Maud wrote to ask for help with her *Carney's House Party* manuscript, Marion responded to long questionnaires with details that show up in the book, such as her favorite dessert at home ("Boiled custard!") and the pattern of her bedroom wallpaper in Mankato (yellow poppies). At the bottom of the letter, Marion scribbled: "I am enchanted with a doll

Reproduction of a photograph of a visit between Maud and Marion in California in 1970

buggy that I bought for [granddaughter] Caroline. I keep it in my living room and push it in off moments. Silly grandmother."

Marion filled her golden years with family, music, and travel, especially to the Western states. She visited old friends from Mankato—including Maud, Rupe Andrews, Tom Fox (Tom Slade), and Connie Davis (Bonnie Andrews)—and continued to correspond with friends from childhood and college until the end of her life. She and Maud Hart Lovelace remained close, even after illness put a stop to visits.

Marion died in Minneapolis at the age of eighty-six on January 16, 1978. Her memory and her connection to Carney Sibley has been kept alive by her children and grandchildren, especially her daughter, Louise. One of the earliest members of the Maud Hart Lovelace Society in Minneapolis, Louise has been a speaker at several Betsy-Tacy events and conventions, drawing on her remembrances of Maud, Marion, and other people behind the book's characters.

—Based on *Future in a Handbasket: The Life and Letters Behind Carney's House Party* by Amy Dolnick. Copyright © 2002 by Amy Dolnick. Published by the Maud Hart Lovelace Society.

About
Winona's Pony Cart

Beulah Ariel Hunt

"*Winona had black eyes that snapped and flashed with mischief. Her face was tanned, and a mane of black hair was always flying out behind her. She liked to be outdoors, to play wild games, and run, and climb trees.*"

—From Betsy and Tacy Go Downtown

WINONA ROOT is the spirited friend of Betsy and Tacy. As she did with the rest of the Betsy-Tacy books, Maud Hart Lovelace based the characters and places in *Winona's Pony Cart* closely on those she knew. Unlike the Betsy-Tacy books in which Betsy is the main character, Winona is the main character in *Winona's Pony Cart*. This book was published in 1953, ten years after Winona first appeared as a character in *Betsy and Tacy Go Downtown*.

Lovelace used the character of Winona in several of the Betsy-Tacy books. Beulah Hunt was the inspiration for the young Winona Root in *Betsy and Tacy Go Downtown* and *Winona's Pony Cart*. However, the character of Winona of the high school books was based on Mary Eleanor Johnson because Maud's editors thought too many characters were being introduced into the series. Since Beulah Hunt belonged to a different crowd in high school, Maud reused the name Winona for her friend Mary Eleanor.

Beulah Ariel Hunt was born October 19, 1891, in

The Frank W. Hunt home, circa 1895. Frank Hunt is standing on the left. Riding in the pony cart is Beulah with her sisters, Bertha and Marion. Beulah's dog, Peter, is also in the picture.

Mankato, and was the daughter of Frank W. and Nellie Morse Hunt (Horace and Agatha Root). Beulah (or Betty, as she was called) had two older sisters, Bertha (Bessie) and Marion (Myra), both born in New York state.

Her parents, Frank (1856–1928) and Nellie (1854–1937), were married in 1877 in Wilna, New York. They came to Mankato in 1887, and Frank and his brother Lewis started the *Daily Free Press* (*Deep Valley Sun*). In March 1902, Frank W. Hunt, Michael D. Fritz, and J. W. True purchased the Free Press Printing Co. Hunt was made president of the company, a position he held until retiring in December 1917.

The Hunts lived in a white house at the corner of

Byron and Clark streets for more than forty-five years. Frank was one of Mankato's most prominent citizens. His obituary stated: "Mr. Hunt was ever a kind father and husband." His description in *Winona's Pony Cart* was probably accurate:

> *He had black hair like Winona's, and white teeth like hers, and perhaps when he was a little boy he hadn't been dignified either. Certainly he always understood what made her [Winona] do the things she did. He had always helped her out when she got into fixes.*

Nellie Hunt devoted her time to her family and her church: "Her [Winona's] mother was very dignified. She was president of the Ladies' Foreign Missionary Society. She was slender and frail and always beautifully dressed, with never a hair out of place." For more than twenty years Nellie held a district office in the Women's Foreign Missionary Society of the Methodist Church and was active in the local chapter of the Daughters of the American Revolution. She is buried beside her husband in Glenwood Cemetery.

Beulah's sister Bertha Hunt (1883–1962) did not marry. Marion married the Rev. Blaine Lambert and had three children: Frank, Lewis, and Louisa. ("Myra was planning to marry a minister. Not any special minister; she just liked ministers.")

In 1952 Maud wrote in the Mankato *Free Press*:

Frank W. Hunt

"Her father was a tall, important-looking man. Across his starched white vest he wore a heavy gold watch chain with a Knights of Pythias fob."
—From Winona's Pony Cart

"Sometimes, if we were lucky, we went to a matinee at the Opera House; on passes, since Beulah's father was the editor of the *Free Press*." In *Betsy and Tacy Go Downtown*, Maud writes:

> *Winona Root did everything first. Just because her father was an editor, she had complimentary tickets—"comps," they were called—to the circus, to the Dog and Pony Show, to the glass blowers, to the lantern slide performances, to all the matinees that played at the Opera House.*

Buffalo Bill's Wild West Show was in Mankato in 1898, so Winona's story about meeting him could very well have been true for Beulah.

Beulah and her dog, Peter
(Winona and Toodles)

Beulah graduated from Mankato High School in 1911. She attended Northwestern University and the University of Wisconsin, where she majored in psychology. She married Edwin K. IlgenFritz on November 13, 1914, in front of the bay window of the library at the Hunt house in Mankato. The couple had two daughters, Bonnie Jean and Beverly. Edwin worked for the Consumers Power Co. in Mankato. In 1920 the family moved to Illinois, and in 1930 they moved to St. Petersburg, Florida, where Edwin had taken a position with Florida Power. Beulah continued studying psychology in St. Petersburg and at the Sorbonne in Paris. She also volunteered as a psychology teacher and for the Red Cross.

Maud Hart Lovelace was honored in 1961 at Betsy-

Tacy Days in Mankato. She spoke to a large crowd at Lincoln School and introduced those who figured as characters in the Betsy-Tacy books. In attendance were Marjorie Gerlach Harris (Tib) of Chicago; Frances Kenney Kirch (Tacy) of Buffalo, New York; Ruth Williams (Alice) of Port Orchard, Washington; Beulah Hunt IlgenFritz (Winona) of St. Petersburg; Mildred Oleson Cahill (Irma) of Waseca, Minnesota; and Mr. and Mrs. Jabez Lloyd (Cab and Irene) and Eleanor Wood Lippert (Dorothy), all of Mankato.

Beulah Hunt IlgenFritz died January 9, 1985, in St. Petersburg at the age of ninety-three.

—Based on *Maud Hart Lovelace's Deep Valley*
by Julie A. Schrader. Copyright © 2002
by Julie A. Schrader. Published by
Minnesota Heritage Publishing.

About Illustrator
Vera Neville

Collection of Patricia Neville-Downe

Vera Neville

VERA NEVILLE was born in Detroit, Michigan, on April 2, 1904. A year later, her family moved to Interlaken, New Jersey, where her father worked as a real estate developer. As a young girl, Vera took ballet, piano, and horseback riding lessons. She spent summers on her grandmother's farm in Canada, where she fell in love with animals and began to craft little drawings of horses, cats, and mice.

The Neville family returned to Detroit in 1916, and Vera began to study art in earnest, taking lessons from Paul Honoré, an American artist known for colorful murals. After high school graduation, Vera moved to New York City and began her studies at the Art Students League. At the League, Vera sharpened her skills and talent, training under renowned American artists George Bridgman and Cecilia Beaux.

In 1928 Vera married fellow artist William B. Hamaker, and they settled in Greenwich Village. Vera first began working in fashion illustration and advertising art but later found steady employment as a children's book and magazine illustrator. Her first children's book, *The Meddlesome Mouse*, which she both wrote and illustrated, was published in 1931.

Over the next thirteen years, Vera illustrated many children's books, including the comical *Lazy Liza Lizard* by Marie Curtis Rains; *The Lonely Little Pig*, a collection of animal tales; and *Highway Past Her Door* by Mary Wolfe Thompson, a young adult romance. Vera wrote and illustrated two books of her own, *Little Bo* and *Safety for Sandy*. She also drew the pictures for stories in children's magazines, such as *Child Life* and *Story Parade*, as well as Christmas cards for the American Artists Group. Her illustrations of animals and children were delightful and lifelike, full of motion and detail.

In 1944, the Thomas Y. Crowell Company, publisher of the Betsy-Tacy books, needed a new illustrator for the high school series featuring Betsy and Tacy, which Maud Hart Lovelace had begun to write. Lois Lenski, the artist of the first four Betsy-Tacy books, declined to illustrate the new longer books as she preferred to work on stories for younger readers. Lenski mentioned Vera Neville as a possible artist for the forthcoming series. Vera was hired in 1945 to illustrate *Heaven to Betsy*, the first Betsy-Tacy high school story.

Vera's illustrations of teenage Betsy and her friends were authentic to the 1900s era. She studied photographs of Maud Hart Lovelace and her friends to create the lovable pictures of Betsy, Tacy, Tib, Carney, Joe, Cab, and all of the other characters in the books. Vera researched fashion, furnishings, and household items to make her illustrations as realistic as possible. Readers fell in love with Vera's charming and sometimes comical, sometimes heartbreaking depictions of Betsy Ray. The high school stories proved to be as popular as the younger Betsy-Tacy books, and Maud wrote a new one each year.

Vera Neville and Maud Hart Lovelace continued their partnership for ten years, which included the four Betsy-Tacy high school books, the Deep Valley books (*Carney's House Party*, *Emily of Deep Valley*, and *Winona's Pony Cart*), and the stories of Betsy's adult years, *Betsy and the Great World* and *Betsy's Wedding*. At the same time, Vera drew the pictures for several more children's books, including *A Lion for Patsy* by Miriam Mason and *Two Hundred Pennies* by Catherine Woolley.

Vera illustrated one more children's book, *Pigtail Pioneer*, in 1956 and then retired from the publishing world. She settled in Michigan and worked in her father's real estate business. She passed away in March 1979.

Vera Neville's remarkable artwork lives on in the

Betsy-Tacy books as new generations of readers become acquainted with Betsy and her friends.

—Teresa Gibson

Sources: Patricia Neville Downe; Lilly Erickson; Elizabeth Riley, Keynote Speech, 1997 Betsy-Tacy Convention; Archives of the American Artists Group, Smithsonian Institution

THE BETSY-TACY SERIES BEGINS

BETSY-TACY

ISBN 978-0-06-440096-1 (paperback)

Set in 1897, book number one is the classic, much-loved tale of the five-year-old Betsy, who finds a friend when a little girl named Tacy moves in across the street.

BETSY-TACY AND TIB

Foreword by Ann M. Martin

ISBN 978-0-06-440097-8 (paperback)

Now eight years old, Betsy and Tacy continue their adventures with the addition of the pint-sized, golden-haired Tib, a welcome third.

BETSY AND TACY
GO OVER THE BIG HILL

Foreword by Judy Blume

ISBN 978-0-06-440099-2 (paperback)

The girls turn 10 in this book and, while venturing further away from home for the first time, meet a real Syrian Princess who lives in the Slough.

BETSY AND TACY GO
DOWNTOWN

Foreword by Johanna Hurwitz

ISBN 978-0-06-440098-5 (paperback)

The girls, now 12, venture into downtown Deep Valley, where Betsy is introduced to the librarian Miss Sparrow, and the girls see their first automobile, and learn about the world of theater.

THE BETSY-TACY HIGH SCHOOL YEARS AND BEYOND

HEAVEN TO BETSY AND BETSY IN SPITE OF HERSELF

Foreword by Laura Lippman

ISBN 978-0-06-179469-8 (paperback)

Heaven to Betsy: In the first of the high school books, Betsy is 14 and a freshman at Deep Valley High. Boys become very important—especially one Joe Willard, a new boy in town.

Betsy in Spite of Herself: It's Betsy's sophomore year and she takes a glamorous trip to Milwaukee to visit Tib.

BETSY WAS A JUNIOR AND BETSY AND JOE

Foreword by Meg Cabot

ISBN 978-0-06-179472-8 (paperback)

Betsy Was a Junior: Julia returns from college and brings back the idea of sororities, which Betsy (unwisely) introduces to Deep Valley High.

Betsy and Joe: Betsy's senior year arrives and finally she is going with Joe! That is, until Tony (her freshman crush) suddenly changes his brotherly manner to a more romantic one.

BETSY AND THE GREAT WORLD AND BETSY'S WEDDING

Foreword by Anna Quindlen

ISBN 978-0-06-179513-8 (paperback)

Betsy and the Great World: Betsy sets off for a year-long tour of Europe to start her writing career and put some distance between herself and Joe.

Besty's Wedding: Betsy returns home as WWI is sweeping across Europe . . . will she and Joe finally find happiness?

THE DEEP VALLEY BOOKS

EMILY OF DEEP VALLEY

Foreword by Mitali Perkins

ISBN 978-0-06-200330-0 (paperback)

Maud Hart Lovelace's only young adult stand-alone novel, *Emily of Deep Valley* is considered by fans of her beloved Betsy-Tacy series to be one of the author's finest works.

"I never grow tired of cheering for Emily, and neither will a new generation of readers." —Mitali Perkins, author of *Secret Keeper* and *Bamboo People*

CARNEY'S HOUSE PARTY AND WINONA'S PONY CART

Foreword by Melissa Wiley

ISBN 978-0-06-200329-4 (paperback)

Carney's House Party: In the summer of 1911, Caroline "Carney" Sibley is home from college, and looking forward to hosting a month-long house party. Romance is in the air with the return of her high school sweetheart, Larry Humphreys, for whom she's pined many years.

Winona's Pony Cart: More than anything in the world, Winona Root wants a pony for her eighth birthday. She's wishing so hard that she's sure she'll get one—at least, that's what she tells her friends Betsy, Tacy, and Tib…